T0044347

Murder
at San Miguel

Copyright @ 2022 Danee Wilson

All rights reserved. No part of this publication may be reproduced,
stored in a retrieval system or transmitted, in any form or by any means without the prior
written permission of the publisher or by licensed agreement with Access:
The Canadian Copyright Licensing Agency (contact accesscopyright.ca).

Editor: Paul Carlucci
Cover art: Tania Wolk
Book and cover design: Tania Wolk, Third Wolf Studio
Printed and bound in Canada at Friesens, Altona, MB

The publisher gratefully acknowledges the support of Creative Saskatchewan,
the Canada Council for the Arts and SK Arts.

Library and Archives Canada Cataloguing in Publication

Title: Murder at San Miguel / Danee Wilson.
Names: Wilson, Danee, author.
Identifiers: Canadiana 20220397287
ISBN 9781989274767 (softcover)
ISBN 9781989274781 (HTML)
Classification: LCC PS8645.I466175 M87 2022 | DDC C813/.6—dc23

radiant press
Box 33128 Cathedral PO
Regina, SK S4T 7X2
info@radiantpress.ca
radiantpress.ca

In memory of Beatrix, Betty,
and all the resilient women who came before them.

For Destiny, the wire fox terrier, who will never read this book,
but who brings great joy to all who know her.

DANEE WILSON

Murder
at San Miguel

Chapter I

MY POSTERIOR HAD long since grown numb as Mauricio, the donkey, slowly and unsteadily climbed the path up Mount Archueta toward the sanctuary. Muffin, my fox terrier, sat primly in front of me, unperturbed by the constant shifting of Mauricio's weight as he plodded along. It wasn't my first journey by four-legged, stubborn ass (pardon my French) up the mountain that summer, and I sincerely hoped it wouldn't be necessary to repeat the experience. At my age, these things were simply impractical, not to mention the gut-wrenching moments when Mauricio clopped so close to the edge that one false step would've sent donkey, small dog, plump old lady clad in khakis and dusty work boots, and all the food we carried with us tumbling over the precipice to become forage for the vultures.

"Bill," I called to my husband, brushing a small insect off the breast pocket of my rumpled work shirt, "perhaps we should consider taking a car 'round the other side of the mountain next time. It might take longer, but it would save us some trouble."

No response.

"Bill! Are you listening?"

I dared not turn around while riding, lest I lose my balance or knock Muffin off. It wasn't uncommon for my husband to be lost in contemplation, completely oblivious to the world around him. On the other hand, I hoped he hadn't fallen asleep at the reins the way he often did in front of the television.

"Bill, did you hear me?" I called again, louder this time.

"Pardon me? Did you say something, Beatrix?" Bill appeared, bringing his donkey, Margarita, in step with mine.

"Yes, dear." I said, "Why don't we take a car next time instead of these obstinate beasts? Mauricio is a doll when I'm feeding him carrots, but he's not exactly complacent with me on his back. I can't really blame him either. In fact, I can quite easily empathize."

"I suppose you're right." He pushed his glasses up on his nose and glanced left and right. "A car would be more practical. It was very kind, however, of Father José María and Father Pedro to invite us to lunch in the village, don't you think?"

"Goodness, of course it was," I said, holding the reins with one hand and stroking Muffin's head with the other. "Father Pedro is a lovely young man and always has been. It's wonderful to see him again, after all these years. I find him refreshingly modern and progressive for a Catholic priest, unlike his mentor. Father José María is traditional to the point of being dogmatic. All his talk of a woman's place. Wives and mothers. The only path for a woman of morals. Suggesting that I and our female students should have stayed home, that education is wasted on us. I'll have him know I've been on more archaeological excavations than most men! I profoundly dislike him and his antiquated ideologies about women and religion. I held my tongue, but only because we are dependent upon his approval for this excavation."

Bill shifted awkwardly in his saddle. "I quite agree with you, Beatrix. However, I don't see that we have much choice in the matter. We're guests here, and though we may disagree with Father José María and many things in this country for that matter, it would be unwise for us to be too vocal about our beliefs. We both knew what this project would entail, and we agreed that we could go a few months without rocking the boat."

"True. Jail wouldn't suit you, Bill. You'd have to give up your pies. You know how much you'd miss those."

"Well, it's not the forties anymore," Bill said, wiping dog saliva on his khakis, which very closely resembled mine. "So as foreigners, I don't think we're at much risk of imprisonment for our beliefs. I suppose they'd simply remove us unceremoniously from the country. If we were Spanish, it would be another matter. Sticking the two of us in a prison as political dissidents would cause an international scandal. I can't believe that would be good for Spain's global relations, surely."

Bill was right. Putting two elderly foreigners in prison might reflect poorly on Francisco Franco's regime. The diminutive dictator famously didn't take kindly to political nonconformists, with his secret police, the Brigada Político-Social, enforcing compliance with the political tenets of his establishment. Yet Spain had opened up to the world after many years as a pariah state. These days, more than two decades after Franco took power, certain repressive tendencies were no longer accepted on the international stage. Especially not with tourists encouraged to visit the country's beaches in droves, flocking like seagulls to the sunny shores, drawn by catchy advertising slogans like "Spain is different." What, precisely, did they mean by that? That Spain had changed? As, indeed, it had. Or did they mean that the country presented a unique experience for visitors? It certainly did. Either way, Spain was no longer what it had been after the civil war and was rapidly developing into a desirable tourist destination, its not so attractive qualities hidden far from the golden sands and glimmering hotels.

Of course, I did try to keep my opinions to myself in public forums, knowing that things here were very different than they were in our own country. Or so I liked to think. Father Pedro insisted that we'd be welcomed in Spain with open arms and Bill could conduct archaeological excavations at the Sanctuary of San Miguel in Excelsis as long as we kept our political views about dictatorships and political repression discreet. I had already maintained my composure for two and a half months. Only one remained. We'd reached the final stretch of keeping our thoughts to ourselves, but it hadn't been effortless.

Bill and I had both been surprised to hear from Pedro the year before, in the form of a politely worded letter. He asked if Bill would be interested in organizing excavations at San Miguel prior to the initiation of construction of a new cafeteria and clerical residence adjacent to the church to replace buildings that had burned down in the forties. Pedro had been one of Bill's students at the University of Toronto, studying anthropology, before his family insisted he return to Navarre to become a priest. His family was extremely religious and had only tolerated his interest in anthropological studies long enough for him to earn his degree. We were sorry to see him leave, as he'd been such a dedicated student. Though a mentorship and friendship had developed between Bill and Pedro, we hadn't really expected to see him again, and Bill was already retired when we unexpectedly received the letter. He was ecstatic at the thought of a new project, but I had my reservations. We'd both essentially given up field archaeology when Bill retired, though he'd kept an office at the university and strong ties to the department. I'd always accompanied Bill on his excavations, for many years with children in tow. I truly felt that we were now too old to take on something new. It was time to enjoy our retirement years, our children, and our grandchildren. We'd experienced enough adventure for more than one lifetime. Bill insisted, however, that studying the remains buried in the cemetery near the medieval church of San Miguel would be fascinating, and Pedro had enticed him, suggesting that the infamous medieval knight and founder of the sanctuary, Teodosio de Goñi, might have been interred at the church. Bill was so excited, the temptation of discovery luring him away from our comfortable home, that I simply could not deny him the opportunity. I told him that this excavation would be his seventieth birthday present. He couldn't have been more eager to add to his collection of skeletons.

Eleven of us travelled from Toronto to Spain to recover skeletal remains from the medieval cemetery before crews of workers descended upon the mountain to do their own excavations and construct the new buildings. Bill was directing the dig with the assistance of Archie Davidson, a doctoral candidate, who helped him supervise the students who'd come to learn field techniques and skeletal analysis from an internationally recognized name in archaeology and physical anthropology. Bill had a reputation among his colleagues for brilliant research, and students still clamoured to learn from him despite his retirement.

Having studied art many moons ago, much to the chagrin of my parents, who believed that cooking and sewing were much more useful skills for a young woman to learn, I took charge of illustrating the project. I drew skeletons, archaeological features, and site maps. Eight students from the University of Toronto's Department of Anthropology also joined us, each writing carefully in neat cursive on his or her application that this project represented the opportunity of a lifetime and they hoped to be chosen to participate. I couldn't disagree with them on that point. They probably wouldn't have a similar opportunity for many years. It wasn't every day that students had the fortuity to work with a leading authority in their field. Most of our students were undergraduates, young and inexperienced; some had never been away from home and their families before. For many, the adjustment hadn't been easy.

As Mauricio stumbled along the uneven path, jostling my poor bones with each tottering step, I recalled our first night on the mountain, when Father Pedro had recounted the legend of the origins of the Sanctuary of San Miguel. It was dark and stormy, as always befits a chilling tale drawn from the early middle ages. Despite the number of people crowded around the long wooden table in the kitchen of our San Miguel accommodations, I shivered and drew my wool shawl tighter around my neck and shoulders as the rain thundered down outside. Though it was already the middle of May, it was still frightfully cold and damp on the mountain, and we were all struggling to transition from Toronto's warm, spring days to the brisk air that seemed to chill even our souls.

"More than one thousand years ago lived a knight called Teodosio de Goñi," Father Pedro began, his English excellent thanks to his having studied and lived in Canada. He sat at the head of the table, and all eyes were directed toward him. "He was a noble from the Goñi Valley, where he lived in a castle with his wife, Constanza, who loved him dearly. However, he spent many years far from home in Africa, fighting the Moors."

"What are Moors?" Janis, one of the students, broke the spell Father Pedro had already cast over the room.

"Very good question." Father Pedro smiled benevolently at Janis, causing her to blush.

I was surprised. Though we'd only recently met the students, it seemed somewhat out of character given Janis's assertive personality. She had her mousey hair cropped short, wore no jewelry, and had a stocky build, wide through the shoulders and waist. I'd noticed her physical strength at the airport, heaving bags around as though they weighed next to nothing.

"Moors are what we called the Berber and Arab people of North Africa," Father Pedro explained, adjusting his glasses and then running his hand over his short, dark hair. "They conquered much of Spain in the eighth century but were gradually pushed out over the next several hundred years."

"What's a Berber?" Janis persisted, propping her elbows on the table.

Before Pedro could respond, I cut in, worried we'd be in the kitchen until dawn if there were too many interruptions. "Perhaps we could leave our questions until Father Pedro has finished the story."

Father Pedro nodded his thanks to me. He had a pleasant appearance, with dark eyes partially obscured by the lenses of his glasses. Beyond new frames and the black priest's cassock he wore, which I'd had to grow accustomed to, he looked much the same as he had when he was Bill's student.

"Teodosio returned from Africa to the Kingdom of Pamplona without giving any notice to his family. He rode his beloved grey steed, Ekaitz, meaning 'storm' in the Basque language, as fast as he could through the forest to arrive home. But suddenly, he heard a terrible cry in the woods, which startled his horse. The cry sounded once again and Teodosio knew he had to investigate. He left Ekaitz on the path and crept through the woods, thinking he'd find an injured animal, but he found an old man with a long white beard wearing a monk's robe. The old man belonged to no order; he was a hermit monk, as we used to have here in Navarre a long time ago. The monk's leg was injured; he'd been shot with an arrow. Teodosio had survived many battles in Africa and seen many war wounds, so he helped the monk remove the arrow and tend to the wound. The old man thanked Teodosio and told him he had some news from the castle in Goñi. He told the knight that Constanza, his loving wife, had been having an affair with the handsome young groom Teodosio hired before he went away."

"What?" Graham, another student, exclaimed loudly. "He goes off to war and she cheats on him? Jeez, what a wife!"

Graham was what the young people these days would call "nerdy." I'd learned the term from my eldest granddaughter, now in her late teens and studying at university. Graham had blond hair slicked back with Brylcreem and a sprinkling of freckles across his nose. His front teeth were large and crooked, giving him a somewhat rodent-like appearance. The girls frequently rolled their eyes when he spoke, which tended to force him to retreat into his shell.

"Maybe she was tired of waiting for him." Miriam flipped her curly dark hair over her shoulder. "I know I'd be."

"Goodness, my dears," I interrupted, holding Muffin close so she wouldn't jump off my lap. I often let her sit with me at the table when there was no food around, but she was sensitive to voice commands and always ready to perform for a treat. "We must let Father Pedro finish his story, or we'll be here all night."

"Thank you, Mrs. Forster," Pedro said. "As I was saying, the monk told Teodosio that Constanza had been unfaithful while he was gone. Teodosio was enraged, running Ekaitz at full speed back to the castle, though they didn't arrive until the middle of the night, when everyone had already gone to bed. Teodosio burst into the castle and went straight to his bedroom, where he found a couple sleeping under the blankets. He swiftly drew his sword and slaughtered them mercilessly."

Father Pedro paused for dramatic effect. I glanced at Bill as the students audibly gasped in shock. It was clear Bill had entered another realm, his eyes fixated on the ceiling and his lips open as though he were about to speak, but no sound came out. We'd both already heard the story of Teodosio prior to arriving at San Miguel, and it was clear Bill didn't feel the need to hear the gory details again.

"When Teodosio pulled back the sheet, now soaked in blood, he realized that he had not killed Constanza and her lover—but had murdered his own parents."

"Holy moly!" Graham said, then covered his mouth as our eyes met.

I gave him a little wink. I was pleased by the students' excitement, but it was already quite late and I was suffering from jet lag, a condition recently discovered in those who travelled rapidly across multiple time zones.

"Keep going, Father Pedro," Janis said, cupping her face in her hands and looking expectantly at the young priest.

"Teodosio was horrified by what he'd done and ran to find Constanza, who was just coming home from midnight prayer at the chapel. He confessed what he'd done, telling his wife that the devil had disguised himself as a monk in the forest to trick him into committing murder. Constanza, who still loved Teodosio, forgave him."

"I wouldn't have if he'd just tried to kill me," Miriam blurted, the others shushed her immediately.

"Teodosio went to the bishop in Pamplona, who sent him to the pope in Rome, for punishment. His castigation was to be bound at the waist by heavy chains, return to Navarre, and roam the mountain range of Aralar, where we are now, until the chains wore down and fell off." Father Pedro took a sip of water from a glass in front of him, looked at each of the expectant students in turn, and continued. "Teodosio did as he was told and came back to wander the Aralar mountains. What he didn't know was that a dragon named Herensuge lived in a cave in the mountains."

"A dragon?" Janis demanded, sitting back from the table and crossing her arms over her chest.

"Janis, be quiet," one of the other students hissed.

"Yes, a dragon," Father Pedro said, smiling. "Remember this is the legend, the myth you might say, of the origins of the sanctuary. There are many fantastical creatures in Basque mythology, and Herensuge is just one of them. Let me continue. Teodosio learned of Herensuge's presence from shepherds who also roamed the mountains in the warmer months of the year. They warned him to stay away from her cave, as she ate anything she could get her claws on. After years of roaming the mountains during all the seasons and growing weak from the chains and lack of food, one day, Teodosio mistakenly wandered right up to Herensuge's cave. There were bones everywhere around the entrance, animal and human."

"Ooh," chimed the students in chorus.

I wasn't surprised. They'd come here to dig up skeletons after all. I looked over at the kitchen window once more, but the inky darkness prevented me from seeing anything outside, and the thundering rain muffled any sound that might have penetrated the dense stone walls. Without any blinds on the windows, I realized that anybody outside would be able to see us clearly without us knowing they were there. I shuddered at the thought, who would brave such terrible weather to spy on our little party? The legend of San Miguel, full of murder and dragons, put me on edge.

"Teodosio found a young woman at the dragon's cave. She'd been offered as a sacrifice to appease Herensuge and stop the dragon from snatching people from the villages and fields. Teodosio told her to run, that he'd take her place. When Herensuge appeared, Teodosio was paralyzed with fear, and the dragon easily snatched him up in her enormous claws. She was just about to scorch him with her fiery breath when Teodosio begged St. Michael to help him."

The room was illuminated momentarily by a strike of lightning, followed by a deep rumbling of thunder. Muffin barked loudly at the noise, her little body shaking with nervous energy. She wasn't fond of thunderstorms, and if not being held, she'd find some place to hide.

"Shhh," I comforted her, and she quieted down. "That's a good girl."

"It's St. Michael come to visit, but Muffin isn't so certain she wants to meet him," Father Pedro joked, the students laughing nervously. In such an unfamiliar, remote location, everyone but Pedro must have been a little anxious. "Well, much like the flash of light we just saw, St. Michael appeared to rescue Teodosio. He held a cross in one hand and a sword in the other. With a quick slash to her throat, he slayed Herensuge, who dropped Teodosio to the ground. Teodosio was in awe of the archangel who'd just saved his life. He got on his knees to thank St. Michael, who used his sword to cut off Teodosio's chains and told him that God had forgiven him for his sins. He gave Teodosio the chains and told him to keep them nearby as a constant reminder of the dangers of the devil. Teodosio was so happy, he rushed home to find Constanza, who was still waiting for him at the castle all these years later. He told her everything and said he wanted to build a church on Mount Archueta in the Aralar mountain range to honour St. Michael for saving him from the dragon. So with the help of many villagers from all around, Teodosio and Constanza built the sanctuary of San Miguel in Excelsis, and they hung Teodosio's chains inside the church. We can go see them tomorrow when we have a tour of the sanctuary."

"Is San Miguel haunted?" Graham asked, leaning forward to get a better view of the priest.

Father Pedro turned his palms up to the ceiling and shrugged. "Perhaps that's something you'll learn while you're here."

I scooted Muffin onto the floor and stood up from the table, my limbs aching from sitting in one place for so long. I was about to send the students off to bed when the door to the kitchen swung open, sending a cool breeze rushing into the room, which was otherwise kept warm with a crackling fire, and setting Muffin yapping again. Everyone turned to look at the door as a white figure charged into the room. Though a small scream of surprise interrupted the barking, we were all quick to realize that it was no ghost who'd burst into the kitchen but a person of flesh and blood cloaked in a white bedsheet. Muffin didn't take kindly to the intruder. Growling, she rushed over and grabbed a pantleg in her mouth. As soon as I saw the blue jeans and cowboy boots below the sheet, I knew very well who'd decided to pull a prank on the rest of us.

"Roger, you jerk!" Miriam cried, pulling the sheet off a tall and robust student who now wore a sheepish grin on his face.

"Sorry, Mrs. Forster," he said, tucking his chin down and peering at me. "I just couldn't resist."

"Goodness," I sighed, realizing that Bill and I were in for an eventful field season.

Chapter 2

"BILL, DID YOU CATCH the name of the lovely young woman who gave us the tomatoes and jam?" I asked, pulling myself out of my reverie of our early days at San Miguel. "I should write her a note to thank her. It was really very kind, and I'm sure the students will enjoy them immensely."

No response.

I realized then that Bill had drifted away from me once more as we ascended the mountain.

"Bill, did you hear me?" I shouted.

I wondered if he was losing his hearing.

Suddenly, two gunshots rang out from the forest in quick succession. I gasped sharply as I nearly toppled off the startled donkey. Mauricio kicked up his hind legs and took off running, helter-skelter, up the mountain path. It was the first time he'd picked up his pace since we started climbing. Initially, all I could do was hold tight, my hands clutching the reins and my legs squeezing poor Mauricio with all my might. Once my wits returned, I pulled hard on the reins, my teeth clenched as Mauricio clattered wildly up the path. I worried he would take off into the forest and knock me out with a branch, but finally he eased off. With shaking legs, I ungracefully dismounted at the first opportunity. I looked back along the path. Muffin was already running toward me, barking excitedly, but I couldn't see Bill. Panic compressed my heart. What if he'd been shot or Margarita had run off the side of the mountain in fear? What if he'd had a heart attack because of the fright? All kinds of terrifying scenarios flashed through my mind as I hurriedly yanked on Mauricio's reins and pulled the willful animal back down the path.

"Beatrix!" Bill's voice broke through my anxious thoughts and soothed the sensation of my chest being squeezed in a vise. "Beatrix, where are you?"

"Bill! We're over here, up the path."

As he ascended and I descended, we caught sight of one another.

"Thank goodness you're both all right," Bill said, dismounting Margarita. Muffin jumped into his arms, licking his cheek and beard. "I thought Mauricio had run off with you for good."

"I'm fine," I said, dusting off my pants. "You know well enough it's not that easy to get rid of me. Are you all right?"

"Not a scratch, but what the devil was that? I nearly went over the edge with that noise. Who in blazes is shooting up here?"

"Goodness, I suppose it must be a hunter, but it would be nice to confirm the hypothesis."

"Agreed." Bill passed me Margarita's reins and walked over to the tree line. "Hola?" he shouted in Spanish, given that it was unlikely many locals spoke English. "Who's there? Anybody?"

Bill and I developed a certain fluency in Spanish thanks to our time working at sites in Latin America and on previous trips to Spain. It was difficult to communicate effectively at first, but we'd pressed on and now both of us could converse with ease in the other language.

The trees swallowed Bill's voice, and at first we heard nothing, only the breeze rustling the leaves. Then came the distinct sound of heavy boots stomping over the ground toward us at a quick pace, snapping branches as they approached. I instinctively began to search the nearby ground for a weapon in case the boots were worn by foe instead of friend, but there were no substantial sticks or rocks close at hand. I could hear a low growl coming from deep in Muffin's throat. As an alternative to a stick, I quickly rummaged in one of the saddle bags slung over Mauricio's back. A heavy glass jar of homemade jam was better than nothing.

As the footsteps drew nearer, a tall, slender figure dressed in dark clothing became apparent among the trees.

"Ignacio, eres tú?" Bill asked when the man drew closer.

"Sí," the sanctuary's caretaker replied gruffly.

He offered no explanation for the gunshot.

"Was that you shooting in the woods?" Bill asked, though the answer was clear, as Ignacio emerged with a shotgun cradled in the crook of his arm.

Ignacio nodded his head and took a long drag from the cigarette embraced in the fingers of his right hand. He wore a black beret over his thinning hair and the appearance of an aged, malnourished Che Guevara, the revolutionary we'd grown accustomed to seeing in the newspapers during the Cuban Revolution in the fifties. He had the same fiercely determined look in his eyes.

Ignacio was an enigma to me. He kept to himself, despite living in close proximity to us and the students. I couldn't gauge whether it was shyness or something else. "I think that man has a secret," I told Bill within the first week of our work at San Miguel. Bill agreed with me, as he usually did, and he seemed unperturbed by the lanky man in his fifties with long, stringy grey hair and a gold tooth that embarrassed him greatly. I'd observed him use every artifice to hide it, from holding his cigarette precisely to obstruct it from view to speaking with dinner companions with a spoon hovering in front of his mouth. Each inter-action I had with Ignacio left me feeling that he was hiding more than just some old dental work. Though, perhaps it was just me.

"Have you been hunting, then?" Bill asked, returning to take hold of Margarita.

Ignacio nodded again.

"Did you catch anything?" I asked, hoping he'd elaborate on his activities in the forest.

"No," he replied, brushing hair out of his eyes with his wrist. I noticed blood on the back of his hand, but I said nothing.

"Where's Francisco?" Bill asked, smiling. "You haven't left him behind, have you?"

I couldn't tell if Bill saw the blood or not. My husband was capable of spotting an auditory ossicle, the minute bones of the middle ear, in a shovelful of dirt, yet he could be blissfully unaware of a leaf of spinach stuck in his dining partner's teeth. Needless to say, I always carried a pocket mirror in my purse.

Ignacio looked over his shoulder and whistled. A large pink shape came trotting toward us, snuffling and snorting with joy. Muffin immediately wagged her tail enthusiastically and jumped up at her friend.

"Hello, Francisco! How are you?" Bill said to Ignacio's pet pig as though he were a fluffy dog. He cupped the pig's face between his hands, letting Francisco sniff his beard, snout burrowing into the coarse white hair. Bill then reached into his pocket and procured a stub of carrot, the likes of which he'd started keeping to feed pigs, horses, or whatever other animal decided to approach for a snack. Francisco gulped down the carrot and then came over to me, probably anticipating more treats, but I had nothing for him.

"Sorry, Francisco, I don't have any tidbits for you today."

I leaned over and patted the enormous beast on the head, and he snuffled at my hair. I smiled. I had to admit Francisco was more social and amiable than his owner.

"Will you be joining us for dinner this evening?" I asked Ignacio.

"Yes, thank you, Señora Forster," Ignacio said, not making eye contact and turning his face so that I wouldn't see his gold tooth. "Very kind."

It wasn't uncommon for Ignacio to join us at the meals shared with the students and prepared by Maite, a local woman from the village of Huarte-Araquil in the valley. She was employed for the summer to help us with food preparation and housekeeping. Ignacio usually kept quiet and disappeared right after dinner. A spectre with a healthy appetite.

After agreeing we'd see each other for dinner at eight o'clock, a compromise between the local and the foreign customs of our party, Ignacio disappeared back into the forest, with Francisco sauntering along behind him. I wondered about the blood on his hand. Had he in fact killed an animal in the forest and lied to us about it? I couldn't be sure.

Chapter 3

I STOOD AT THE KITCHEN counter preparing Muffin's food while the students diligently helped Maite set the table. Dinner was typically a raucous event at our sanctuary lodgings. Father Pedro organized accommodation for us in the archaic twelfth-century house annexed to the church that once belonged to the Brotherhood of St. Michael. It was quite dilapidated, full of cobwebs, creaking floorboards, and rusty hinges. But it was a roof over our heads, even if we did occasionally wake to find that flakes of white paint slowly peeled off the wall in the night and floated down to rest on our faces, reminding me of childhood, when I'd catch snowflakes in my mouth as they drifted down from the sky. It was, however, better than waking to find a spider on your nose, which also occurred and resulted in much screaming until the poor terrified creature was squashed into non-existence.

Maite prepared simple meals for us, often consisting of beans or lentils and vegetables. If there was meat, she cut it into small pieces and mixed it into whatever stew she happened to be making. Given the rumours we'd heard of the wide variety of animals consumed during the difficult post-civil war years, known as the hunger years, we dared not ask what kind of meat we were eating. Some things were best left unknown. Sometimes, though, there was spicy chorizo to go with the lentils, procured from a farmer in the valley. Those meals always got rave reviews from the students, who were tired of the monotonous diet.

I'd noticed that even the students brought up in the wealthiest households lent Maite a hand without complaint, as Archie, Bill's teaching assistant, impressed upon them, before their arrival at the sanctuary, the importance of good behaviour, respect for local culture and people, and hard work. His speech must have been powerful because it seemed to have worked, at least on the surface. Bill and I were treated with reverence, something I admit I didn't mind in the least, even if the fawning was often exaggerated, the politeness superficial. A good recommendation from Bill could help ensure a place in a respected graduate program or a job after their degree, and Archie made that perfectly clear.

Archie was a good-looking young man, tall and fit with the fiery red hair of his forbears. Bill and I attended his marriage to the daughter of a prominent businessman the year before. The reception was lavish, held at the beautiful art deco Arcadian Court in downtown Toronto just a stone's throw from both the old and new city halls. At the time, some people questioned Archie's motivations for marrying a somewhat plain girl, but when Bill and I met her, we found her delightfully charming. Archie always had Bill's respect, and I pushed the money-grubbing rumours, common in Toronto social circles, aside.

Once everyone was seated at the table, the chatter began.

"Professor Forster, would you mind if we went into the lab tomorrow night after supper to do some extra studying?" Helen, our youngest and most outspoken student, asked sweetly when everyone sat down to eat. "I just want to make sure I'm making the most of my time here."

Helen came from an affluent family, much like Archie's wife, and I knew she was used to getting her way at home. She flashed Bill a wide grin, teeth straight and brilliantly white. She'd carefully painted her lips a deep blush before dinner to match her outfit, and she'd also lined her eyes with kohl, giving them an exaggerated, cavernous appearance. She was a beautiful girl nonetheless, with or without enhancement. I wondered if the makeup, which she diligently applied each day after work in the field, was for her own benefit or that of someone else.

"I APPLAUD YOUR DESIRE to advance your studies, Helen. Are you all wanting to spend extra time in the lab?" Bill set his spoon down and directed the question to the other students, who'd fallen silent after Helen's request.

"Not me," Eduardo piped up, pushing his heavy glasses up the bridge of his nose with his index finger. "I've already asked Mrs. Forster if I can help with the illustrations tomorrow night."

"That's because you don't like real work," Roger, a graduate student and our resident prankster, huffed under his breath. He must have realized I heard him, as he apologized immediately and profusely, then became quite interested in the contents of his plate, turning the bowl around a quarter at a time. "Sorry, Mrs. Forster. I meant physical work, not real work. You know what I mean. I didn't mean...I'm sorry."

"No offence taken, Roger," I said as graciously as I could. "Just remember, as we've said before, that all elements of a project are as important as the others. We need to put as much effort into intellectual work as physical work if the research is to have merit."

It wasn't the first time I'd heard similar discourse from the mouths of male colleagues, as though my sex made me impervious to comments intended to deride my contributions to the field. Roger was a muscular young man from out west, more used to wrangling steers than making polite dinner conversation. He'd learn to censor himself, as I had. I comforted myself with the image of his mother paddling him with a wooden spoon each time his remarks were unappreciated, citing the old English proverb that children should be seen and not heard. It didn't matter if the image approached reality or not; it gave me an airy sense of lightness and an increased ability to forgive his crass comments.

"Eduardo has indeed asked to assist with my work tomorrow evening," I continued, addressing everyone this time. "Of course, anyone is welcome to join. We want you all to get a comprehensive picture of all types of work that go into an excavation, not just digging things up, which I know many of you enjoy a great deal. Some a great deal too much."

They chuckled and the mood lifted. Spoons began, once more, to clink against the ceramic bowls.

"Mrs. Forster, if you don't mind, I'd like to join," Angela said quietly, tucking her long blond hair behind her ear. If she leaned any further forward, her hair would've been in her stew.

She was a shy girl, bright, and though she was quiet, she seemed to get along with everyone at the excavation, which could not have been said of all the others.

"I'd be glad to have you help out, Angela," I replied, noticing that Muffin came to sit beside me, having finished her own dinner and hoping to get some of mine.

Miriam, Angela's best friend, dropped her fork on her plate, pouted, and whined, "I thought we were going to wash our hair tomorrow night. We had plans."

"We can do that tonight. It's not such a big deal, is it? Come do illustration with us."

"Fine. I'll come too."

"I'll come to the lab if that's an option," said Graham his mouth full of half-chewed lentils.

The girls across from him groaned and rolled their eyes in unison, obviously not impressed by Graham's table manners.

"I'll join the lab people too," Janis said, scratching at her hair, which lay quite flat against her head, having been covered by a sunhat during the day.

Bill's eyes turned to Patrick, who hadn't spoken yet, which wasn't a surprise. He nodded his head, and I took that to mean he'd join "the lab people" as well. Patrick was generally quiet and had adopted the hippie culture, wearing his hair long and shaggy and dressing much of the time in loose tunics and bell bottoms.

Archie enthusiastically volunteered to supervise them, and Bill gave his blessing for after-dinner study on the Friday evening. Usually, the students had evenings free to do as they liked, but as we drew closer to the end of the season, we saw some of them work harder to be noticed, likely because they sensed the impending end of their time at San Miguel and, hence, the end of their practical experience in the field. Bill didn't like the students to be in the lab alone, given the propensity some had for getting distracted while chatting, which led them to mix things up or unintentionally break the fragile bones of the specimens.

While talking to the students, I failed to notice that Maite and Ignacio were leaning across the table toward one another, deep in quiet conversation. Neither spoke English, so it was no surprise that they kept their own company at the end of the long table in the kitchen. However, they straightened up and immediately stopped talking when the loud chatter from the rest of the table suddenly died out. They were usually polite enough to each other, but I hadn't ever seen them exchange more than a few words at a time. I wondered if their conversation was related to Ignacio's hunting expedition in the forest that day.

"Maite," I said in Spanish, taking advantage of the lull in both conversations to see if I could finagle some information out of one of them. "Father Pedro and Father José María will be joining us tomorrow for lunch here at San Miguel. Is there any chance you've got something special, some meat perhaps, for the meal?"

"Meat? But Beatriz, tomorrow's Friday." Maite always used the Spanish version of my name. After living together for months at San Miguel, we'd grown quite familiar, and though I was older, she addressed me informally, unlike Ignacio, who continued to use a formal honorific when he spoke to me. "We can't eat meat."

Maite smiled and almost laughed, the wrinkles at the corners of her eyes and mouth crinkling pleasantly. I imagined her thinking of Father

José María, extremely strict in his doctrine, being served meat on a Friday. She was, like me, not a great admirer of the elder priest, though she was never outwardly impertinent in his presence.

"Of course! Very true. I forgot that Catholics don't eat meat on Fridays. And I suppose fish is out of the question at the last minute. I expect it'll have to be beans then. I hope you didn't catch anything today that will go to waste, Ignacio."

"No, señora," Ignacio replied bluntly.

With that, he began to eat again. It was clear he wasn't about to relinquish any details of his day to me, his secrets safely tucked behind lips that minced words at every turn. I pushed the incident in the forest to the back of my mind, deciding it was of little relevance to myself or the excavation.

After dinner, I accompanied Bill to the lab to check on the materials and how the students progressed while we were gone to the village much of the day, leaving Muffin to beg from Maite in the kitchen as she cleared the dishes away. No dogs in the lab—that was a long-established rule at our excavations. Although we referred to it as "the lab," the rooms we'd designated for post-excavation study could hardly be called such. They were dimly lit chambers with one window each on the western side and a narrow hallway separating them. Long ago, the walls were painted white, but much of the work began to chip and flake off, leaving plaster exposed in some places, and where the plaster was also damaged, the stones of the house's original construction showed through. On the mountain, we were often enveloped in the clouds themselves, and stone walls were no buttress against the humidity that infiltrated the decrepit old house. Mold grew in many nooks and crannies, forming patches of dispersed black spots in some places and wispy growths of white crystalline filaments in others. The windows in the rooms consisted of double panes held together by frames of decomposing wood.

When we'd first arrived, Ignacio explained to Bill that a severe snowstorm had blown the windows in one winter and caused much of the damage we saw in the house. There was no money available to repair the resulting deterioration. It was 1967, and the economic situation of

Spain had greatly improved since the impoverished, desperate years of the forties, after the end of the Spanish Civil War. However, it was still evident that even the church here suffered the strains of the isolation of the rural parishes. Once you added the skeletons themselves, laid out in anatomical position one at a time on the makeshift tables, their empty orbits gaping and their teeth bared in grotesque, eternal grins, the rooms took on a particularly eerie feel. All the unseeing eyes and unfeeling fingers made me appreciate the liveliness of the students. After spending nearly half a century around human remains because of my and Bill's work, I didn't believe in ghosts, but there was something about the lab at San Miguel that gave me goosebumps every time I visited, and the students most certainly conjured up an entire cast of ghosts and spirits who haunted the halls and chapels at San Miguel.

Chapter 4

THAT NIGHT, AFTER we checked on the lab, Bill and I retired to the room we shared on the third floor of the house. It was cramped and furnished with nothing more than two army cots pushed together in the centre and two small wooden tables that acted as nightstands on either side of the makeshift double bed. Above the beds hung a simple wooden cross on a nail hammered into the plaster. It was sparse and dreadfully cold at night, but we'd experienced much worse on previous excavations. I, however, insisted that Bill and I spend a few nights at La Gran Perla, a luxury hotel in Pamplona, before we returned to Canada. The Perla was known for hosting Hemingway on several occasions; he'd died just a few years before the excavation. Bill and I were both familiar with the author's works, and I was eagerly awaiting those nights in a quality bed after more than two months on the mountain in our dreary accommodations.

"What's your plan for tomorrow, Bill?" I asked, each of us sitting on our own bed.

"I'll have Archie extend the excavation area another metre to the east," Bill replied, reaching over to pat Muffin on the head as I worked on brushing the long hair of her front legs. "We have some skeletons half-exposed, and I'd like to get them out in their entirety. Unfortunately, they go past the section beyond the limits of our trench. I'd also like to get a start on opening the sarcophagi inside the church. Since Pedro and José María are coming up tomorrow, it'll be good to have them there when we open the tombs so they can participate in that aspect of the project."

"I can adjust the site plan when Archie's finished the extension," I said, glancing up from my work. "You'll have to choose the students to help you with the indoor tombs wisely, or they'll be fighting about it until we go home. You know how jealous they get of one another when they think something's a privilege. Maybe you can find a way to have everyone involved."

"I can manage that." Bill yawned and stretched his arms up above his head. "Even if some are just standing around watching. It'll be more about brute strength than technical expertise to get those lids off, anyway."

"Very true," I said.

"What do you think, Muffy?" Bill asked, leaning in and holding his face close to her long, bearded muzzle. Muffin tilted her head and her pink tongue darted out to kiss him on the nose.

"Lights out?" I asked.

Bill nodded and stood up from the cot. The light switch that controlled the naked bulbs above our bed was closer to the door in the short hallway that led to the room than to where we slept. Bill's daffodil yellow pyjamas hung loosely off his body as, unlike myself, he had a propensity for losing weight during an excavation. I turned on Bill's flashlight so he could return to his bed without stubbing a toe. When I switched it off, we were cloaked in darkness except for a sliver of moonlight that peeked through the gap between the shutter and the window. As I lay back on my cot and pulled the blankets up to my chin for warmth, I felt the familiar sensation of Muffin circling, once, twice, three times, until she curled up between me and Bill.

I WASN'T SURE how long I'd been asleep when a shriek startled me awake. Muffin growled and instantly stood up. I reached out and felt her little body rigid in anticipation.

"Bill."

No response.

"Bill, did you hear that?"

My question was met with a low grumble. I leaned over and shook my husband awake.

"Bill, I just heard someone scream."

"What? Where?"

"Goodness, I don't know. Somewhere down the hall. It sounded like one of the girls. Maybe it was just a nightmare, or another spider, we'd better make sure."

"Pass me the flashlight please, Beatrix. I'll go."

"I'll go too."

I handed Bill the flashlight and we got out of bed. My joints felt stiff and my eyes heavy with sleep. I felt around on the table until I located my glasses. The room was frigid, and I shivered as I grabbed a sweater I kept at the foot of my bed for nighttime excursions to the bathroom. Bill turned on the weak lights, and I pulled my slippers out from under the bed with my foot. We went out into the hallway toward the bedrooms occupied by the students. Girls in one room and boys in another. I was nearly certain by then that the scream came from the girls' room. There was a muffled sound of excited young ladies all talking at once. By the time we arrived at the room shared by the four girls, Eduardo and Graham popped their heads out into the hallway, much like pocket gophers peeping out of their holes. They looked dishevelled, wrenched from a deep sleep. I must have looked the same or worse.

"What's going on?" Eduardo whispered, squinting in the half light of the passage. He wasn't wearing his glasses, and I wasn't sure what he could distinguish without them.

"Stay in your room, please," Bill said with kind firmness. "We'll handle this."

Bill knocked on the girls' door. Helen opened it, wide eyed.

"Thank goodness you've come!" She nearly shouted. "We weren't sure what to do. We were so frightened. I just...we thought she was going to kill us. We didn't know what to do."

"Slow down, Helen," I said as Bill pushed the door fully open. "We can't make sense of what you're saying. What's happened?"

I gasped when I entered the room and saw Janis, broad shouldered and muscular as she was, kneeling on the floor with her hands tied to her cot with a bedsheet. She didn't seem to notice Bill and me as we entered. There was a pillowcase tied around her mouth as well. Angela and Miriam sat on another cot across the room, their pale hands intertwined, Angela with her head on Miriam's shoulder.

"Goodness," I said, covering my mouth. What could've happened?

"Good Lord!" Bill exclaimed, shoving his glasses further up the bridge of his nose. "Ladies, I need an explanation, please." He immediately resumed his even, calm tone, but I knew he was as shocked as I was. "What on Earth is going on? Why is Janis tied up?"

"It's her own fault!" Miriam declared, shaking Angela's head from her shoulder with a quick shrug. She was visibly agitated, speaking rapidly, the words tumbling from her mouth. "She was standing over me in the middle of the night. She had a knife! What was she going to do? She might've killed me and everyone else in this house! She's bananas, that one. She belongs in an institution. I screamed, and then Angela and Helen helped me tie her up so she couldn't hurt anyone."

I went over to Janis, crouched down, and carefully removed the pillowcase from her mouth. Muffin sniffed at it as it hung around her neck.

"Janis, dear," I said softly, gently touching her arm. "What happened? Why were you out of bed tonight?"

Her eyes were unfocused, and she seemed to look right through me as though I weren't even there.

"I went to the kitchen," she said, suddenly struggling with her bound hands.

Her efforts to free them didn't last, and she let her arms go limp. She was a strong girl, though, and I decided to leave her hands safely tied up until we could resolve the issue.

"Please, give me the knife," Bill said to Miriam.

Ignoring the fact that Bill spoke directly to Miriam, Helen leaped across the room toward the windowsill. She picked up a butter knife and handed it to Bill.

"Not my murder weapon of choice," a male voice sneered from the doorway.

"Shut up, Roger!" Helen shouted.

I looked up to see his large frame blocking the doorway; the heads of the other male students, plus Archie, Maite, and Ignacio filled in the gaps left around Roger's body. Only Patrick was absent, perhaps he'd slept through the bedlam. They all peered in at us, but none dared enter the room. Miriam's scream must have woken nearly the entire household.

"Please, all of you, go back to bed," Bill insisted, facing the door with the knife in his hand. "We'll speak with the girls."

He repeated his instructions in Spanish for Ignacio and Maite.

"Janis," I tried again. "What were you doing with a knife?"

"I just wanted to make a sandwich," she said casually, her voice relaxed and dreamy.

"Bill," I said, beckoning for him to come over. "Janis isn't really awake. I think she's been sleepwalking. I imagine she's been to the kitchen and got the knife there. I don't think she meant to harm anyone."

"She goes to the kitchen all the time in the middle of the night," Miriam blurted.

"Is that true?" Bill turned back to look at her.

The girls all nodded.

"So she's been sleepwalking all this time, and you didn't say anything to us?" I stood up using the cot for support, my knees creaking under the strain.

Nobody said a word.

"Goodness," I scolded. "This could've been extremely dangerous for Janis. She could've fallen on the stairs or worse. You should've told us what was going on."

Helen still wore the appearance of a startled animal as she drew closer to me. "I only knew because they told me, Mrs. Forster. I'm a deep sleeper."

"It could've been dangerous for us too," Miriam protested. "She did have a knife, Mrs. Forster."

"I'm really sorry, Mrs. Forster," Angela whispered. Muffin somehow made her way into Angela's arms and was soaking up the agitated caresses she was receiving. "We should've said something. Maybe it wouldn't have come to this if we had."

"All right," Bill said, moving to put an end to the discussion. "I think everyone should go back to bed. We'll discuss all of this in the morning,"

"Janis, it's time to go back to bed," I said, leaning over to untie her hands.

"Okay," she meekly replied.

"I'm not going to sleep in the same room as her," Miriam declared loudly, standing up from her cot and crossing her hands over her chest. "She might kill us. Sleepwalker or not, she's a danger to everyone here."

"I agree with Mrs. Forster, Miriam," Bill said. "I don't believe she meant to hurt anybody."

"Come on, Miriam," Angela said softly. "She wouldn't hurt anybody. She can't help what she does when she's asleep."

"Angela, stop protecting her. She's not even your friend. She isn't normal, Professor Forster, Mrs. Forster. She sits around talking about death and dying all day. That's all she talks about. It's not normal."

"Well," Bill said, a sly smile on his face, "I can't see that being so abnormal when we're dealing with skeletons every day."

The expressions on their faces made me think the girls didn't appreciate his making light of the situation, and I couldn't help a small grin. The situation was so absurd that I could hardly believe it was real. I bit my lip so nobody would notice my amusement.

"It's not like that," Helen jumped in, putting her hands on her hips. "Janis is strange. And she doesn't like us. She told us that there's no point in our being here since we're all just going to get married and never work anyway. She said that this education is wasted on us, that *she's* not going to marry and *she's* going to be a professor at a university.

She's going to do something with her life. She said we would just be housewives, so why bother? Pretty faces but no substance."

"Goodness, Helen," I said. "You shouldn't take these things to heart. You, Angela, and Miriam will do whatever you want with your lives, married or not. And no education is ever wasted. It wasn't kind of Janis to say these things, I agree, but not everybody sees eye to eye all the time. It's very difficult to live with strangers and adapt to their personalities. We must try for the good of the team."

"Mrs. Forster is right, ladies," Bill added for emphasis. "We do have to try to get along, even if we decide never to speak to one another again after the excavation."

"I don't feel safe," Miriam stated, adopting a pose much like Helen's. "I don't want to sleep in the same room. Please, Mrs. Forster, you must understand."

"I do," I said, taking a moment to think of a solution to the problem. "Bill, what if we put Janis to sleep in the kitchen tonight? There's plenty of room for her bed down there."

The kitchen was an enormous room on the main floor of the house with its own fireplace. Despite the long wooden table that easily accommodated twenty people, there was a vast empty space between it and the kitchen cabinets and outdated appliances Maite used to prepare our meals.

Bill nodded his assent. "I don't see why not."

Janis was already lying on her bed with her eyes closed. I had no idea if she was really asleep, pretending to be asleep, or still in an altered state of sleep. Regardless, we'd have to get her up to move her into the kitchen for the night. I hoped it would be a temporary solution, the girls seemed quite shaken by the incident, and I anticipated that Janis would be even more excluded than she'd already been for the rest of our time here. Perhaps it would be her preference, if what the other girls said was true.

"You girls help Bill move the bed when I get Janis up," I said, taking charge of the situation. "I'd like to get her and everyone else to sleep as quickly as possible."

Although Bill was exceptionally good at dealing with the academic concerns of his students and the black and white of professional and educational matters, the personal and emotional issues of young people were areas in which he did not excel. Even with our own children, he'd tended to let me deal with the tears and wild ranges of emotions children and teenagers are known to exhibit. Fortunately, he'd always agreed with my methods, even when our children attempted to try to play us against one another. "What did your mother say?" he always asked them, and they knew their efforts would be fruitless.

I helped Janis down to the kitchen, holding her arm as we descended the stairs, as though she were an invalid. I was worried Janis might fall, though I knew she'd apparently done this repeatedly without incident. Bill, Miriam, Angela, and Helen brought the cot with all the bedding down and set it up in an unused corner of the kitchen. Then we sent the three girls back to bed. When I tucked Janis in, I still wasn't sure if she was fully awake or not. It was difficult to tell — her features were blank — and she wasn't particularly expressive during the day either. I wondered about blocking the door to the kitchen somehow, but my fear of Janis being stuck in the building in the event of a fire was greater than my fear of waking up to find her standing over me. I closed the door quietly after confirming she hadn't moved from her bed, and Bill and I went back upstairs.

"Bill," I said outside our bedroom door. "Go check on the boys, and if they're awake, tell them what happened and that Janis is sleeping in the kitchen. Tell them there's nothing to worry about. I'll go tell Maite and Ignacio. Maite won't be thrilled about our using the kitchen as a bedroom, but the only other room available is the one for the priests, and we can't use that."

Maite answered nearly immediately after I knocked. She must have expected some news of the commotion. As I'd anticipated, she wasn't pleased about the new sleeping arrangements, but I indicated that the only other possibility was for her to share her own room with Janis, and she hastily agreed that the kitchen was the best place. Next, I climbed the stairs to the attic room, where Ignacio lived all year round. I couldn't fathom the isolation and loneliness of living here alone in the winter months, when the snow could block access to the mountain for days or weeks at a time. Though for someone as withdrawn as Ignacio, perhaps it was a haven of sorts. I knocked on his door.

No response.

I tried again, louder this time.

Nothing.

There was little else I could do, so I returned to my room and climbed into bed next to Bill. I felt sure that I wouldn't be able to go back to sleep. I was wide awake. I just hoped there'd be no further disturbances in the night.

Chapter 5

WHEN BILL AND I ENTERED the kitchen the next morning, we were met by an ominous silence. Despite the occupants busily preparing the first meal of the day, no one said a word. Breakfast typically consisted of toasted bread with olive oil and tea or coffee. The students had to adjust to simple food during the excavation, as there were no shops nearby. The remote location of the sanctuary meant we relied entirely on Ignacio's weekly trip, by beat-up fifties SEAT, down to a village in the north valley. Occasionally, a shepherd or visitor to the mountain would bring us cheese or some other provisions that they very generously contributed to our meals. We were aware of the poverty of many of the people living close to San Miguel, even with the ameliorated economic conditions of the country. Mostly, the improvements could be seen in the cities, while the rural areas continued to languish.

Though nobody spoke, they did, however, take notice of the jar of jam I'd received in the village the day before, as I placed it on the counter.

I started preparing Muffin's breakfast at the counter. As I set her bowl down I scanned the kitchen and saw that the male students, Archie, Maite, and Janis were present.

"Where are the other girls?" I asked no one in particular.

I saw shoulders shrug and eyes avert.

"They're sick," Eduardo offered helpfully, if a bit conspiratorially. "I went to check on them this morning. That's what they told me."

Though they had occasional tiffs, Eduardo was quite fond of the girls, so it was no surprise to me that he'd been the one to check up on them that morning.

"Angela wasn't in the room," he continued. "She was in the bathroom. But Miriam told me that she was sick and that they'd been throwing up during the night. Really, Mrs. Forster, it's a real downer. You shouldn't go in there, or you might catch whatever they've got."

"Thank you, Eduardo," Bill intervened, setting a plate of toast and cup of coffee on the table. "Sounds as if it could be a stomach bug, or we'd all be sick. We all eat the same food every day, and everyone else seems fine. Mrs. Forster and I will speak with the girls, but most likely, they won't come out to work today if they're unwell."

"Stomach bug or Janis," Roger scoffed, already seated on one of the benches at the table.

"I'll go, Bill," I said to my husband quietly. "But maybe see if you can have a talk with Roger. We don't want to ostracize Janis. It won't help things."

I left the kitchen and climbed back up the stairs to the rooms where we slept. My stomach gurgled in protest, as I hadn't eaten. The old wooden stairs were awkward, and by the time I reached the third floor, I was out of breath. Next time, I decided, I'd send Bill.

The door to their room was closed. I knocked softly and heard Helen call out for me to come in. The room was still chilly from the night, but it smelled of stale air. I immediately went over to open the window a crack.

"Goodness, it's a bit stuffy in here," I said. "If you've got a stomach bug, the fresh air will make you feel a bit better. It's no colder outside than inside now."

"Thank you, Mrs. Forster," Helen said weakly from bed, where she lay under the covers. Her eyes still bore black streaks near the lash line, remnants from last evening's eyeliner.

"Now," I said, resting my posterior on the windowsill and examining the girls from my temporary perch, "tell me what's wrong."

"Well, it started last night." Helen spoke rapidly, her words tumbling out with hardly a breath in between. "After the Janis thing, we just all started to feel unwell, but Angela's got it worst. She hasn't come back from the bathroom this morning. I only threw up once, and Miriam a couple of times too."

"Any other symptoms?" I wasn't a medical doctor, but you learn a thing or two as a mother.

"Just upset stomach," Miriam replied from her cot. There was a sour look on her face and purplish skin under her eyes.

"No fever, then?"

Both girls shook their heads.

"Strange that Janis isn't sick," I said, contemplating the situation out loud. "She was sharing a bedroom with you up until last night."

"She doesn't spend much time with us," Helen said quickly.

"I see." I stood up from the windowsill and moved into the middle of the room The students' rooms were much larger than mine and Bill's because of the need to accommodate more beds, but the décor was just as austere. "And what about work today? Do you feel up to it or do you need some time off?"

"I can't work today," Miriam stated with conviction, turning her head on the pillow to look at me. "I'm too sick."

She did look a bit off, her skin sallow and eyes dull. Her curly, dark hair was splayed in disarray on the pillowcase.

"I don't think I should either," Helen said, less confident in her response. There didn't really appear to be anything wrong with Helen. "I mean, unless you think Professor Forster will be angry. I don't want him to think I'm skipping work." She looked at me nervously and started chewing a fingernail.

"Goodness, Helen, dear," I said firmly. "If you're sick, you're not skipping work. If you don't feel well, it's best to stay in bed and rest. But it you feel fine, then you should certainly not miss a workday. I'll leave it up to you girls. You're old enough to decide if you should or shouldn't work today. I'll go check on Angela. You girls come back to work when you're ready. I'll have Maite check in on you, and I'll see if she can bring you some tea this morning."

"Thank you, Mrs. Forster," the girls chimed in unison.

I left the room a little suspicious at the sudden illness of all three girls just after the incident with Janis. Perhaps they were just tired and felt the need to embellish their situation to justify missing work. I flicked the light switch in the hallway, as it was always dark in the passage regardless of the time of day, and went to the bathroom. I knocked on the door.

No response.

I knocked again.

Through the door, I could hear some muffled movements and then a deep groan. Angela certainly didn't sound well.

"Angela," I called through the door. "It's Mrs. Forster. May I come in?"

I could hear some scraping over the tiled floor, and then the door opened. Angela looked dreadful, her blond hair limp and hanging in her face, the skin around her eyes dark, her lips dry and cracked.

"Goodness, Angela, are you all right?" I was shocked by her appearance. "How long have you been sick?"

"I'm so sorry, Mrs. Forster. I didn't mean for you to come up. I just... I just..." Angela didn't finish her sentence. She turned back to the toilet and kneeled down. Her body shook and she clutched her stomach, but nothing came out.

I went over to her and rubbed her back as I'd done many times with my own children. She collapsed beside the toilet and began to cry.

"What are your symptoms, my dear?" I kept my voice low and calm.

"I have terrible cramps and I feel nauseous, but I can't throw up," she moaned. "I think I'd feel better if I were able to. I'm so sorry, Mrs. Forster, I didn't mean to be sick."

"Of course you didn't, dear," I placed my hand on her bare arm and realized she was terribly cold. "Angela, there's no need to apologize for being sick. It happens to everyone. The other girls are also sick, though it would seem this bug has hit you the hardest."

Angela laughed a little through the tears.

"Now, what do you think ails you, my dear? You've been a bit pale these days. Is this the first time you've been ill?"

"The cramps started in the night, after Janis went to sleep in the kitchen, but I don't think what happened has anything to do with me feeling sick today. I really don't think Janis would hurt anybody, Mrs. Forster, she's just a bit of an odd duck, that's all."

Angela began shaking harder and I knew she couldn't stay longer on the frigid bathroom floor.

"I think it would be best if you went back to bed, Angela. You'll be warm there, and you can sleep some more."

"I'm not sure I can leave . . ." she mumbled, looking at the toilet upon which she was supporting her right shoulder.

"I'll find a pot in the kitchen that you can use if you need it, and we can wash it out afterward if your body does decide to purge itself. I don't think you'll get better if you stay here. You might even get worse. You need to stay warm."

I told her I'd meet her back at her room with the necessary receptacle. I hoped Maite wouldn't mind my taking one of her pots away for alternative purposes. There really wasn't much choice. It wasn't good for anybody in ill health to sit on a cold tile floor. I got to the top of the stairs, sighed at the thought of going down and back up again, and started my return journey to the kitchen. As I descended, I wondered at the contradictions in the girls' stories. Miriam and Helen said they'd all been vomiting, while Angela, who was clearly in pain from her cramps, said she wasn't able to vomit despite some nausea. Perhaps they'd misunderstood one another and assumed they all had the same symptoms. I would've asked about their monthlies, but it seemed odd they would all have a difficult period at the same time when they hadn't had one previously at the excavation. It was all incredibly odd, but other than helping them get better, there was little to do.

I wasn't been gone long, so there were still people in the kitchen, including Bill, finishing up breakfast. He got up when I entered.

"How are they?" he asked quietly.

"Angela's quite sick. I'm going to get her something she can use for vomiting so she can stay in bed."

"I'm sorry to hear that."

"Yes, it's unfortunate, but this is life. Not the first time someone has been sick at an excavation. At least it isn't food poisoning this time. Remember Mexico?"

Bill chuckled at the memory of the entire team getting food poisoning on a Mesoamerican archaeological expedition. Montezuma certainly wreaked his revenge on us, hapless archaeologists that we were. We were all dreadfully sick for days, and it wasn't the kind of excavation where we had access to indoor plumbing. It hadn't been funny at the time, but we'd learned to laugh about most of our misadventures over the years.

"How could I forget?" Bill asked, his eyes twinkling with delight. "I'll go ahead and take the students out and get them started working. Archie can keep them in the field, and I'll go have a look at the sarcophagi inside the church when the priests arrive. I guess it'll be a reduced group today with the girls staying in. Once Father Pedro and Father José María arrive, they can give their assent and we can remove the remains today. I presume they'll be skeletonized, but you never know if conditions might have been right for mummification or partial mummification to occur. Though it does seem a bit damp here for that to have happened, unfortunately. Yet it would be quite interesting if we were to have a desiccated body here for the students to see. Don't you think, Beatrix?"

"Yes, Bill, but you've gotten off track," I said. "First things first. And don't get the students excited about something that probably won't happen. I'll come over once I've got the girls settled."

"Don't forget to have some breakfast, or you'll be hard pressed to last until teatime. That toast is for you." Bill motioned at a plate with some toast, next to a cup of black tea. "It might be a bit cold by the time you get to it, I'm afraid."

"Thank you, dear," I said. "Now off you go."

When Bill wasn't consumed by thoughts of skeletons and mummies, he was a thoughtful husband. I stooped to look under the table and spotted a fluffy, cotton-ball tipped tail quivering next to a pair of stockinged legs. When I straightened up again, my eyes locked with Maite's and she gave me a guilty smile.

"Madre mía, Maite," I pretended to scold her. "Have you been giving her treats again?"

Maite held her hands up. "What can I do, Beatriz? Who can resist that face?"

I shook my head and went over to the kitchen cabinets. While I rummaged through the contents to find a suitable container, Maite approached me to ask what I was looking for. I explained what happened.

"I'll help you," she said kindly. "Those girls, though, running around at all hours of the day and night. No wonder they're sick now."

I knew the students often went hiking in the mountains. "To have some alone time," they always said. I understood the desire to escape the madding crowd when we lived in such close quarters, spending all our time together. Had I still been able to hike extensively, I would have considered doing the same myself on a regular basis. There were extraordinary views from the mountain, with the blue-tinted Pyrenees visible to the east on clear days. The valley itself was cut into neat squares and rectangles of agricultural land to the south, which were frequently illuminated by celestial beams of sunlight that pierced the clouds. To the west were the Basque mountains, lush and verdant. To the north, you could climb higher up Mount Archueta, to the highest peak, and look out over grazing lands and achieve a bird's eye view of the sanctuary. Bill and I climbed up once or twice to watch the sunset. However, though the path was short, the climb was steep, and I didn't make the excursion regularly.

"The students have been out at night?" I asked, surprised.

I wasn't aware. I wasn't their mother, but I didn't like their going out late at night. The mountains could be dangerous, especially in the dark. A false step could prove fatal, and there were plenty of animals about. The vipers didn't often venture out at night, but they were certainly present, hidden among the rocks. The wild boars, however, were nocturnal.

"Yes, I thought you knew, or I would've said something," Maite told me, sincerely. "The boys and the girls, I think. I don't know if they go off together. I mean, not all of them go out, I suppose. At least, not all at once. I don't see them, but I hear them in the hallway sometimes at night if I can't sleep. The doors opening and closing, footsteps, muffled voices. That kind of thing. I suppose they don't go together to the bathroom, so what else could they be doing?"

I knew that Maite cared for the students, despite the language barrier. She often snuck them treats if there were any to be had. Food was, in my experience, a more powerful tool of communication than words. Sometimes, she'd ask me or Bill to interpret so she could tell them little stories about life in the village. Caricatures of the interesting characters she encountered were her favourite, but sometimes she told stories of the history and culture here, the witch trials, the mythology of the Basque people. We encouraged her to tell them anything she wished, especially about the culture. They were budding anthropologists, after all, and they had little contact with local people because of the isolation of the sanctuary. I doubted very much she wanted to see them in trouble for their youthful adventures in the night.

"Goodness, I had no idea," I said. "I'll have to speak to Bill about this, and maybe we'll have to have stricter rules. I thought any noises I heard at night were just visits to the bathroom. Apparently, I was wrong. I know they mean well, but they're young and away from home. I don't want them to get into trouble here."

Maite found a large ceramic basin in the cupboard and passed it to me.

"Perfect," I said, standing up, thankful to be able to straighten my knees again.

"Good luck, Beatriz," Maite said, and she smiled ruefully before she went back to the kitchen table to start clearing away her own breakfast dishes.

Then, as I marched back to the staircase, I called out to Maite: "I'll be back in a moment for my toast." I already knew that it would be a trying day as I mustered my strength to ascend the two flights of steep steps without a break halfway up.

Chapter 6

AFTER I LOOKED IN on the girls, still wondering about their symptoms and inconsistent stories, I left the old stone house through the door on the south side with Muffin trotting along beside me. We circled behind the house and walked past the water cistern on the north side toward the entrance of the church, which was facing east. It was a roundabout route to the front of the church, it meant avoiding the ruins of the fire-damaged buildings that once stood on the south side. A few goats were nibbling at the overgrown vegetation near the sanctuary, the heavy bells around their necks clanging as they lifted their heads to examine us as we passed. Muffin barked at them, causing them to scatter, but she quieted down when I snapped my fingers in her direction. The goats and the horses were problematic at times; they had a tendency to steal things from the site. They dragged rope and small tools off while the students charged after them to recover the stolen items. We couldn't easily replace materials at San Miguel, so each element was crucial, and we couldn't afford to lose a single one. Though the animals were mischievous, I took pleasure in their presence. They were a source of entertainment far from the world of cinemas and restaurants.

I stopped off at what constituted a stable for the donkeys, a rickety old shed made of rough wood open to the south to avoid the tempestuous northern winds. I'd smuggled a carrot from the kitchen for Margarita and Mauricio. I snapped it in two and they gobbled up the treats from the palms of my hands. I wiped the donkey saliva on my khaki pants, already stained with dirt and other unidentifiable substances. I remembered the days when we used to excavate in long skirts, the only appropriate garment for women in those days, and thanked heaven that we'd advanced enough to accept women in pants. I didn't dig much these days, nor did Bill — our backs and knees were not what they'd been — but I still appreciated the comfort of not having to tuck my skirt up when I crouched down to examine something.

I left the donkeys and continued east, the sun already high in the sky, the clouds dispersed. I could see the dark blue outline of the Pyrenees, and I smiled at the sensational view. The small things made life enjoyable.

As I rounded the corner of the church, I saw Archie, Janis, Roger, Patrick, and Graham busily extending the excavation, as Bill instructed. They worked within the newly demarcated area, removing the topsoil with pickaxes and then shovelling the dirt out and into a waiting wheelbarrow. The exposed skeletons were covered with a tarp to protect them while the students carried out the work.

"How are things going here?" I asked, surveying the students as they exerted themselves to dig down to lower levels.

"Great, Mrs. Forster." Archie placed his pick over his right shoulder and wiped some sweat from his brow with his left hand. "I hope we can get down to the legs today if we work fast. Would you be able to add the extension to your site plan this afternoon?"

"I don't see why not," I said, feeling a slight twinge in my lower back as I swivelled to examine the area to be added to the site plan. "I'll check back in a little bit and see how things are progressing."

I also needed to draw the skeletons in situ. We photographed everything these days, but having a detailed illustration could sometimes be more effective than a photograph. I liked to have a separate drawing of each individual for our records. With practice, I'd become quite efficient over the years.

"Janis." I saw that she was taking a momentary break from digging and decided to ask her about the events of the previous night. "Could I speak to you a moment, please?"

Janis stepped up and out of the excavation area, and she joined me on the grass under a tree.

"Yes, Mrs. Forster?" She sounded hesitant as she brushed some dirt off her arm with a gloved hand.

"Janis, did you know you were sleepwalking last night?" still by my side.

"Well, I guess so." Janis pushed her sun hat back so that it hung from the adjustable string around her neck. "Roger said something this morning. Well, there were a few comments this morning. I guess I scared the other girls this time."

"So you know you've been sleepwalking?"

Janis nodded. "Miriam has mentioned it a few times. She says I go down to the kitchen sometimes. I don't actually mean to, Mrs. Forster. I can't help it."

"I understand, dear." I felt sorry for her. I knew sleep alterations were not well understood. "Do you remember what you did when you were sleepwalking?" I wondered if she knew she retrieved a knife from the kitchen and held it over Miriam as she slept.

"You mean the knife?"

I nodded.

"I mean, I don't remember when I wake up—maybe I feel like I had a dream or something, but I don't have specific memories of what I've done. I do know about the knife, though. Roger told me about that too."

"Well, mind you, don't take what Roger says too seriously," I said, swatting a fly away from my hair. "Now off you go back to work, Janis"

One of Bill's silly literary references, this time to Mary Shelley's most famous work, it was Muffin's signal that she was free to roam and terrorize the mountain's four-legged dwellers. Though certainly less hideous than Frankenstein's monster, Muffin had the ability to strike fear into the hearts of many a critter minding its own business in the mountains. She knew she wasn't allowed into the excavation area, but she loved to explore, chase, dig, or even just sunbathe when the weather was nice.

"I'll go see what's happening in the church if you've got things under control here, Archie," I shouted back to him before I left.

"No problem, Mrs. Forster." Archie smiled and walked closer to me, his freckles wrinkling under his eyes. "I saw Father Pedro and Father José María arrive just a few minutes ago. Oh, by the way, how are the girls?"

I could tell he was trying to sound casual, but it was clear he was concerned.

"They're a bit under the weather, but I think with some rest they'll be fine. Who knows? They might even make an appearance for lunch. It's rare for students to skip a meal."

I winked at Archie knowingly, and he chuckled. At the beginning of the excavation, both Helen and Graham had been unwell for a morning, saying they were ill and needed to rest in the house. It was evident they were just tired and sore from the physical exertion the day before, something they weren't at all used to. They were accustomed to spending their days at the university, where the most vigorous exercise was walking from one class to another. Their brief illnesses hadn't surprised me in the least, and it wasn't the first time I'd seen tender muscles exaggerated into an ailment. Needless to say, they'd emerged from their rooms when lunch was served. It's hard to ignore a rumbling stomach, regardless of one's aching body.

I'd taken only a few steps away from the perimeter of the excavation when I bumped into a young couple with two small children. The woman wore a kerchief over her dark hair and carried a wicker basket in one hand. I couldn't see the contents, as they were covered with a linen cloth, but I guessed that the basket contained either a picnic lunch or mushrooms. It was common for people to pick mushrooms in the woods, though I had been told it was still early in the season. Families also climbed the mountain to visit the church, making an excursion of it and bringing provisions for a meal. The man looked athletic and carried a wooden walking stick in his hand. They smiled, nodding their heads in greeting, but said nothing. Not suffering from the same reserve as his parents, the little boy approached me, reached up, and tugged the sleeve of my work shirt.

In earnest Spanish, he asked me, "Are you looking for the dragon, señora? Is this where they buried the dragon?"

"Don't be stupid," the little girl proclaimed, crossing her arms in contempt for her younger sibling. She was, I guessed, two or three years older than her brother. "There are no such things as dragons."

"You're stupid," the boy responded, sticking his pink tongue out at her.

"I'm sorry," the mother said, her cheeks rosy. She grabbed the boy by the arm with her free hand and pulled him toward her. The girl ran to her father, grasping him around the waist. "Do you speak Spanish?"

People here always recognized Bill and me as foreigners, our very pale skin common among northern Europeans, whereas people in southern Europe tended to have darker, more tanned skin. That and the way we dressed; we simply couldn't blend in. It wasn't common for visitors to speak Spanish, or at least not fluently. Bill and I were often asked if we spoke the lingua franca.

"Sí, claro," I told her. "And there's no need to apologize. Children are a joy even when they misbehave. We don't see enough children up here on the mountain!"

"Thank you," the woman said, looking relieved.

"Do you like dragons, then?" I asked the little boy.

He nodded his head, suddenly shy and leaning into his mother's skirt.

"Well, we're not actually looking for the dragon here," I told him. "But you never know what you might find when you start digging. If we dig deep enough, we may find things that are very, very old! This is the exciting thing about digging. We don't know what we'll find."

I said this knowing that, in our case, it was an exaggeration. We'd already realized that we couldn't dig down very deep into the mountain, that the cemetery was shallow in depth, because the limestone of the terrain was quite close to the surface. In some cases, those that buried the dead were forced to chip away at the rock to create graves that, in another location, might have been cut into the earth alone. Nevertheless, I didn't think a little invention would hurt a young boy whose imagination was surely more fertile than my own.

He smiled at me, encouraged once more. "Have you found any coins?"

"Yes, we've found lots of coins. Some new and some very old."

"Enough to make you rich?"

"Oh no," I said. "Not as many as that! They'd not be worth many pesetas, I don't think."

The little girl stepped forward, her eyes now glittering with curiosity.

"What about swords? Did you find any swords? We have a sword in the house and Ama says it's fold." She puffed her chest out in pride.

"That's very exciting. We haven't found any swords here, unfortunately. We have found some arrowheads. Can you imagine the knights here with their bows and arrows?" I watched for her delighted reaction, knowing how much children love the imagery of medieval life, accessed through the pages of books and, if they were lucky, at the cinema or on television.

I wondered if this family had a television in their home, if they gathered together in the evenings to watch the black and white images dance across the screen. This was a privilege reserved only for families with sufficient wealth to purchase the box that had become the primary glue of family life in many homes back in Canada. Even Bill and I sat in our armchairs in the evenings, fascinated each time the CBC brought the world into our living room, no travel required. We watched, as though there in person, as our own country transformed into a new, more progressive nation than we'd known before. We laughed together when Prime Minister Lester B. Pearson announced a new Canadian flag before an emphatically disappointed audience. The new symbol, a great controversy of our time, brought with it significant emotional upheaval. But Bill and I hadn't felt quite as sentimental about the old flag as some of our countrymen.

"Uyyy!" The little boy broke away from his mother and stood next to his sister, unconsciously grabbing hold of her hand. She didn't resist. "I wish I had a bow and arrow." He then wrenched his hand away to point an invisible bow and arrow up to the sky.

His parents laughed at his moxie.

"Why don't you come back to visit us one day so we can show you some of the things we've found?" I asked. "How does that sound?"

I glanced at the parents, and they nodded. It was good for the local people to see what we were up to. Modern archaeology was meant for the benefit of the many, not the few, as it had been in the beginning.

"Thank you, señora, for your time," the mother said, once again collecting the children with her free arm. "It's very kind of you to offer. They'll have much to keep their imaginations active this week, and we'll return to see the treasures soon, I promise!"

I waved goodbye and continued toward the church. I noticed then a donkey loosely tied to a tree near the entrance. The animal would have been for Father José María to ride up the mountain, Father Pedro leading it by a rope attached to the halter. The donkey munched happily on the grass and took no notice of my approach. I imagined the two priests arriving at the sanctuary. The scene had a biblical quality to it, though I knew very well that José María wouldn't have appreciated my likening him to the Virgin Mary arriving in Bethlehem.

Chapter 7

THE HEAVY WOODEN DOOR to the church protested as I pushed it open, its rusty hinges groaning and squealing. I had a copy of the skeleton key, which I always hung on my belt so as not to lose it, but Ignacio had already unlocked the door for visitors. Although San Miguel was generally considered a safe place because of its inaccessibility, over the centuries, there were several attempted and successful burglaries of precious items from the sanctuary. The punishment for stealing from the sanctuary had traditionally been hanging, or at best a life in chains, as Father Pedro recounted when we first arrived. In one case, the hands of the thieves had been chopped off and nailed to the outside of the church, a visceral warning to those entertaining similar notions of an easy payday. It was a rather gruesome punishment. An object of particular interest to thieves was the effigy of St. Michael, a gold and silver statue of the archangel holding a cross above his head that contained a piece of the Lignum Crucis, the True Cross, brought to San Miguel in the eleventh century by the son of the King of Navarre from the conquest of Jerusalem during the Crusades. It was one of the most prized and emotive possessions of the sanctuary. It wasn't on display inside the church, rather locked up for safekeeping until mass was given and the congregants could line up for their turn to kiss the face of the relic, the officiating priest wiping St. Michael with a cloth after each pair of soft lips caressed the cold, hard glass that covered the angel's wood-carved face.

A burst of cool air from the hallway ruffled the short curls of my hair and made me shiver. The long, wide passage before me was dim because of the lack of natural light between the impenetrable stone walls. I'd expected to find Bill and the others here in the hall since the sarcophagi to be opened that day were located here. Yet the vast hallway was empty. I let the door close behind me and walked along the smooth stone floor, the sound of my rubber-soled work boots muted against the solid surface. Steps at the end of the hall led me to a large antechamber. Thanks to Father Pedro's research, we'd learned that the earlier pre-Romanesque church, built in the ninth century, was believed to have been destroyed the following century during an attack by Islamic forces. The current church dated to the eleventh century, when it was initially reconstructed, though it had seen many changes and additions over the years. What survived, if anything, of Teodosio de Goñi's original construction was uncertain. From the expansive antechamber, which was relatively bare, I could hear men's voices carried from a distance. I followed the sound up a few stairs and into the nave of the church. A small chapel, walled off by thick limestone blocks, obstructed the central area from view. To the left of the open entrance were two chains of distinct lengths and varying links, said to be the chains worn by Teodosio as punishment for parricide. I'd often seen local people who entered the church pass the chains over their heads, from shoulder to shoulder, three times for luck. Inside the chapel, there was a stone missing in the wall to the right of the altar. Legend had it that the hole went deep into the mountain to the cave of the dragon. Those who were free of sin could safely place their heads in the hole, but those who'd sinned would be scorched by the fire-breathing lizard. Nobody ever seemed to question the contradiction in the origin story of San Miguel: St. Michael had, in fact, killed the dragon. Myths have a way of captivating our imaginations without the need for critical appraisal. The hole leading to the dragon's den did, however, result in some amusement for the students. On the second day after our arrival, on a tour of the sanctuary organized by Father Pedro, every member of the team enthusiastically placed their head inside the cavity and retreated unscathed, suggesting that the dragon deep within must have been fast asleep and therefore ignorant of our virtue-testing endeavours, for surely we weren't all without sin.

I continued past the chapel to the wooden pews lined up before the altar where the faithful gathered to hear the priest give his sermon. Upon the altar was an enamel triptych dating to the twelfth century, said to have been commissioned by the King of Navarre. The metalsmiths and enamel artisans travelled all the way from Limoges in France to Pamplona to complete the work on the altarpiece. It was considered to be a great masterpiece of Romanesque goldsmithing. Father Pedro had been an invaluable source of information on the sanctuary and the treasures it contained, having done a great deal of historical research before we arrived. Though the documentation was limited, his work illuminated certain peculiarities about the place that we might not have discovered on our own.

The voices in the sacristy adjacent to the nave roused me from my thoughts. I climbed the stairs to the entryway and stepped in through the open door. Everyone turned to look at me: my husband, the two priests, and Eduardo. I noted that Eduardo had a certain knack for avoiding heavy labour, in spite of its prevalence in archaeological work. "Muy bien, Beatrix, estás aquí," Bill maintained the language in which they were already conversing, despite addressing me. "How are the girls?"

"Some are worse than others," I said. "But I think they'll be fine given some time to rest."

I didn't feel comfortable discussing the situation in front of Father José María, who was against having women as part of an archaeological team. I knew that Father Pedro interceded on our behalf and managed to obtain José María's tolerance, if not acceptance. Father Pedro seemed to have a calming effect on Father José María, who had an inexplicable fondness for Pedro despite their ideological differences. I couldn't understand Pedro's influence over the older priest, but he often acted as a buffer between the objectives of science and the traditions of religion.

"I'm so very sorry to hear that they're sick," Father Pedro said wholeheartedly. "Professor Forster told us they were unwell. If there's anything we can do, please let us know."

"This is what happens when you bring the weaker sex out of the domestic sphere and into environments where they simply do not belong," said Father José María, repeating the same arguments he had the previous day, and many times before that. "It's God's intention that women stay at home and take care of their families. They're simply not the equal of men. It's a medical fact. Many respected doctors have testified to this."

I wasn't certain in what decade exactly he'd heard these medical "facts" he put forward each time he made his arguments, but the idea seemed to have planted itself in his mind, never to be uprooted. Pedro told us he was the same age as Bill, but he appeared much older because of his stoop, his wrinkle-creased face, and his knobby fingers, the joints of which were swollen with arthritis. Had I guessed, I would've said he was at least eighty years old.

"I can't agree with you there, father," Bill objected, but his tone was soft, not aggressive. I admired his ability to remain composed when vocalizing his disagreement with another person, even if they were wildly out of touch with reality. "Women bring alternative perspectives to the world of archaeology, some that men simply wouldn't have considered. Beatrix has been instrumental in the excavations we've carried out, and I don't know what I would've done without her."

"Probably lost your glasses once or twice," I teased, hoping to move the subject of the conversation to something that didn't involve whether God intended me to be involved in a field I'd participated in for many decades.

When I was young, women were actively discouraged from pursuing many careers and pushed instead into domestic life upon marriage. Friends that studied to be teachers gave up their careers the moment they were married. Of course, the same rule didn't apply to male teachers, and some of my friends wound up choosing work life over married life. When Bill and I were married, I devoted myself to family life, as I was expected to do. Though I'd considered working in some capacity or other, societal norms were ultimately stronger than personal convictions. I was fortunate, though, that Bill always asked me to accompany him on his excavations. I learned about archaeology and physical anthropology from him, though it had never been my aim to work in the field. In the end, with my background in art, I unintentionally carved out my own niche within the discipline, making myself an essential member of an excavation team. Yet I could never shake the prejudiced comments of the majority of our male colleagues. I'd been fortunate that Bill was oblivious to many social expectations and never once questioned my abilities or right to work alongside him as an equal partner. Sadly, it seemed most women would never stop having to fight for acceptance in male-dominated environs. Women in archaeology had been fighting this ideology since the birth of the discipline. I'd used my influence to ensure that we had as many female students as male for this project, that in the hopes of giving these young women a leg up in a world that would rather see them with a baby in their arms than a pickaxe.

"Things are changing, José María," Pedro said, putting his hand on the elder priest's shoulder, accentuating the difference in height between the young priest and his stooped mentor. "Women have important roles both within and outside the home. We must not restrict their potential to contribute in many ways to society. You know very well that God hasn't blessed all women with children, so what would you have these women do? Should they not have some other fulfilling role?"

The ability or inability of a woman to bear children has nothing to do with what she could contribute to society, so at the least, Pedro was on the right track. "Progressive" was a relative term.

"Well, in that you are perhaps correct, Pedro," José María admitted, running a hand over his freshly shaved chin. "However, the current doctrine indicates that women and men are not equals and that for society to function, we must have a separation between the roles of women and men. But perhaps this is a discussion for another time and other company."

I knew especially well that I was the only one in the room that José María didn't welcome into the discussion of the value of women outside the domestic realm, regardless of whom it affected most. As I stood next to him, I examined his hunched shoulders and twisted neck. His grey hair was neatly cropped, still thick and wiry despite his age. His bent frame and priest's cassock, the traditional long black robe worn by much of the clergy, gave him a peculiar appearance, like a character from a gothic novel. He seemed pulled from another era, dropped into the sixties from the time of the Brontë sisters. I conjured up an image of him, solitary, on the edge of the mountain, his cassock at the mercy of the fierce winds, the age-old story of man battling nature. It was a romantic notion, to be sure.

"Let's get back to the task at hand, shall we?" Bill interceded. "Pedro, did you receive permission from the archbishop in Pamplona to open the tombs within the sanctuary?"

"I did, Professor Forster."

"And the archbishop understands that we may or may not find what's expected in the sarcophagi? They may be the remains of Teodosio and Constanza, or they may be the remains of other people altogether. Findings of a scientific nature cannot be altered to suit the desires of the church."

"The archbishop," Father José María stated, staring unblinkingly at Bill, "is certain that your scientific findings will coincide with the belief of the community, that the burials within the sanctuary belong to Teodosio and his wife. He has no doubt of it. Faith guides his decisions."

"I understand he has faith," Bill explained further, "but it's important to keep in mind the destruction of the original church in the tenth century, of which Father Pedro has found documentation. Assuming the remains of Teodosio and Constanza were in fact here at that time, there's no telling what might have happened to them. And we have no real way of being certain that whatever remains are in the tombs are actually those of Constanza and Teodosio without an inscription or some material finds that suggest the identity of these individuals."

The study of skeletal remains advanced a great deal in the past decades, although it was not an exact science that could provide all the answers people hoped to gain from their study.

"It will be them," José María assured everyone.

"We have faith it's Teodosio and Constanza," Pedro amended the older priest's statement. "And with scientific advances, we hope that one day there will be irrefutable evidence of their identities. Until then, the archbishop wishes to ensure that the remains are safe. When construction begins, there will be many people coming to the mountain to work, and keeping all the valuable objects secure here will be difficult. Many things will be sent to Pamplona for security reasons, including the remains."

I knew Bill was sceptical about even the existence of Teodosio and Constanza. The details of their story had been greatly distorted through the centuries. Of course, Bill hadn't said this to either priest, given their seeming belief in the veracity of the tale. Had Teodosio de Goñi actually existed? It was a fascinating tale, but perhaps we'd never know if truth had espoused legend at San Miguel.

"Well, let's go and have a look, shall we?" Bill said, starting toward the door. "They're not getting any younger, and neither are we."

"Professor Forster." Eduardo was one step behind Bill, a question on his lips. He spoke Spanish fluently, unlike the other students, and he could follow the conversations in both languages, giving him a distinct advantage at this site. His father was a colleague of Bill's, in the area of Mesoamerican archaeology. Though they had different specializations, they'd maintained an antagonistic relationship during Bill's years at the university, a tense professional rivalry that escalated a few times into verbal jousting matches. It was uncharacteristic of Bill to get into that kind of argument, but Professor Reyes Iglesias seemed to strike a nerve. When Eduardo applied to join the excavation in Navarre, I had my reservations, despite my feelings about his father, I rather liked the bespectacled young man with tanned skin and shiny black hair. "How are we going to lift the tomb lids? Won't they be heavy?"

"We'll be lifting together, Eduardo, with the assistance of some rollers. Not to worry. I certainly won't be lifting a stone lid by myself, and I don't expect anybody else here wants to either."

"Do you think he'll have been buried with his sword?" Eduardo continued, following Bill in much the same way Muffin did. Given Bill's height, and Eduardo's small stature, he was forced to look up at Bill as he walked.

"I don't know, Eduardo." With Bill's long stride, Eduardo, Father José María, and I had to scurry to keep up. Father Pedro, on the other hand, was not vertically challenged and easily matched Bill's gait. "It's hard to predict. You've seen the burials from the medieval period, and they have few or no grave goods in them. Christian belief was that we don't take our worldly possessions with us to heaven, so it didn't make sense to bury people with objects of value. Perhaps, when Teodosio was originally buried, when not everyone converted to Christianity yet, he might have been laid to rest according to local customs, not necessarily Christian traditions. However, we do not know if this is his original sarcophagus. That might have been destroyed during the attack on the church. We simply won't know much until we open things up."

"The people here have been Christian from early times...Professor," Father José María interjected, out of breath as he struggled to keep pace with the group. "We had a Bishop in Pamplona as early as the third century...San Fermín himself was the first bishop of Pamplona...Teodosio was most certainly a Christian...St. Michael would not have saved him otherwise."

"Of course, Father José María," Bill replied, unaware that some of us laboured to keep up. "The story of Teodosio does indicate that he was

Christian. But the person that was in charge of his burial didn't necessarily follow all the traditions of Christianity. Many pagan customs carried on despite mass conversion. In fact, we'd be very much in luck if he'd been buried with grave goods, as they give us clues to the identity or status of the person and the period during which he was buried. This would be quite fortunate."

"Perhaps," Father José María replied brusquely.

We exited the church and stood in the passage facing the northern wall that contained two alcoves with carved stone sarcophagi. The lids were of dimpled, ivory-coloured limestone, with some decorative details around the edges but no other distinctive markings. Not even an inscription to convey to the generations of visitors to the sanctuary the identity of the persons laid within. We observed some social stratification in the burials at San Miguel. We knew the sarcophagi inside the sanctuary belonged to exceptional people, since they were tucked away safely inside rather than in the graveyard east of the church's apse, where most people were buried in humble graves lined with irregularly shaped stones or simply in a shallow pit dug into the ground. The people in the tombs within the church had most likely been of importance and rank at the time they died. We'd seen some distinction between graves in the cemetery, as some burials were evidently created with more care than others, even made with shaped stones. However, despite differences in how they were buried, the bodies we exhumed from the graves were much the same.

Bill examined the edges of the sarcophagus lid, which was greater in dimension than the stone box beneath.

"Perhaps we should call Roger and some of the others," Bill said, seeming to have forgotten our discussion of the night before about including all the students in opening the tombs. "There's something to be said for brute strength in archaeology."

"Brute is right," Eduardo said under his breath.

"Eduardo, could you please run outside and get the others to come in?" Bill asked. "The lid will be quite heavy, and we don't want to damage it."

I was glad he was getting help. The last thing I needed was for him to put his back out.

"Young people are extremely useful for this kind of thing," Father José María mused.

Within a few minutes, all the students who'd been working outside were eagerly loitering around the first tomb.

"It's a shame not everyone is here for this," Father Pedro lamented.

"Your concern is appreciated, Pedro," I said, assuming he was referring to the missing students. "You shouldn't worry. They can come out when they feel better and have a look first hand. They're really only missing the first moments of excitement, the moment of discovery, before the real work begins."

"Of course, of course," Pedro said, casting a smile in my direction. "I'm really very pleased that you invited us here today."

Certainly, this was a lesser event in the history of great finds in archaeology. It would be of most importance to the local people, who venerated St. Michael and could actually be descendants of the people buried at San Miguel. Unless we made some extraordinary find, it would be of little relevance to the international archaeological community. Bill didn't take into consideration the attention and recognition a project would garner when he decided where to excavate, and I was glad of it. It wasn't funny when your derriere showed up more than your face in a newsreel. I'd learned my lesson about the press.

I heard footsteps in the hallway and turned to see Maite. I was surprised. Prior to today, she'd shown almost no interest in the excavation whatsoever, except as related to our schedule and dietary needs.

"Maite," I greeted her. "Have you come to see the opening of the tomb?"

"Curiosity got the best of me, Beatriz," she grinned abashedly. "Dead bodies give me the willies, if you know what I mean. But who could resist seeing something that's been untouched for so long?

"All right, Roger," Bill directed, returning the general conversation to English for the benefit of the students. He collected two metal cylinders that were resting against the wall. "You take the east end with

Janis. Archie, you take the west with Patrick. You'll have to stand perpendicular to one another because of the lack of space. We'll lift one end of the lid at a time, and when you lift it up, I'll slide the rollers into place so you can rest the lid on them gently. There's not enough space in the alcove to roll the lids off entirely, but it's a start. We'll roll the lid to the west until there's no longer room for Patrick to stand. Then we'll have to do some maneuvering if we don't have clearance to tip the lid vertically. Everything clear?"

Those involved nodded and wrapped their fingers around the cool stone of the lid. Archaeologists were always aware of the cardinal directions on site, as it was crucial for descriptions of location. On day one, everyone became well acquainted with north, standing in the cemetery and looking up toward the highest peak of Mount Archueta.

"Archie and Patrick, you lift on three," Bill said, preparing to slide one of the rollers into position. "One, two, three, lift."

With some effort, they raised the west end of the lid up long enough for Bill to slide a roller into the gap. At Bill's command, Janis and Roger repeated the process on the east end. The team then began to slowly roll the lid toward the west. I realized I'd been holding my breath. My chest, ready to explode, compressed the air out in a rapid, audible, hiss. Bill turned to look at me, his mouth taking a round shape, ready to speak, but he didn't have the chance. Roger released a blood-curdling scream. He bumped into Janis in his effort to escape from the tomb, causing her to put all her weight on one of the rollers. I watched in shock as the sarcophagus lid toppled to the ground, the collision of limestone against limestone smashing it into dozens of pieces.

Chapter 8

"GOOD LORD!" Bill exclaimed, his face contorted in disbelief. "What in blazes happened? Is anyone hurt? What happened?"

We all instinctively approached the now open tomb to see what lay inside, except Roger, who was already a good distance away, a horrified look on his face as though he'd seen the very dragon of Aralar. Janis inspected the contents first and started to laugh as soon as she looked inside the open sarcophagus. I couldn't imagine what could be funny as I stepped over shards of broken stone and peered over the edge of the coffin.

"Goodness me," I whispered.

"They're just snakes," Janis proclaimed, a smile on her face. "Nothing to scream about."

Inside the tomb, where a skeleton ought to have been, was nothing but a squirming mass of long, thin, black and tan bodies knitted into a complex, writhing corpus that brought to mind a certain mythical woman. I heard Maite gasp beside me, then she crossed herself. It was the first time I'd seen her do it.

"Don't touch them!" Father Pedro shouted in English as Janis reached inside the stone coffin. "Those are vipers, and they are poisonous!"

"Venomous," Janis whispered, correcting Pedro's misnomer as she quickly withdrew her hand.

He didn't seem to notice.

"How on Earth did they get in there?" Bill asked. "There's no opening to the sarcophagus, no crack, nothing. And where in blazes is the body that's supposed to be here?"

"Goodness, Bill, let's not worry about that now," I said, standing next to him and placing my hand on his arm. "First, how are we going to get rid of them? We can't just leave them there, for our sakes and theirs. We can solve the mystery of the missing body and the appearance of the snakes later."

"Just kill them," Father José María said coldly in his mother tongue, glancing momentarily at the vipers and then turning his back on them as though they were unpleasant weeds growing in the garden. "You can use a shovel to chop their heads off. We've had to do it before when they had their nests too close to the sanctuary. For the safety of our congregants, of course."

José María stalked off down the passageway, presumably to obtain a shovel from the work site.

"Wait, José María!" Father Pedro demanded. "Don't forget that these are God's creatures too. They do more good than evil, keeping pests away from the sanctuary."

"Yes, but they're extraordinarily dangerous," Father José María insisted, turning back to face his junior, his eyes flashing a warning. "They can easily kill us if we can't access the necessary medicines quickly enough. You know this. The Bible also suggests a different interpretation of snakes than your own, Pedro."

"True, perhaps we can move them quite far from the sanctuary, somewhere in the forest. Spare their lives. Ignacio is used to dealing with these kinds of things. We can ask him to help us."

"Fine, Pedro. Deal with this as you wish."

Father José María turned and trudged away from us, his head awkwardly preceding his body because of his spinal disfigurement. At that moment, I had to admit I agreed somewhat with José María. If we killed the vipers, at least we'd be certain they couldn't hurt anybody. I hoped Ignacio would see to that.

"Archie, please take the students for their tea break and then continue working outside at the excavation area until lunchtime," Bill said, having gotten over the shock of the absent skeleton. "We'll get things sorted here."

The students obediently followed Archie toward the wooden door. I wondered what chatter would ensue once they were out of earshot.

"I'll go find Ignacio," Father Pedro said, his shoulders slumped and his smile strained.

I imagined this would have been as disappointing for him as for Bill, yet he remained composed, putting the well-being of the vipers ahead of his frustration. As I watched him follow the others down the hallway, I realized this was one of the things I admired most about him.

"I'll go with you," Maite said quietly, she looked anxious and was rolling her thumb over the beads of a rosary. She must have had it in the pocket of her apron.

Bill and I were left alone with the snakes, the empty sarcophagus, and the smashed lid. I put my hands on my hips and sighed. I'd seen precious artifacts crushed into thousands of fragments before. This was just a piece of stone, no matter how long ago it had been carefully shaped by the hands of an artisan. I'd learned not to overthink the things that were beyond my control.

"Beatrix, I can understand the removal of a skeleton from a grave. It could have happened anytime in the last millennium. It wouldn't be unheard of. Bodies disappear all the time, for many reasons, as we know well. There's no way that these snakes arrived here on their own. It's impossible. Someone must have put them there on purpose, knowing that we'd find them at some point. The question is: is this a bad joke, or is someone trying to scare us off?"

"Goodness, if it's a joke, it's in poor taste at best. Only Janis found it amusing, and I can't say that her sense of humour is standard issue. I don't know what to say. There haven't been any other incidents to suggest someone wanted us gone, have there? Have we become oblivious in our old age? There's always the possibility that someone wants to ruin the excavation."

I tried not to jump to conclusions, but my thoughts danced around Professor Reyes Iglesias, his smug smile, his arrogant voice. I wouldn't put it past him to use his son to tamper with our work, but Eduardo didn't seem the type to cause mischief, at least not something serious like this. I went over to the tomb and examined it without leaning in too close. Bill was right, there were no holes or gaps that would've permitted the snakes to enter. The lid had been on tight, so the vipers hadn't slipped between it and the coffin either. At some point, and recently, someone placed them inside the tomb. Most likely, they'd also known we'd discover the vipers within a reasonable amount of time, assuming their intent was to frighten us. A living snake elicits quite a different reaction than a dead one. There was also the weight of the lid to be considered. It was incredibly heavy, so the culprit probably hadn't acted alone. This made me further doubt Eduardo's involvement – who would he have enlisted him to help? The students wanted to impress us, not undermine months of their own hard work. It was clear to me that no ordinary person would be able to lift the lid without assistance, though I recalled then that Maite regaled us with tales of the Basque strongmen, and sometimes even women, whose sport consisted very simply of lifting the heaviest of stones, weighing hundreds of pounds each. The *harrijasotzaileak*, they were called in Basque. I'd asked Maite to write the word, a complete tongue-twister for English speakers, on a piece of paper. She acquiesced, but after I looked at it, she crumpled the paper and threw it into a pile of garbage. Her action didn't surprise me, as she'd spoken often of the repression after the civil war. After coming to power in the late 1930s, Franco outlawed the minority languages spoken in Spain. Basque, Galician, Catalan, and many other languages became a liability if spoken in the public realm. For some, it was their only language when the Franco regime began. People were forced to abandon the language they'd spoken since words first graced their lips; they had to learn Spanish instead. Though I knew that the linguistic politics of the postwar period had relaxed greatly, people still carried the paranoia and fear from those early years with them even decades later, despite hearing the language bandied about in public once more.

"Who even has access to this area?" I asked. "It's locked at night and in the mornings until Ignacio opens up for any visitors that make the trek. Except for Sundays, that's usually very few people. A few families for a picnic here and there or the odd shepherd checking on the sheep and goats. We aren't exactly on the main tourist circuit here at San Miguel."

"It may be few people, but anybody that comes up the mountain can access the church from nine in the morning until six at night."

"Yes, but Bill, someone would've noticed something, would they not have? Ignacio comes and goes throughout the day to check on things. Surely he would've said something if he'd seen someone tampering with the tomb."

"I don't know. Ignacio has lots of work that keeps him outside. And as for us, we're almost always working outdoors or in the house. We might not have noticed who went in or out of the church. The farmers sometimes stop by when they check on the animals. And the priests and nuns come to visit. But they all seem unlikely candidates. The archbishop has given his express permission for this work, so it doesn't make sense for anyone with an association to the church to go against his wishes. And the farmers and shepherds have no reason to want us gone. We don't interfere with the animals in any way, other than Muffin's occasional attempts at herding, which we have tried to keep under control. She hasn't caused injury to any animals—she just spooks them from time to time. Don't you think if there were a problem they would simply come speak to us about it rather than resorting to what equates to vandalism?"

"I agree. But you should speak to Ignacio to find out who comes and goes anyway. Just in case. It makes me uncomfortable that someone could do this right under our noses and nobody saw a thing."

"Yes, I'd certainly like to get to the bottom of this," Bill said, stroking the bristly white hairs that populated his chin.

He paced back and forth in the hallway, lost in thought, while we waited for Father Pedro to return with Ignacio. I kept an eye on the vipers to make sure they couldn't slither up the side of the stone coffin and escape. Not that I would've stopped them if they'd tried, but it would be good to know just how many snakes were loose in the church if we did have to hunt them down.

Sunlight streamed into the passage as the door creaked open, and two dark silhouettes appeared in the entryway, backlit by the brightness of the natural light. They hurried toward us, and I recognized Father Pedro and Ignacio as they approached.

"How did they get in?" I heard Ignacio ask Pedro.

"We haven't figured that out yet," Pedro replied, his cassock flowing behind him as he strode toward us.

Ignacio carried a wooden box in his left hand and a shovel in his right. He nodded in greeting when he reached us.

"Excellent," Bill said, motioning for Ignacio to approach the open tomb. "Thank you for coming."

"It's a nest," Ignacio said, peering into the sarcophagus. His long hair dangled in front of his face. He wasn't wearing his beret, so I guessed that Pedro found him inside the house. "These are all young vipers."

"Any idea how they came to be here?" Bill asked.

Ignacio looked at him for a moment. "No," he said, setting the box down on one of the fragments of stone lid and then pushing the hair out of his face. "If I find a nest near the sanctuary, I burn it. Kills a few, and the rest disappear and usually don't come back. It's a good way to get rid of them."

"You won't be burning these, will you?" Pedro asked. He looked concerned. "Just take them far enough away, and they won't come back."

"I'll do what I can," Ignacio said unfeelingly.

He appeared unmoved by Father Pedro's plea to save the vipers.

Ignacio went to work, scooping the snakes out of the tomb with the shovel and putting them into the uncovered box. He made a quick job of it, placing the lid on the box once the last viper was dropped inside. He nodded and then disappeared without saying anything more.

"I hope he doesn't just kill them," Father Pedro said, staring after him.

Chapter 9

EVERYONE APPEARED in the kitchen for lunch, except Miriam and Angela. Even Helen descended, looking a little sheepish as she took a place at the long wooden table. Father José María had a brooding expression on his face. Ignacio made eye contact with nobody, staring vigilantly at the table. Fortunately, the students didn't seem to notice the tension in the air and chatted away about why there was no skeleton in the tomb and about how close they'd come to being bitten by a venomous snake. Helen, forgetting how sick she'd been earlier, whined that she hadn't seen the vipers. Maite prepared lentils with vegetables for lunch, using a ladle to scoop the round, flat legumes out of the pot and into the dishes held out by hungry priests and archaeologists.

"Looks delicious," said Father Pedro as the steam wafted up toward his face from his bowl. "Thank you, Maite."

She smiled at him kindly. As she did with the students, she had a soft spot for the young priest. Father Pedro was always polite, always grateful.

At the table, the students clustered at one end, the rest of us at the other. I could tell Bill was deep in thought as he made figure eights in his stew with his spoon, over and over again, never lifting the utensil to his lips.

"Pasa algo? Is something wrong?" Maite asked Bill, noticing, as I had, that he wasn't eating.

No response.

"Seems he's entered another dimension," I teased, switching from Spanish for Maite to English for my husband. "Bill! Bill, dear, eat up!"

He was startled out of his reverie and dropped the spoon, which clanked against the ceramic bowl.

"Oh, yes...of course. Lunch." He obediently took up his spoon, dipped it into the lentils, and lifted it to his mouth.

Everyone raised their eyes when the kitchen door, which was left ajar, slowly squeaked all the way open. For a moment, I thought it would be Miriam or Angela, hungry and wanting something to eat. But no person walked through the doorway. I had to raise my derriere off the bench and look down to see that the intruder was pudgy and pink, its flattened snout turned up as it sniffed out the source of the smell that drifted outside the house. Francisco trotted into the kitchen as though it were his home and we were the visitors. I had to stifle my laughter with my napkin to my face when Maite jumped up from the table and used a towel she usually kept tucked into the waistband of her apron to try shooing Francisco out of the room. The circus didn't need an additional act.

"Go on, Francisco, you're not supposed to be in here. Out you go."

But the pig ignored her towel and scooted around her.

Father José María, his face flushed in anger, stood up, hovering over the table, his eyes fixated on Ignacio. "What is that pig doing in here?"

"He's just looking for food," Ignacio replied, maintaining his composure, not lifting his eyes to meet the forbidding gaze of the priest. "I didn't have time to feed him. I was looking after the vipers."

"You show a clear lack of respect for the Caudillo by calling that beast Francisco," José María shouted. "You should be locked up for such an offense. Pigs don't need names. They're animals put on this Earth by God for consumption by man. To keep such an animal as a pet, giving it such a name, is profane. You should be ashamed."

I glanced at the students. All were staring, most wore blank looks on their faces. Only Eduardo could understand exactly what was being said.

"Come now, Father," Maite intervened, turning her back on the ungulate who, thus far, refused to leave the kitchen. "Franco is not the only Francisco to have existed. Ignacio gave his pig a common name. There are many Franciscos. I'm sure he meant no offense by it."

Although Maite didn't seem particularly fond of Ignacio, she had a certain affection for Francisco, as many of us did. I'd seen her often secret kitchen scraps to the pig outside when she thought nobody was looking, speaking to him softly and caressing his head and snout with her hands. Eventually, we'd all begun to treat him as though he weren't much different from Muffin, though he wasn't actually allowed inside the house.

"I'll take offense to that which is offensive. And I deem this to be repugnant. We must uphold the utmost respect for the highest authority after God in this country. Ignacio, you'll get that swine out of this kitchen at once, or you can pack your belongings and you and your pig can leave the sanctuary immediately. Is that clear?"

"Perfectly, father," Ignacio said quietly, rising from the table. He called for Francisco to follow and the pig scurried happily after him.

No one dared say anything to Father José María, whose face revealed that the absence of the pig did nothing to diminish his foul mood. We were all here with José María's permission, and he could revoke it as easily as he'd given it. I had no doubt that there was a point where Father Pedro's influence reached its limit, and I hoped we'd not discover it in the near future.

I glanced once more at the students and saw that Eduardo was quietly summarizing the scene that just played out for the others who hadn't understood, though I imagined that they'd gathered the essence of the situation without their speaking a word of Spanish.

"I think we should go ahead and open the other sarcophagus after lunch," Bill said suddenly, breaking the muted atmosphere of the room. "I'm curious to see if that one's empty as well, and since Father Pedro and Father José María are here today, it's best not to wait, in case there should be something of interest there."

I looked across at Bill, wondering if he'd been lost in thought during the entire argument between the priest and the caretaker. It was certainly a possibility.

Chapter 10

AS SOON AS I FINISHED my lentils, I excused myself and went upstairs to check on the girls. I knocked softly and entered without waiting for them to reply. Both girls were in bed. Miriam was reading a book and looked startled when I came in. Angela was asleep and remained so despite my sudden appearance.

"How are you?" I whispered softly as I approached Miriam's bed and crouched down next to her.

"I'm feeling a bit better than before," she replied, placing the book on the rough blanket that covered her.

"I'm glad to hear that. What about Angela? She looks rather pale, even for her."

"She's been asleep for a while. She vomited a lot this morning. She's been sleeping since. I was only sick a few times, but now I feel better. I think she has it much worse than I do, whatever it is."

"Goodness," I said, noticing that once again Miriam said Angela had been vomiting when Angela told me she wasn't able to. The inconsistencies between their stories concerned me, but I didn't feel it right to accuse either of lying. I wondered if this had anything to do with the tombs in the church, but I couldn't immediately conceive of a connection. "I'm a bit worried about her. But if you both have the same thing, and you're on the mend, then she should feel better soon too. Now, if you're feeling well enough, we're going to open the second sarcophagus this afternoon. Would you like to come down for that?"

Miriam smiled briefly and then looked over at Angela, the smile fading from her lips. She wasn't a sweet girl like Angela. She was tough and opinionated, but it was clear that she cared deeply for her friend.

"Let her sleep for now," I said to Miriam, seeing the conflict in her eyes. "A good rest will give her a chance to recover, and we'll check back on her later."

Miriam nodded, already pulling the blanket and sheets away from her. "I just need to get dressed and I'll be right down, Mrs. Forster."

"Good, you know where to find us," I said standing up, the familiar pinch in my knees making me wince.

As I descended the stairs, I bumped into Father Pedro and Father José María deep in conversation in the darkened stairwell. They both stopped talking as soon as they saw me. I knew I'd intruded on a private exchange. Muffin, oblivious to the awkward encounter, dashed down the stairs to paw at Father Pedro's cassock.

"Mrs. Forster," he said, addressing me in English and smiling despite my inconvenient appearance. He bent over to oblige the small dog begging for attention, pausing momentarily to adjust his glasses as they slid down his nose. "We were just taking our bags up to our room. We'll stay the night here, if it's no inconvenience to you. There's so much happening. We wouldn't want to miss anything important!"

I hadn't noticed that both priests held small overnight bags. Of course, it wasn't up to me whether they stayed the night or not. It was their prerogative, and they stayed often enough at the sanctuary to avoid the awkward trip up and down the mountain. I did, however, appreciate Pedro's efforts to make us feel at home when we were in fact the guests.

"Goodness, of course! We're always glad to have the company, and we wouldn't want either of you to miss any important discoveries. We had some bad luck this morning. Perhaps we'll find something of interest this afternoon."

"I certainly hope so," Father José María said peevishly, his sour mood little improved from lunchtime. "Otherwise, this entire expedition will have been for nothing. We must find Teodosio for this to have any value."

"Remember what I told you, José María," Pedro said, placing a hand on the older priest's stooped shoulder. It was a gesture I'd seen Pedro employ frequently when José María became vexed for one reason or another. "There are no certainties in archaeology. We can only find what's there to be found, not that which we hope to find. We must prepare ourselves both for the joy of discovery and the anguish of disappointment."

"If it's God's will, we'll find him."

"Exactly. If it's God's will."

Father Pedro seemed to drift between the worlds of anthropology and theology. Though he was familiar with anthropological methodologies and had an understanding of archaeological practice, I could tell he also believed in the teachings of the church and that God had some role to play even in scientific activities.

"Perhaps Bill could show you some of the other remains we found in the cemetery," I interjected. "They may be of interest as well. Bill hopes they'll tell us more about the population that lived here in the medieval period. Pedro indicated that there's little historical documentation. Perhaps these excavations will illuminate what life was like at San Miguel a thousand years ago, who lived and died here on the mountain. There'll be time later to visit the lab, since you're staying the night."

"Thank you, Mrs. Forster." Pedro's smile was soft and genuine. "That's very kind of you. We'd like that very much. We'll meet you in the church once we've dropped our bags off upstairs."

I left them and made my way out, around the back of the house, and toward the entrance to the church. The donkeys brayed as I walked past the stable, but I had nothing to feed them this time. Mauricio and Margarita were now sharing their shelter with the donkey brought by the priests that day. I ignored their plaintive calls for attention. As I walked past the cemetery excavation site, I noticed Ignacio headed down the mountain with his shotgun, Francisco jogging behind. I wondered if he'd catch anything this time. Or whether he'd tell us if he did. I waited until they were out of sight before releasing Muffin to explore. I didn't want her following them into the woods. Not when Ignacio had a weapon with him.

I grimaced at the screeching as the wooden door to the church scraped over the ground. One could never grow accustomed to such noises. Inside, I found most of the students gathered around Bill, chattering excitedly about what the second sarcophagus might contain. Bill always loved the enthusiasm of the students, and his excitement matched theirs. It was as though the disappointment of that morning dissipated like steam from a kettle into the surrounding atmosphere. Nothing could be so exhilarating for Bill as making a new discovery. In that sense, I was different. I liked to take my time with any artifacts, analyzing the minute details, the incredible things that humans were capable of creating. It was in the gradual revelation of ancient secrets that I attained the maximum gratification.

"It's going to be empty, just like the other one," Helen stated matter-of-factly, putting a damper on the conversation.

"You weren't even here for the other one," Janis retorted.

"Plus, it wasn't exactly empty," Roger added. "We did find something." The students who'd been present laughed nervously.

"We'll cross our fingers for better luck this time," Bill said. Then, noticing I'd joined the group: "Beatrix, have you seen the Fathers?"

"They were just dropping their bags off upstairs and said they'd be right down. Miriam will be joining us shortly as well."

"I'm here, Mrs. Forster." Miriam's voice echoed in the passage behind me. I hadn't heard her come in since I'd left the door wide open for the others.

"Good," I said, smiling at her.

"Miriam, glad to have you back," Bill said. "Are you all better, then?"

"Just about, Professor Forster," she said timidly, which was unlike her.

"You look well," Archie added, giving her arm a quick squeeze. "We were all sorry you missed the entertainment this morning."

Miriam blushed but didn't reply.

Archie was our first choice to help supervise the field school, and we'd been pleased when he accepted without hesitation, though it meant leaving his new wife behind for several months. He was one of Bill's undergraduate students, and after a master's at another university, he'd returned to Toronto to do his PhD with one of Bill's colleagues. Though Bill was officially retired, he took an interest in Archie's work, and Archie frequently went to Bill for advice. He was such a responsible young man that we'd often had him look after our house when we were away and our children couldn't help. Graduate students always appreciated a little extra money, though Archie no longer suffered from financial constraints. We'd been able to trust Archie completely with our dogs. He was a well brought up young man.

"Archie, how much longer do you anticipate it will take to finish the extension?" Bill asked.

"I'd say at least another couple of hours. I've had the students switch to small tools above where the legs should be so we don't damage the bones with the larger implements."

"Good. I'd like to have those skeletons out by end of day tomorrow, if possible. So make sure you've got each of the levels above the skeletons excavated and recorded, and we'll get to those skeletons tomorrow. We were lucky it didn't rain last night and things were dry this morning. Let's hope we don't get any rain tonight so we can keep up the momentum."

"We'll get that done, Professor Forster. Don't worry." Archie smiled confidently, holding his wide-brimmed excavation hat in front of him.

A few minutes later, the priests arrived, followed by Maite.

"Back again?" I asked her.

She nodded, but her demeanour was more subdued than usual. I noticed she was holding the rosary again in her hand and that her thumbnail clicked over each bead as she pulled it through her fingers with her other hand.

"Well, let's see what we discover this time, shall we?" Bill rested his hand on the lid as though trying to get a sense of what might be inside. "Who wants to do the honours?"

Roger piped up first: "I will."

"Remember, we don't want to smash the lid this time," Bill stepped away from the sarcophagus and adjusted his glasses.

"I can handle it, professor," Roger said assuredly, flexing his biceps for everyone to see. "Even if we do uncover a nest of vipers, I'll be ready this time."

"I can help too," Pedro volunteered.

He was quite fit, despite a studious rather than active profession. I guessed it might have something to do with walking rather than riding up and down the mountain, an unforeseen benefit bestowed upon him by Father José María.

"I'm in," Archie proclaimed.

I looked over at Janis, expecting her to jump at the opportunity, but she kept silent. I wondered if she was afraid of dropping the coffin lid again.

"Go on, Janis," I encouraged her. "They'll need your help too."

It seemed all she needed was a little encouragement. She stepped forward and wrapped her fingers around the edge of the lid. Patrick stayed back this time, leaning casually against the wall of the passageway, keeping the silence that created his somewhat veiled persona.

"All right, let's get started then," Bill said. "Same procedure as last time. Anybody not lifting, let's give our labourers a bit of room, shall we?"

The rest of us stepped back compliantly. Bill counted, and they lifted the east end of the heavy lid up so Bill could slide a roller in. Next, they worked at the west end. Once both metal cylinders were in place, they rolled the lid west until Pedro had to step out of the alcove and hold the lid on the south side with Archie. Through a series of rolling and tipping maneuvers orchestrated by Bill, they were able to bring the lid down to the ground safely this time. There was an audible, communal sigh of relief. Everyone remained immobile and silent as Bill stepped around the lid to examine the contents of the sarcophagus. Being small of stature, I stood on tiptoe to see what was inside, but the effort was fruitless. I needed to get closer to see over the edge of the burial structure. Bill's expression told me he wasn't pleased with what he saw.

"What is it?" Janis burst the hush that fell over us.

"Come on over and have a look, but please don't touch anything," Bill warned us.

I went over to the edge of the tomb and looked inside while bodies all around me pushed and jostled for a position to see what it contained. My heart fell a little when I saw what was there.

Chapter II

I'D HOPED TO SEE a single skeleton, with luck carefully laid out inside the tomb. The arms crossed over the chest or pelvis, or perhaps straight along the sides of the body. The legs straight, side by side, or crossed at the ankles. What I saw instead was a jumble of bones, all mixed together as though someone dumped boxes full of body parts into the sarcophagus. I could clearly see two skulls on the surface of the pile, but a closer look told me there were at least three bodies, or parts of bodies. I counted three right femora, the largest bone in the body and, thus, easy to identify and even determine the side of the body from which it came without touching it. Of course, a person had only one right leg.

"We'll need to photograph this," Bill began, brushing his hand over his hair. "Beatrix, could you draw this?"

I nodded. It would take some time, as there were so many bones all scrambled together.

"What are we looking at?" Father José María asked in Spanish, staring with uncomprehending eyes at the skeletal remains.

I'd forgotten that not everybody could decipher the contents as quickly as we could, though of course we'd seen hundreds of thousands of bones in our lifetimes.

"We have multiple bodies all mixed together," Bill explained. "I can count at least three at a glance, but we'll have to move the remains to the lab to determine exactly how many and how complete each skeleton is. If we're fortunate, we may be able to piece together each individual skeleton, but it might be complicated."

"So is one of these people Teodosio?" José María reached toward one of the skulls as though to grab it.

Everyone gasped as a hand reached out and slapped Father José María's fingers away.

"What?" Maite proclaimed in self-defence. "The Professor said not to touch."

José María looked at Maite in disbelief but said nothing. I stifled my laughter by pinching my arm and gave Maite a conspiratorial wink when nobody was looking. She smiled back at me, but I could tell something was weighing on her mind.

"Yes," Bill replied, stepping forward protectively. "We don't want to move the remains so that we can precisely record their position within the sarcophagus. It may give us some clues about how these remains ended up like this."

"Is one of them Teodosio?" Father José María insisted.

"We don't know yet," Bill said. "We may never know. We need time to analyze what comes out of this tomb."

Bill was right. We might never determine who was buried there, nor why there were multiple bodies in what should've been a single burial. We'd already found clear evidence of the reuse of graves in the cemetery at San Miguel. It had been common practice to remove a previously buried body from its grave and place a new one inside to avoid the task of creating a new grave. In some cases, if the burial itself had space, a second person was simply placed on top. But mostly, the remains of the original occupant were unceremoniously dumped back on top of the newly buried individual. In this case, it wouldn't have been incomprehensible for there to have been an additional body in the tomb, but for the bones to be mixed the way they were was perplexing based on the importance that would've been placed on the interior burial structures. Was this perhaps a secondary burial resulting from the destruction of the original church? Why leave one sarcophagus empty and put three individuals in the other? Or had those tasked with burying the dead wanted to create an ossuary? A secondary burial place for decomposed bodies in order to make space in the cemetery for the newly deceased, where the positioning of the disarticulated remains had no importance? Was the missing body from the other sarcophagus here? That made sense, but what about the third body? Where had it come from? Were they creating space for a new burial that never occurred? Yet, if what we saw here happened in the past, what could explain the vipers in the first sarcophagus? Archaeology was often a puzzle with most of the pieces missing, never to be recovered. It was, however, difficult to convey that to people who expected answers to all their questions.

"At least there are bones in this tomb," Archie said optimistically.

"Lots of them," Janis added pushing back the sun hat she was still wearing despite being indoors.

"It's like a mystery for us to solve," Eduardo said.

With that, the students began to talk elatedly once again among themselves about the possible reasons for the cryptic contents of the sarcophagus. I went over to talk to Bill about the work that needed to be done. When I looked at the group, still hovering over the bones, I noticed that both priests and Maite had disappeared.

Chapter 12

I SPENT THE REST of the afternoon drawing the bones that were visible on the surface. Bill took most of the students outside to work, Eduardo stayed behind, having volunteered to help me. It was a scale drawing, so he took measurements for me as I directed him. I was glad to have a moment alone with him to ask him about his father. As far as Bill and I knew, Professor Reyes Iglesias was excavating in Mexico, I wondered how far he might go, both literally and figuratively, to obstruct Bill's own excavation halfway across the world.

"Mrs. Forster, I think I might like art better than doing other things," Eduardo said as he pulled a measuring tape taught across the open sarcophagus. "You know, like digging and that kind of stuff."

I'd assumed Eduardo avoided physical tasks because he was slight of frame rather than simple indifference toward the more laborious aspects of archaeology. He seemed to enjoy helping me with more detail-oriented work. For the others, the skeletons and field excavation were the major draw of this project. Eduardo didn't quite fit the mould in that sense. I wondered now if his father has pressured him to come on this excavation.

"Well, there's nothing wrong with that," I told him. Not wanting to bring the subject of his father up too abruptly, I let him guide the conversation. "There's something for everyone in archaeology, assuming you like it in general, as a field."

"I do. I do like archaeology. Or at least, I like the idea of it. You know, travelling the world, making discoveries. I don't mind being outdoors, so much. I just don't like getting dirty. And I really love drawing."

"Well, Eduardo, I don't know that you'll ever get away from dirt if you get into archaeology. Unless you want to be an armchair archaeologist, more into theory than practice. If you like art and archaeology equally, then why not exploit that speciality?"

"Are there even jobs in archaeological illustration?"

"Of course, there are! Photographs can only give us so much information. It's crucial to have good site drawings, and drawings of artifacts and skeletons too. And as much as I love my husband and would certainly continue illustrating without pay if it came to it — which for years it did — I insisted some time ago that the university start paying me for the work I do on excavations. Well, the university doesn't so much pay me directly as Bill hires me with funds it provides to pay the excavation team. Either way, illustration is a paid job. Many large and even some small-scale excavations have specialized illustrators on site in order to ensure the best records are kept. Remember what you learned in your first archaeology class: archaeology is destructive; once you've dug away the dirt, the context of any artifact is gone forever, and all you're left with are the drawings, photographs, and written records to tell you the details of where and how the artifact was found. Good documentation is crucial. So if you really like both fields, art and archaeology, I'd encourage you to pursue what you love. It might sound impractical, but the reality is that you can combine both and have a job that you enjoy. Sometimes, Eduardo, the cake and the fork are provided."

Eduardo smiled at me as though he were Prometheus and I'd just knocked the eagle out with a solid rock and the precise snap of a slingshot. I hadn't realized these things weighed on him for months or, perhaps, even years. Our students didn't often open up to us, especially about anything we might have perceived as a weakness in terms of their potential for advancement. It was as though an impenetrable glass of professionalism hung between us and them. We could know them as they projected themselves to us, but those projections were superficial. As a mother, I didn't mind their dropping the generally expected pretense of civility, as I hoped to have more of an impact on them than simply teaching the impersonal methods of archaeology. It was true that we saw more of the real people behind the façade of academic competence and absolute respectability embodied by most students at university simply by living with them for months on end. Yet, in most cases, I felt we'd merely scratched the surface of who these young people really were, the essence of their characters.

"Thanks, Mrs. Forster. My father won't like it at all if I take up any form of art, even if it is archaeological illustration. He wants me to follow in his footsteps, to become a Mesoamerican archaeologist, and he thinks most artistic endeavours are a waste of time. He can be really straitlaced, not at all like you and Professor Forster. But I do feel a lot better now knowing that there's work out there if I decide to change my direction."

I wondered how much he knew about the conflict between his father and Bill. It certainly seemed he didn't idolize his father, another reason to doubt his involvement in meddling with the tombs.

"How's your father's excavation going in Mexico?" I asked, tucking my pencil behind my ear and focusing my attention on Eduardo. "Does he write to you to keep you updated?"

Eduardo shook his head. "I don't know, Mrs. Forster. He writes home to my mother, but I think I've been a bit of a disappointment to him. He really wanted me to go with him to Mexico this summer. You wouldn't believe how mad he was when I applied to come here with you."

Eduardo's story sounded genuine. He'd chosen to join us of his own volition, and his father hadn't been pleased. Yet, if raiding the tombs had been premeditated, planned carefully before we left Toronto,

Eduardo certainly had time to practice a fib such as a disagreement with his father.

"Why did you choose to come here instead of Mexico?"

He looked away from me and fiddled with the tape measure. "I've already been to Mexico so many times, Mrs. Forster, and I've never been here. And when I heard that you would be coming on the excavation, I knew I could learn a lot from you, you know, about illustration and that kind of thing."

He certainly knew how to win me over.

"Goodness, that's very kind of you to say, Eduardo. I hope the experience has been as you hoped. Now, enough tittle tattle, we have work to do."

Eduardo removed his black, plastic-framed glasses and wiped the lenses on his shirttail while I began to outline the shape of a rib that was tossed haphazardly on top of the pile of skeletal remains. That's when I noticed something distinctly modern among the old bones. I sucked in my breath, but Eduardo didn't notice. A cream-coloured plastic button lay beneath the rib I'd started to draw, resting in the concave blade of a scapula. It was hardly noticeable, the colour of it blending seamlessly into the monochromatic background of the bones. It certainly confirmed that the second sarcophagus had been disturbed recently too, but I didn't want Eduardo to know the culprit left evidence behind. Not yet anyway. I quickly slipped the button into my pocket before he put his glasses back on. I'd discuss the anachronism with Bill later. It made sense that the remains from the first tomb were tossed into the second one. The question still lingered: who would have done such a thing and why?

Chapter 13

LATE IN THE AFTERNOON, I returned to the house to check on Angela again. Though she was still in her room, I was relieved to see she was dressed and looked much better than earlier. Some of the colour had returned to her cheeks, and her long blond hair was brushed neatly and tied back as she usually wore it for work.

"I feel fine now, honestly," she told me. "Just a bit weak. Miriam brought me something to eat a little while ago, and I feel much better."

"That's good news," I said gently, sitting down on Miriam's cot so that I could face Angela. "But you didn't look well earlier, so please take it easy for the next few days. You don't want to overtire yourself."

"I will, Mrs. Forster." Angela touched her stomach as though recalling the pain from that morning. "I think it must've been something I ate because I'm okay now. It seems to have passed."

It seemed unlikely it was something she ate, given the circumstances, but if she was on the mend now, the cause of the acute illness was of minimal importance unless the rest of us also got sick.

"Good. When you're ready you can join the others in the lab, if you feel up to it. Professor Forster will be showing the priests some of the things we've recovered from the cemetery. You can get up to speed on today's activities as well."

"Oh, Miriam already told me. About the snakes and the commingled bones and everything. I'll go down right away. Thank you, Mrs. Forster."

I left Angela in her room and went to the lab myself. The first room that we'd appropriated for our work was full of warm bodies milling about while trying not to disturb the skeletons that were laid out with care on the tables. When the students first arrived from Toronto, they'd been careless at times in the lab, bumping tables and causing all the tiny bones of the hands and feet to roll out of position, sometimes even falling to the floor. The little mishaps ended quickly enough when Archie reprimanded them for their clumsiness. He made them put each of the bones back exactly where they'd come from, using textbooks and handouts from their lectures as references in the early days before they'd mastered all the bones of the skeleton and their correct placement in anatomical position. They'd certainly come a long way in the time we'd been at San Miguel, but despite their great strides, Bill preferred they work under supervision.

I decided that an additional plump body in the room wasn't going to help the issue of space. Bill kept me up to date on all findings anyway, so I didn't need to hear the information intended for the priests and students again. I nodded to Bill to indicate my departure and stepped out of the first room and into the second. Here, there were two more tables with skeletons on them. I glanced around the room. The electric bulbs were dim, but the bright afternoon sun still generated a diffuse light through the grimy window, illuminating the cobwebs that were missed when we first cleaned these rooms on arrival. Or perhaps they'd been created since. I didn't spend much time in the lab, so I couldn't be sure. A quick scan of one of the skeletons laid out told me that this person, in life, might have suffered back pain or numbness of the limbs. Bony growths protruded from the vertebrae. I put my hand on my lower back, wondering if I had similar growths on my own spine and to what extent they'd formed. Certainly, I already experienced pain and stiffness, especially at night. The terribly thin mattress on the cot didn't help matters much.

"Happens to the best of us," I commiserated with the skeleton lying before me. "At least you can't feel it anymore."

I walked over to the window, looking out over the valley bathed in the glow of the late afternoon light. I heard the clanging of a bell and looked just below to see a few horses scrutinizing the flora that grew behind the house. I loved the horses, heavyset and plodding in comparison to the lean, nimble horses used for riding. Sadly, I knew that their ultimate destination was an abattoir. People here ate a broader range of foods than what we were used to in Toronto. Maite told me that people had even eaten cats when times were particularly bad. I didn't like the idea much, but I could fully understand the desperation of an empty stomach. We ourselves lived through the thirties, the mass exodus of the farmers on the Canadian prairies, the drought that seemed endless. None of us who'd suffered during that time could cast judgement on others who'd endured even greater trials.

A sudden bang emanated from the hallway and roused me from my thoughts. Startled, I clutched my hands to my chest. Recovering my composure, I consciously relaxed my shoulders, took a deep breath, crossed the room, and gingerly stepped into the darkened hallway. Then I flicked on the lights. To my relief, despite their blinking and sputtering, they came on and remained on. I could hear Bill talking about medieval coins in the other room. Had they not heard the noise?

I tiptoed down an adjacent hallway that had rooms we didn't use for lab space. Ignacio said that these rooms were used as storage for the sanctuary and that the students should keep out of them since they contained old furniture and hadn't been cleaned in years. I thought everyone followed the rules and stayed out, but the noise suggested otherwise. I paused to listen again, but all was quiet once more. I opened the first door on my right. The air smelled of dust and mildew. A narrow beam of light filtered through one small pane of glass in the window on the far side of the room. The other glass panes were replaced with wood and allowed no natural light to pass. As expected, cobwebs hung from every corner, dangling wispy, dust-enshrouded threads reaching toward old wooden tables and chairs stacked up against the walls, which glistened with moisture that accumulated on the bubbled, peeling, discoloured paint. Among the amassed furniture were broken panes of glass scattered over the wooden floor, creating a labyrinth of sharp edges that posed a danger to anyone careless enough to venture too far into the room. There were several pairs of footprints of varying sizes on the dusty floor, suggesting more than one person was in the room recently, despite its overall appearance of years of disuse.

I couldn't see anything that would've caused the banging sound, so I decided not to go farther. At the entrance, however, there was a closet next to the door where I stood. I was concerned that some trapped animal might burst forth the moment I opened the doors, so I stood aside, inching the folding doors open little by little until I was certain that nothing with teeth nor claws would suddenly emerge. I peeked around the corner to find it full of ceremonial robes worn by the clergy. They'd been long forgotten, despite the luxuriousness of the fabrics, with creamy ivories, radiant greens, and brilliant gold adornments set off against rich crimson tones. They were dusty and smelled of decades of abandonment, but the garments were striking. Above the hanging robes, I could see strips of white sheets stuffed into the back corner of the top shelf. I lifted my heels from the ground and drew myself to my maximum height to pull at the ragged, torn edges that were within my reach. They tumbled down to the floor before me in a heap. It was clear they were stained with blood, and the blood was fresh, the stains still reddish in colour rather than of the rusty brown tinge they took on when exposed for some time to the air.

"Goodness me," I mumbled as I looked down at the tangle of stained cotton.

Was it the closet door banging shut that I'd heard? Who would hide bloody, torn sheets here? I couldn't help but think of the bloody sheets from the legend of Teodosio.

Uncertain what to do, I stuffed them back into the closet and closed the door. I went back into the hallway and tried the next brass doorknob I came across. It wiggled in my hand, but I couldn't turn it. It was locked. The door was weak and I decided not to force it.

With questions churning in my mind, I returned to the safety of the lab, still full of lively chatter.

Chapter 14

AFTER DINNER, with everyone present, Maite, Ignacio, and the priests left the kitchen while the students and I all settled into our work as agreed upon at dinner the previous evening. I stayed behind in the kitchen with Eduardo, Angela, Miriam, and Patrick, who'd changed his mind about going to the lab to work instead on some of the illustrations of the skeletons uncovered that week. The other students followed Archie upstairs to the lab, and Bill set out on a short evening walk.

The students and I sat around the kitchen table, tracing and graph paper strewn before us. Through the window, I could see it rain was falling, heavy droplets rapping intermittently against the glass, patiently seeking entry into the warmth of the kitchen. The grey clouds intercepted the last rays of sun, making the use of the electric lights necessary to see our work. I hoped it wouldn't rain into the morning hours; if it did, the students would have to work indoors the next day. They always got a bit quarrelsome when they were cooped up inside for too long, and I supposed I couldn't really blame them.

We spoke little, the crackling flames of the fire creating a cozy atmosphere as we focused on the task assigned: adding details to sketches started in the field. When the wind was blowing, which happened frequently on the mountain, field drawing was a miserable activity. The air currents mulishly aspired to rip the pages from the clipboard while the illustrator battled to take measurements with one hand and keep everything from flying away into the abyss with the other. It could be unpleasant, to say the least. I'd learned many years ago that sometimes it was best to take down only the essential information in the field and complete the drawings indoors, where the greatest foes to archaeological illustration were sticky fingers and cups of coffee.

I left the students, their pencils scratching across the transparent paper, and went to the stove to heat some water for tea. A soothing, warm drink with a splash of milk before bed helped me to sleep in the dank room I shared with Bill. As soon as I was away from the table, the students began to talk in low voices. I couldn't help overhear.

"How are you feeling, Angela?" Eduardo asked. "Miriam said you were worse off than she and Helen were."

Angela smiled sweetly, her eyes leaving her work momentarily to meet Eduardo's concerned gaze. "Much better, thanks, Eddie. Whatever it was seems to have passed now."

"Let's hope the guys don't get it next, right, Patrick?" Eduardo looked over at Patrick, who lifted his head at the sound of his name but said nothing, maintaining his sullen silence despite Eduardo's efforts to lure him into conversation. "Helen was telling me today about her chauffeur dropping her off for school each day," Eduardo changed the subject to the gossip du jour. "Did she mention that to anybody else?"

"Of course," Miriam said. "Do you think she'd miss an opportunity to flaunt her family's money to the rest of us? I swear that girl has a new mini dress on every night for dinner. How did she even manage to get here with so much luggage?"

"No clue with those skinny arms," Eduardo replied. He sighed heavily. "The things I could do with that kind of bread. I mean, not that my family is poor or anything, but I most definitely walked to school every day of my life. It was a real bummer in the winter, that's for sure. A nice, warm car would've made all the difference."

"I'm sure she doesn't mean anything by it," Angela intervened, tapping her pencil against the table. "For her, it's just a normal thing. She doesn't know any different. Helen just wants people to like her. Remember she's the youngest one here. She just wants to have friends, like anybody else would."

"You're too nice, Angela," Miriam scolded, flipping her dark curls over her shoulder and away from the paper in front of her. "One day you'll get into trouble for being nice to everyone. It may seem like the right thing to do, but people will take advantage of your kindness and belief in their goodness. Not everyone's intentions are pure. They aren't all like you."

"That's a bit of a dark opinion, Miriam," Eduardo said. "I'd like to think that good things happen to good people."

"Then I'd say you're a bit naïve, Eddie. Then again, you're a bit like Angela, taking lost souls under your wing."

"What's that supposed to mean?"

"Oh, please. You know I mean your best buddy Graham. I don't know what you see in that kiss-up. He's a bit of a panty-waist if you ask my opinion."

"Miriam, you don't need to be so cruel," Angela chided her friend.

"Miriam, Graham's a nice person," Eduardo said, his cheeks visibly flushed. "If you even tried to get to know him, you'd see that. Who made you queen of the excavation anyway?"

"I never said I was, Eddie," Miriam crossed her arms over her chest.

The students no longer seemed to care that I was in the room and that their voices had risen to a pitch that I could clearly hear from the stove. Patrick stayed out of the conversation, engrossed in his work, or pretending to be. Angela, who was listening intently, began to chew on her pencil and shift her weight back and forth in her chair. The conversation made me uncomfortable as well, and I was well aware that young people, though highly sensitive to the opinions of others, often felt the need to cast judgment.

"Graham isn't the only one kissing up to Professor Forster," Eduardo retorted. "You know that, and you shouldn't talk either. I've seen the way you stare at Archie all day."

"Baloney," Miriam said sharply.

"Oh, that's right, Helen called dibs on Archie day one. I forgot." Eduardo was really twisting the knife in Miriam's side.

"Dibs?" Miriam swung her hair over her shoulder again, her eyes wide and unblinking. "She can call dibs if she wants. It doesn't change the fact that Archie's married."

I guessed she was sore about Eduardo using her very personal feelings to vex her. Though they were mostly on friendly terms, every once in a while Eduardo and Miriam had a little tiff.

"Well, I guess it's better than having a crush on Roger," Eduardo said, pulling in the reins somewhat.

Miriam rolled her eyes and they both laughed, their argument suddenly over as they settled on someone they could mutually dislike."Oh stop, you two!" Angela finally cried. "You're one just as bad as the other. He's just a bit rough around the edges, but he's not a bad person."

"You don't need to defend everyone, Angela," Miriam said. "Unless you've got some reason to. Anyway, I'd say that if his parents shipped him off to Toronto to go to university thinking it might refine him, then they wasted their money."

"He's just lucky he's strong and good-looking..." Eduardo's voice dropped off.

My return to the table put an end to the conversation.

Chapter 15

VOICES BREACHED the stillness of the kitchen from the hallway. The other students returned from the lab. One last chance to socialize before bedtime.

"Goodness, time flies," I said, standing up from the table. "Sounds like the others are back already. Let's gather up our things. We can finish off tomorrow."

"Thanks, Mrs. Forster," Angela said, smiling demurely and smoothing some loose hair back from her face.

"Not at all. Thanks to all of you. I'm always glad to have a little help."

Before I could praise their work, which, from a pedagogical standpoint, I believed was important, Helen burst through the kitchen door, her cheeks aglow.

"Patrick, will you sing for us tonight?" she spoke loudly, rushing into the kitchen before the others. She wore a bright pink, sleeveless mini dress, the kind that was all the rage among young women these days and caused quite a stir as the hemline was well above the knee, much to the shock of older generations.

"Sure," Patrick said. "I'll grab my guitar."

As Patrick stood up from the kitchen table, I noticed him squeeze Angela's shoulder and whisper something in her ear. She nodded but didn't get up from her seat.

"Wonderful," I said cheerily before he left the room. "That's very kind of you, Patrick."

Although the students always requested songs for Patrick to play that were not quite to my taste, I did enjoy our occasional intimate gatherings in the evening to listen and even sometimes sing along to the melodies he produced on his guitar. When I'd first seen him at the airport in Toronto, guitar case in hand, I was surprised. It wasn't the usual equipment expected at an excavation, but we'd all had good fun when Patrick could be convinced to serenade us. He was very talented, he was such a taciturn young man, keeping his own company most of the time and saying little in spite of the animation of several of his peers. Despite this, he was always agreeable, and the others seemed to like him.

Bill returned before Patrick came back to the kitchen. He gave me a quick peck on the cheek and a brief rundown of where they'd gone. Maite came into the kitchen and went to the stove to prepare some tea. I wasn't the only one who enjoyed a warm beverage before bedtime.

"What do you want him to play?" Helen demanded of the others once we were all seated at the long table and Patrick returned with his guitar, sitting where he could be seen by all.

"Fab four," Graham suggested.

Janis, across from me, rolled her eyes. "Graham, don't you remember? Patrick played The Beatles last time. What about The Rolling Stones?"

A few of the other students shook their heads.

"Bob Dylan!" Maite piped up, pronouncing the folk singer's name with a marked Spanish accent.

I turned to look at her, and though she smiled at me, her spirits seemed diminished, as though something were weighing heavily on her, and I wondered if it was about what happened with the sarcophagi or something else entirely. I knew she hadn't heard some of the songs

Patrick played. For her, they were mysterious tunes with foreign words. She didn't understand the lyrics, but each chord Patrick strummed and each verse he sang were small forms of dissent for her. Maite explained to me that the Franco regime's censors were always hard at work, and many American pop songs didn't make the cut, deemed as promoting sex, drugs, subversion, or even homosexuality. The list of themes unacceptable to the church and the government was long, and the censors made sure the minds of the people wouldn't be contaminated with heretical ideas. Maite learned a great deal about foreign popular music from the students that summer. Because they all liked her so much, if she requested an artist, Patrick complied.

"Groovy," Patrick said quietly and began to strum his guitar. His long, shaggy hair fell over his eyes as he leaned over his instrument, but a sharp flick of his head tamed the unruly mane.

I smiled to myself at the familiar word he used, popular among the young people. My grandson began to use the term with the frequency employed by youths testing the lengths to which their parents will tolerate colloquialisms in their speech. Considering Bill and I were declared to be "groovy grandma and grandpa," I myself had a high tolerance for the word, even if our daughter did not. I looked across the table to see if Bill was thinking the same thing, but he was intently staring into a void, tapping his finger on his bottom lip in time with the music.

I looked around at the others, all mesmerized as the cobra before the flute, their eyes wide and unblinking. Some mouthed the lyrics, a silent accompaniment to a popular anthem. Even I knew the words, memorized subliminally through endless repetition on the radio. Only Janis, picking at the wood on the table, was not enraptured by the familiar tune. I could see she was sore about not getting her way, and I felt sorry for her. It wasn't the first time.

I turned back to Patrick, focusing on the words he sang, the universality of the theme that could've been written about human struggle the world over. Perhaps the songwriter meant to intimate the civil rights movement or Vietnam when he penned the song, it could as easily have been written about the Spanish people themselves. Would they ever be free? Or would Franco and his legacy somehow live on forever? I turned once more to glance at Maite. Her eyes were moist, but she had a faint smile on her lips. Forbidden pleasures were sometimes the most enjoyable.

Chapter 16

AFTER PATRICK'S CONCERT, Bill and I were on our way to bed when I heard footsteps approach rapidly from behind. I turned around to find Maite hurrying after us, her eyebrows knotted into a frown. She tugged at the sleeves of her floral dress as she ascended the stairs to meet us.

"Ay, Professor Forster, Beatriz," she spoke rapidly in Spanish. "Please, may I speak with you a moment in private?"

Bill led us all into the lab I'd been in when I heard the banging noise. I realized that Muffin followed us into the lab, where she wasn't supposed to be, but given Maite's distress, I said nothing. I pointed at the ground and she lay down quietly to wait.

"¿Qué pasa, Maite?" Bill asked.

We all stood in the centre of the room, below the buzzing light bulb. There were no chairs in the labs. Maite looked nervously at the skeletons, positioned exactly as they were in the afternoon.

"It's about the tombs," Maite began, crinkling her nose and twisting one gold hoop earring repeatedly through the hole in her earlobe. "I'm worried, to be honest. I think I may know who, or not exactly who, but what put the vipers into the tomb and probably stole some bones too."

I had no idea what she was talking about and shook my head. "What do you mean, Maite? How did the vipers get there?"

"I think it must have been witches," Maite said, a look of concern in her eyes. She glanced again at the skeletons, inert and lifeless as always. "There have always been witches here in Navarre and in the Basque Country. When I saw the vipers, I knew it must be their familiars, and they probably took some bones to carry out their rituals. With the bones all mixed into one tomb, it would be hard to know what was missing. I knew it was a terrible idea to disturb the dead here at San Miguel, but Father José María was so intent on finding Teodosio. It brings bad luck. The dead should rest in peace. And now look, the witches have come and they probably made the poor girls sick too. It's known that they have strange abilities."

"I know you've mentioned witches before," I said, running my fingers through my hair, "but I thought that was hundreds of years ago, not now. Tell us again about them and why you think they've come to San Miguel."

I didn't believe in witchcraft in the sense of groups of women communing with the Devil in the form of a goat and having familiars, but there was a distinct possibility that people who believed themselves to be witches could've tampered with the sarcophagi in the church if they felt that it served some purpose. What we'd seen required physical strength and an ability to handle venomous snakes without being bitten, but it didn't require supernatural powers.

"There's a long history of witchcraft here. There was a very important auto-da-fé held in the city of Logroño in the early seventeenth century. It's incredibly famous here. The Spanish Inquisition was investigating cases of witchcraft, torturing many and burning some at the stake. With so many accusations, they decided witchcraft must be widespread among the Basques, and they offered a pardon to those who confessed and named their conspirators. The village of Zugarramurdi, near the border with France, was of particular interest. There were rumours of *akelarre*, the Basque term for a gathering of witches. Thousands confessed and made accusations against their neighbours, even their families. Men and women were arrested. The witch-hunts ended a few years later, and they say there are still witches in these parts. Not many because they were persecuted for so long, but they still exist. The bad ones are capable of great mischief, like what we saw today."

"Do you know anyone that practices witchcraft?" I asked, wondering what stance the church took on the subject.

"No, but I have my suspicions," Maite rubbed her hands over her arms. It was cold in the room, with the evening temperatures dropping and the sun's powerful rays lost to the rain clouds. "There are some who are very secretive in the village. Witchcraft is not all bad, of course, and just like people, not all witches are good. What if these witches, Beatriz, aren't the good kind?"

I nodded, mentally compiling a list of odd occurrences at San Miguel in the past few days. Supernatural powers or not, at this point, Maite's assumptions of what happened to the tombs were as plausible as mine.

Chapter 17

WHEN BILL AND I were alone in our room together, I told him of the button I'd discovered in the sarcophagus with the remains. I pulled it from my pocket and handed it to him.

"Definitely plastic, definitely modern," he murmured, turning it over between his fingers and lifting his glasses away from his eyes to inspect it more closely. "So this confirms our suspicions that both sarcophagi were opened recently, and probably the bones were also mixed at the same time someone put the vipers into the tomb. All very curious. I don't know about Maite's story about the witches, I also can't imagine who'd want to disturb our investigation like this. Who'd benefit from such mischief?"

"Well, I have my own ideas about that too, but it's not the only strange thing that happened today." I lay down on the cot and rested my head on the pillow. I was plain worn out after the day's events. "It could be unrelated, but while you were talking to the students and the priests this afternoon, I went over to the other lab room and heard a loud bang.

Did you hear it too?"

"No, I don't recall any strange noises."

"Well, anyway, I went into the next room to have a look, the one Ignacio told us was full of old furniture."

"Was it?"

"Yes, it was. But I found some torn sheets stuffed in the closet with fresh blood on them."

"Bloody sheets?" Bill turned to look at me, his eyes wide as he ran a hand over his beard. "That's odd. I haven't noticed anyone with an injury today. Not that I'm fully sold on Maite's story, but my imagination does jump to animal sacrifices. Is that something witches do?"

"I suppose each culture has a vastly different idea of what witches do and don't. We'd have to ask Maite. That does remind me, though, that Ignacio did have blood on his hand yesterday. It wasn't that much, and the blood on the sheets was fresh. Ignacio is, however, the only one that would use that room. At least, he should be the only one. It wasn't actually locked."

"I could have a chat with him tomorrow," Bill suggested, lying down beside me. "Maybe find out if he knows anything. Unfortunately, we can't distinguish between human and animal blood just by looking at it. I suppose that if nobody's actually injured, it's less of a concern. It may have nothing at all to do with what happened in the church today, but I'll talk to him."

"I don't know," I rolled onto my side to look at my husband. We'd been a team for so long I didn't know what I'd do without him. "Perhaps we should say nothing and keep an eye out for odd behaviour. See if anything else happens. Other than vandalism, we don't know that a crime has been committed here. It just makes me feel uneasy, all these strange things happening one after the other, and Janis's sleepwalking doesn't make things any easier."

"Odd behaviour?" Bill started to laugh, reaching out to hold my hand. "And how might you define odd behaviour for Ignacio?"

I laughed, too, at the absurdity of my idea. Bill was exactly right.

Ignacio's comportment from the day we met him was anything but ordinary.

We lazily got up from the cots to change into our pyjamas and climbed into bed after Bill switched off the light. I kept the flashlight on so we could see each other.

"Let's hope we get a full night's uninterrupted sleep tonight," Bill said, pulling the blanket up to his neck. "I'm too old for theatrics before dawn."

"As am I."

I switched the flashlight off and placed it on the nightstand. I closed my eyes and then opened them again, seeing little but the shadows of the objects in the room. I wondered if Janis would remain in the kitchen all night. I hoped she wouldn't be inclined to make another nighttime excursion, for everyone's sake, including her own.

After a short silence, Bill asked: "What did you mean you have your own ideas about what happened with the sarcophagi?"

"Ah, yes," I said quietly. "I'm a little ashamed to have jumped to conclusions about it, I simply couldn't discount the possibility that Domingo Reyes Iglesias might be involved. He may be in Mexico, but he does have indirect access to our excavation."

"You don't think Eduardo is capable of something so malicious, do you?"

"I don't want to, Bill, but I just don't know."

Chapter 18

I WOKE EARLY the next morning. My back ached, and I wondered if it was worth staying in bed or if I should just get an early start to my day. There was always something to be done. I hadn't quite finished drawing the bones in the sarcophagus, and I knew Bill would be anxious to remove them for analysis in the lab. I looked over, expecting to find him fast asleep, his eyes were open, and he was staring at the ceiling.

"Bill," I whispered. "How long have you been awake?"

No answer.

"Bill!" I said, more loudly this time. "Bill, are you awake?"

I poked him in the arm with my index finger.

He groaned in protest. "What is it?"

"How long have you been awake?"

"A little while. Why?"

"Just wondering. Shall we get up? Get something done?"

"Care to watch the sunrise?"

"Why not? The drawings can wait an hour."

"They can indeed. There's nothing like a sunrise on this mountain."

It wasn't the first time we'd risen early to see the dawn. The spectacle was magnificent, especially when the clouds hung low in the valley. A sea of white surrounded the mountain, and one could see only the tops of the surrounding rocky peaks and plateaus. Being above the clouds provided an ethereal sensation that couldn't easily be equalled. The sun rose over the Pyrenees, casting its warmth in a blushing, hazy glow. I was glad we had colour slide film for the camera to capture these breathtaking moments, even if a photograph could never quite compare to the real thing, because a photo has a way of conjuring memories from the recesses of one's mind.

We snuck out of our room with Muffin, like teenagers slipping away from home in the middle of the night, hoping we wouldn't wake the rest of the household. Outside, the grass was covered in dew, and the leather on our boots darkened with the moisture. It was damp, but I noticed the rain stopped before we went to bed. There was a crisp breeze, and I pulled my coat tighter around my neck, eager to keep the chill out. Fog swirled around our legs, brushing its gossamer mist over our khakis. We walked quickly and silently around the house, past the side of the sanctuary and toward the east, where the sun was already making an appearance on the horizon.

As we approached the cemetery, Bill suddenly halted, staring over at the excavation area. I stopped directly behind him.

"Goodness, Bill, you can check on the excavation later. We're out here now. Let's not miss this."

"There's something wrong, Beatrix." He stood frozen, as if paralyzed by some invisible force.

"What? What is it? Is it your heart?" I looked at Bill, starting to panic as my mind raced to think of the fastest way to get to a hospital.

Muffin emitted a low warning growl, flattening her tail over her rear. I knew then that it wasn't Bill's heart I needed to be worried about, but Muffin's sudden change in demeanour made my muscles tense in anticipation. It wasn't a small animal that caught her and Bill's attention, or she would already have begun the chase.

"No, it's not me," Bill said breathlessly. "Look over at the grave there. The one built with sandstone slabs. What's that?"

Released from his momentary paralysis, Bill pointed at one of the more elaborate graves we'd excavated the month before. It remained untouched since the skeleton it contained had been exhumed. I saw immediately what concerned him. It should've been empty, exactly as we'd left it. Yet white fabric billowed over the edge of the grave, twisting in the breeze. The nebulous light of the sunrise and the empty graves of the cemetery, partially obscured by the whirling fog, gave it an eerie, ghostly appearance.

"Perhaps it's just some washing that blew away and got caught on the grave," I said hopefully, though I knew nobody hung any washing out the night before because of the humid conditions.

"Let's have a look, then, shall we?" Bill said, already marching toward the undulating fabric. Muffin ran after him, reaching the grave as he did. Bill stood over it, looking down. He was silent for a moment. Then, in a quavering voice: "Good Lord."

I was only a few steps behind, but his tone made me shiver, and I wished I could turn back. But it was too late. I could already see the form that filled the grave.

"Goodness, it can't be..." My words caught in my throat as Bill wrapped his arm around my shoulders and squeezed me tightly.

Chapter 19

ANGELA'S BODY LAY motionless within the grave that was built for someone who died a thousand years before. She fit inside perfectly, as though it was designed for someone precisely her size. I didn't need to check her pulse to know she was dead. It was clear. Her pale skin was nearly translucent in the morning light, and her lips were blue. Her arms were carefully crossed over her chest, her fingernails also the colour of glacial ice. Contusions formed a ring around her throat. I couldn't find the words to speak, and it seemed like breaking the silence might somehow make it real. Instead, I quietly brushed a tear away from the corner of my eye with my finger. We stood mutely, aghast by the scene before us.

Angela was dressed in a white cotton nightgown. I wracked my brain. Had I seen it before? Had she been wearing it yesterday when I saw her in her room? I couldn't recall. My mind was as foggy as the morning mists that still swirled around us, like whirlpools in a river.

Bill knelt down and used his index finger and thumb to carefully open her eyelid. I knew what he was looking for. Petechiae. Little red dots on Angela's eyes. Sadly, this was not the first time Bill and had seen a case of strangulation, but I pushed those memories away. I noticed that the skin on Angela's body was moist with morning dew, just as the grass had been. Her body had been here for some time. Muffin leaned over the sandstone slabs that formed the northern wall of the burial and licked Angela's cheek.

"No, Muffin, don't touch her." I scooped her up as quickly as I could, the camera banging on my chest as I bent over. I folded her tail under and rested her bottom on my hip as I always did, then I squeezed her and kissed her on the head. I needed her comforting presence more than ever. "Who could have done this?" I finally spat out, my emotions wavering between anger and sadness. "She was such a sweet girl. How could anybody hurt her? I just don't understand."

"I wish I had an answer, but I'm as shocked as you are," Bill said, removing his glasses and holding his hand over his eyes. He remained like this for a few moments, without speaking. Then he said: "Angela was a bright student. A lovely young woman. I cannot fathom why anybody would want to harm her. And who? Was it one of us? Did somebody that knew her do this? Or was it a stranger?"

I shook my head, shivering at the thought of strangers or Maite's witches coming to San Miguel. It was only slightly more comforting to think that Angela was killed by someone we didn't know than someone we did. Neither Bill nor I had any answers.

"We should cover her until the police come," Bill said, anxiously scratching his beard. "We'll have to make sure nobody comes outside this morning, and we'll have to tell the others what happened. They shouldn't see this. It'll only make things worse. It'll be difficult enough for everyone."

"Especially Miriam," I said. I wiped my eyes with the back of my hand and replaced my glasses.

Bill handed me a dusty handkerchief from the breast pocket of his vest.

"Thank you, dear," I said.

"Let's go," Bill said, already moving away from the body. "We'll find some canvas with the tools. We need to ensure that nobody comes out early. I don't want any of the students to see this. It'll be too upsetting. We can ask Maite to phone the police."

I turned back once more to look at Angela. Her long blond hair was spread out around her head like the rays of the sun at the east side of the grave.

"She's backwards," I said, suddenly realizing that there was something wrong about her position within the burial structure.

"Pardon?" Bill asked, returning to the grave.

"She's backwards. Look, her head is in the east, but it should be in the west."

"You're right," Bill said. "Angela's facing the church."

In Christian tradition, the dead were buried facing the east, to rise at the second coming of Jesus. The pagans often buried their dead facing the east too, but this was for them to face the rising sun.

"What could it mean?" I pondered, not really wanting to know the answer.

"Perhaps nothing, or perhaps it was deliberate. The person who put her here might have been in a hurry and didn't notice that the direction was wrong. Or he wasn't aware of Christian customs. Or he didn't want her to rise at the second coming. I suppose only the person who did this knows why her body is the way it is."

"Goodness, how awful to think about it." I looked again at Angela lying there, her life extinguished long before her time. "Notice, Bill, that she's been placed here carefully. Her hair. Her arms. Even her nightgown has only a little dirt on it. It's all very strange."

"It's beyond comprehension is what it is. Let's go get the canvas, Beatrix."

Chapter 20

BILL AND I HURRIED back toward the house. There was no time to be in shock; we'd have to look after everyone else. I hoped nobody other than Maite was up yet. She always rose before the rest to prepare breakfast. Bill went to the tool shed to find a canvas to cover Angela's body, and I went directly to the kitchen. Maite was bustling around, whistling softly to herself when I entered. Janis was also in the kitchen, snoring quietly on her bed in the corner, where we'd set it up two nights before. I'd nearly forgotten about the new sleeping arrangements with that morning's tragic revelation. I wondered if she'd been sleepwalking last night. If she saw something, would she even remember?

"Maite," I whispered, walking right up to her. She turned, startled. She clutched her chest but smiled at me. "Maite, algo muy grave ha ocurrido," I continued in a whisper before she could speak. I didn't want Janis to wake. "We need you to call the police. There's been a murder."

Maite gasped, shaking her head. "A murder, Beatriz? Here? On the mountain?"

"Yes, I'm afraid there has been."

"Ay, Dios mío. I can't believe it. Who? Was it...Ignacio?" She covered her mouth, eyes blinking furiously.

I wasn't sure why she thought it might have been Ignacio. Perhaps the thought of a student being killed here was as unfathomable to her as it was to me. I shook my head.

"Not Ignacio. It was Angela." I glanced over at Janis to confirm she remained asleep. I noticed her hair was damp and wondered if she'd been up early to shower before the others.

"My God. Angela? That sweet girl? My God." Maite crossed herself, just like she did when we opened the first sarcophagus.

"Maite, I know how shocking this is. But we must call the police."

"The police? The Guardia Civil." She shook her head passionately. "They're no good," she whispered, fear obscuring her normally good-humoured features. "Some are dangerous, others just stupid. And stupidity is dangerous, Beatriz."

"Perhaps," I said, believing what she said, though I had minimal contact with the Civil Guard. "What choice do we have?"

Maite nodded. A murder has to be investigated by the proper authorities, regardless of her feelings toward them.

"I will call them."

"And, Maite, we must not tell anybody. Not yet. We'll tell everyone together."

She nodded, but I noticed her gaze was fixated on my chest in the way people can't help but stare at a dinner party when you've spilled something on your blouse. They don't say anything, but you become self-conscious and aware that something is amiss. I reached up and patted my chest, my fingers bumping into the hard surface of the camera. I forgot it was slung around my neck. I'd meant to photograph the sunrise. Her eyes were questioning, as though she were wondering what I was doing out early in the morning with a camera and discovering a dead body. Did she think I had something to do with it?

"The camera," I said, looking down at it. We hadn't even had a chance to use it. "Bill and I were going to watch the sunrise when we found the body."

She looked relieved by my explanation.

"I understand," she said simply. "I'll make the phone call."

She left the kitchen without saying more. She'd have to go to the sacristy to make the phone call. There was only one telephone at the sanctuary.

"Do you need keys?" I called after her.

"No," she called back from the hallway.

I took one last look at Janis, who continued to breathe rhythmically, sleeping as though nothing were wrong. I left her as I'd found her, but I wondered how peacefully she'd slept in the night.

Chapter 21

I RETURNED WITH BILL to the cemetery, now gradually clearing of the early morning fog and bathed in the radiant light of daybreak. It would've been beautiful if I was not acutely aware of what awaited us, concealed by the slabs of stone that formed the walls of the grave. Bill carried with him a heavy olive green canvas to cover Angela's body. She'll be cold, I thought. No, she won't, I corrected myself. It was still difficult to process the grim discovery. She'd been unwell yesterday, but she'd been very much alive.

Seeing Angela's body a second time was nearly as alarming as the first. This time, however, my thoughts went to her parents. How would we tell them of this tragedy? As a mother, I knew it would destroy them.

Bill began to unfold the rough material. I wished there was something nicer, something softer, with which to cover her body, but this would have to do until the police arrived. The stones of the grave walls were high enough that the canvas wouldn't touch her body anyway.

Muffin sat dutifully at the edge of the grave, watching over Angela as the sphinx guards the tomb. I didn't have to remind her not to touch the body, and I didn't bother to tell her she wasn't supposed to be in the excavation area at all. At this point, what did it matter? As Bill smoothed the creases in the tarp, I wished desperately that Angela wouldn't be subjected to an autopsy. I wished many things in that moment, but again, what choice did we have? There were procedures that needed to be followed.

While Bill placed one end of the canvas over the foot of the grave, which should have been the head, stretching the fabric over the sides of the walls and placing heavy stones at each of the corners so that the wind wouldn't carry the canvas away, I noticed something I hadn't seen before.

"Bill!" I nearly shouted. "Bill, look at her neck."

Bill stopped what he was doing and knelt down near Angela's head. I watched as he ran his hand over his beard while examining her more closely. He was deep in thought.

"The ligature marks," he said finally. "The pattern, it's unique. I've seen it before."

"Exactly. We've seen it many times before. Every time we walk into the church."

"The chains! One of the chains. Somebody strangled her with it."

"Goodness, yes," I said, imagining the scene. I shivered at the thought. "Someone used one of Teodosio's chains to murder Angela."

"Good Lord," Bill said, still crouched beside her body.

My mind raced, so many questions forming that I couldn't hold on to any one thought long enough to formulate a reasonable answer.

"Beatrix," Bill said quietly. "This may sound macabre, but since you've got the camera here, I think we should photograph the body, especially these ligature marks. Just in case."

"Won't the police do that?" I asked, knowing as I spoke that he was right, however much I wished he wasn't.

We didn't know how long the police might take to arrive, and visual documentation of the body could prove critical for an inquiry. It was standard procedure in archaeology, and though I wasn't a detective intimately familiar with criminal investigations, the steps to be taken were very similar. I had seen them carried out in the past, though I would never become accustomed to the sadness of seeing the recently deceased. I knew well enough that we should carefully record everything just as we would at an excavation. I pulled the camera strap over my head and passed it to Bill. I didn't have the heart to photograph the scene myself.

"Do you have a scale?" Bill asked me.

I patted my pockets but felt nothing except the church key hanging from my belt.

"I don't."

"We'll make do without," he said. "The burial structure can always be used as a reference after the fact."

I picked Muffin up and held her so she wouldn't be in Bill's way as he began to take photographs, some detailed close-ups, some from farther away giving an overall view of the grave with Angela's body within. I watched him work, feeling distinctly disconnected from my body. I pinched my right arm, hoping I might wake up. But all I felt was pain.

Chapter 22

THE KITCHEN WAS BRIMMING with people when we returned. Maite arrived before us. I wondered why we didn't see her leaving the church, but I brushed the thought aside. Perhaps we were too distracted by Angela's death to notice any activity. Maite's nose and eyes were pink as though she'd been crying, but she maintained a composed expression as she busied herself with the breakfast dishes. It was evident from the chatter that nobody noticed anything amiss yet. We were about to crush the excitement of a new day's endeavours. Bill cleared his throat loudly.

"Could everyone please sit down?" he asked over the din.

"But, professor," Roger complained, "we don't all have our breakfast yet!"

"It doesn't matter. You can have breakfast after. We have something very serious to discuss with everyone. We will do this in English and in Spanish so that everything is clear for everyone."

"Is this about the mixed-up bones, Professor Forster?" Graham asked, seating himself immediately at the wooden table, his blond hair freshly slicked back with pomade, his face recently shaved with care.

"No, this is another matter." Bill moved his watch back and forth on his wrist, a clear sign he was stressed. "Is everyone here? It's important that everyone be here."

I realized immediately the mistake Bill made, but I kept quiet. It would only take a moment for them to have a look around and determine who was missing.

"Where's Angela?" Helen asked loudly. "She's not here, and she wasn't in our room when we got up this morning either."

Bill glanced at me. "Angela won't be joining us this morning. She..."

"Ask Miriam," Roger said, looking across at her. "She and Angela are joined at the hip. She should know where her best friend is."

"I don't know where she is," Miriam said quietly, looking up at me from her seat on the bench. "I assumed..." She didn't finish her thought.

"Assumed what, Miriam?" I asked gently.

Perhaps she knew something.

"Oh, nothing," Miriam said, looking away. "I thought she was in the bathroom, that's all."

There was no point in pressing the issue. Perhaps she truly thought Angela was in the bathroom, but something about her hesitation told me otherwise. Maybe she'd be willing to tell us in private, it was clear she didn't want to say anything in front of everyone.

"Please, no more interruptions," Bill said to regain everyone's attention. "We have terrible news. We know how difficult this will be for everyone to hear. Mrs. Forster and I found Angela's body this morning in the cemetery. We believe she was strangled during the night."

The sound of gasping washed over the room, waves of sharply inhaled breath reverberating from one person to the next. Then everyone fell silent, many covering their mouths to keep from uttering a sound. I saw the priests, both of whom spoke English, cross themselves. Ignacio was the only one who didn't yet know what happened.

He looked perplexed, glancing nervously at those reacting to the tragedy around him. Bill quickly paraphrased in Spanish what he'd said in English. Ignacio nodded and looked down at the floor.

Miriam was the first to burst into tears.

"I don't understand," she stammered, making no effort to wipe the moisture off her face.

I went over and wrapped my arms around her, and she nestled her face into my coat. I could feel her shoulders shaking. I held her as tightly as I could.

"I know this is a great shock to you all," Bill continued. "Maite has contacted the police, until they arrive, it's important that you stay inside the house. We ask that you do not go outside until we receive further instructions from the authorities. This is very important. Is this clear for everyone?"

Nobody said anything, but some heads nodded in agreement.

"Isn't that dangerous?" Eduardo broke the silence. "I mean the killer could be one of us." He looked meaningfully around the room at the others.

"Or it could not be," Bill replied calmly. "We don't know anything yet. It's important not to speculate about these things. We don't have enough information to make any informed guesses at this point. Speculation will only lead to discord, and that can be just as dangerous."

"The Guardia Civil is sending someone from one of the garrisons," Maite offered helpfully in Spanish. "They said probably before ten o'clock they could get someone up the mountain."

Bill translated for the others. It would feel like forever before the police arrived, I thought, but there was enough time for Bill and me to look at the chains in the church before anyone arrived. At this point nobody knew about the murder weapon except us and the person who'd used it. I wanted this solved as quickly as possible, and given Maite's reservations, I couldn't help but feel concerned about the effectiveness of the Civil Guard. The priests left the kitchen immediately, which was no surprise to me.

"Is there anything I can do to help?" Archie asked.

"Thank you, Archie," I said. The skin around his eyes was damp, but he wasn't crying. I felt for him and the others. Angela's death was a terrible shock in a place where they were supposed to feel safe. Now nobody would feel at peace until the killer was caught. "Bill and I have everything outside under control, if you could keep an eye on the students, that would be a great help to us."

Archie nodded sadly. "I can do that, Mrs. Forster."

I gave his arm a quick, reassuring squeeze before taking Muffin's dish to her corner. She gobbled it up as she always did, and then Bill, Muffin, and I left the kitchen.

"Beatrix," Bill whispered when we were in the hallway, away from the others. "I put the camera in our room while you were in the kitchen, for safekeeping. We wouldn't want the police to get any ideas and confiscate it."

I nodded. It was best to keep some things to ourselves at this point.

Chapter 23

THE CHURCH WAS UNNERVINGLY QUIET, and I shivered involuntarily in the cold and damp. We made sure to lock the door behind us so that nobody could enter. As we passed by the sarcophagi, I wondered if Angela's death had something to do with the vipers and commingled remains. There was no clear connection between the two at this point, but we knew so little about Angela's demise.

Just outside the chapel, the chains hung ominously, inert as they'd always been, now an omen of death rather than a symbol of good fortune. Bill crouched down to examine the chains without touching them, shining his flashlight over the links in case the killer left behind some physical evidence. There were two chains with different link patterns. The longer one matched the bruises that encircled Angela's fragile neck. The police would have to dust for fingerprints when they arrived, but I guessed it would be of little use. People touched the chains whenever they visited the church, and I doubted that Ignacio cleaned them regularly. All these people would have unwittingly left a trace of themselves on what was now a murder weapon.

"Anything?" I asked after a few minutes peering over Bill's shoulder.

I was anxious that he find something conclusive, some key that would tell us without a doubt who'd committed this terrible crime. I knew very well that murder investigations could drag on or never be solved, and I wasn't prepared to accept that possibility.

No answer.

"Bill, do you see anything?" I repeated loudly while tapping him on the shoulder.

He jerked his head away from the chains in surprise. "Hmmm?"

"Anything?"

"Nothing." He stood up. "At least nothing visible to the naked eye. Maybe the police will find something more. The pattern certainly looks the same, don't you agree? And it doesn't appear that the chains could be removed from the wall, so this has to be where the perpetrator killed poor Angela."

"Goodness, what a thought." I shuddered as my mind raced over the details of the crime. "That does raise the question though: who had access to this area last night? Not everybody has a key to the church."

"Indeed. That could rule out a stranger. It's unlikely anybody not associated with the sanctuary or our dig would have known where to get a key in the middle of the night. An outsider wandering the mountain wouldn't have been able to slip into the house unnoticed and take a key from someone, nor would he have a key unless he had some prior association with San Miguel. I suppose that remains an option, but it seems unlikely."

"Hmmm . . . 'he,' you said."

"Pardon?" Bill peered at me through the now dusty lenses of his glasses.

"You said 'he.' You assume it was a man, then?" I reached over and took the flashlight from him so he wouldn't have to carry the dog and the torch.

"No, I'm not sure we should make any assumptions just yet. It could as easily have been a woman, I imagine."

Chapter 24

THE CIVIL GUARD ARRIVED in a four-door Renault, painted green with white front doors. The doors were emblazoned with the coat of arms of the military force that conducted policing duties in the rural areas of Spain. The officers came from the northern valley, which was accessible by car. Ascending the mountain on foot or by donkey from the southern valley wouldn't have been very practical, considering the circumstances. The officers stepped out from the car, their polished black boots glistening in the sun. They approached us briskly, climbing the stairs toward the sanctuary, one slightly behind the other. It was clear who was in command here. Bill and I waited near the entrance to the church, a bewildered and haggard welcoming committee.

Both men wore olive grey uniforms, carefully pressed, and the black patent tricorn hat that made them instantly recognizable as members of the Civil Guard. The older of the two men reached us first, the younger close behind.

"Buenos días. I am Capitán Sánchez Barrios and this is Sargento Ortega Velasco. We were told that a student attending an educational program here has been murdered. Who's the person responsible for this program?"

The captain's moustache perched straight as an arrow above his lip. The younger officer, the sergeant, had kind eyes and smiled softly when his superior introduced him.

"I'm in charge of the field school," Bill stated. "I'm Professor William Forster, and this is my wife, Beatrix Forster."

"Good," the captain said brusquely and without looking at me. He kept his eyes fixed on Bill as he spoke. "I'll see the body now, and we will commence our investigation. Ortega, you'll take notes."

"A la orden, mi capitán," the sergeant replied.

I noticed that Captain Sánchez Barrios's uniform belt was drawn taut over an ample belly. Not that I was one to judge, as I was abundant in that department as well, but I'd expected him to be in better form given that he couldn't have been much older than forty-five and I imagined his job demanded fitness. Sergeant Ortega Velasco was, on the other hand, the polar opposite of his commanding officer. He was tall and lean, and his face had been shaved that morning, revealing the smooth skin of youth.

"Of course," Bill said kindly. "We're very shocked and saddened by the incident. Angela was a kind and intelligent young woman. She was well liked by everyone here at San Miguel. We'll show you where we found her."

"Perhaps your wife would like to go back to the house and have some tea...to comfort her," the captain suggested, his face showing no emotion.

"She's already seen the body and has noticed some peculiarities about the scene. I don't believe she wants tea at the moment, do you, Beatrix?"

Bill's response was so innocent, it could've been interpreted as stemming from the oblivion that men often suffered when faced with the prejudice of their counterparts. It was clear, though, that the captain didn't believe murder to be the purview of a woman.

"As you wish," Sánchez replied.

"I'm very sorry for your loss," Ortega said, placing his hand over his heart.

"Notes, Ortega. No talking. Just notes."

I nodded at the sergeant in understanding. Perhaps Maite was wrong. Maybe they weren't all bad, though she seemed to have hit the nail on the head when it came to the captain.

The four of us tramped over the still slightly damp grass toward the cemetery, where the canvas was stretched taut over the grave where Angela's body laid since sometime in the night.

"Ortega, remove this canvas," the captain ordered, trampling over the excavated area in his heavy boots.

"A la orden."

Ortega tucked his notebook into his pocket and began to move the heavy rocks that Bill placed earlier to weigh down the thick fabric. Sánchez made no effort to assist him, so Bill and I helped remove the other rocks and roll up the canvas. Ortega nodded a silent thank you.

Captain Sánchez crouched down near the body, careful not to kneel in the dirt and sully his clean uniform.

"Strangled," he stated when he stood up.

"Yes," Bill agreed. "That's what we thought as well."

"The doctor will have to perform an autopsy, anyway," Sánchez said.

"Of course," Bill replied. "We understand."

"Have the girl's parents been informed?" Sánchez asked.

"Not yet," Bill said, stuffing his hands in his pockets. "We were waiting to confer with you, and waiting until morning in Canada."

"Fine. I'll leave that up to you. I don't speak English. Maybe it would be a good job for your wife." Sánchez motioned toward me with his hand. "I imagine she has a comforting voice on the telephone. Women often do."

I didn't take his suggestion as a compliment.

"We'll discuss what will be best for the family," Bill said. "There's something else, though. We've located the murder weapon."

"Murder weapon? Where? Did you remove it?" The captain became visibly agitated, looking around near the grave as though it might have been carelessly discarded near the body.

"Of course not," Bill replied, maintaining his poise. "Beatrix noticed that the pattern on Angela's neck matches the chains hanging in the church here."

"Curious," Sánchez said, tranquil once again as he twisted the hairs of his moustache. "I will want to see those right away. Excellent observation, Professor."

I ignored his jab, anticipating that I'd have to endure many more of his attempts to not so subtly undermine me.

"We can go inside and show you," Bill said. "Perhaps we should cover the body first. The sun's getting strong already today, and we don't want the body to be exposed any longer than necessary."

"Not to worry, Professor. As soon as we've looked at your chains, we'll remove the body and take it to the doctor."

"You're going to leave?" I blurted.

"It'll only be for a few hours. If you are afraid, señora, you can come with us." Sánchez laughed, the first time I saw him smile. Somehow his moustache remained linear, despite the movement of his lips.

"That will not be necessary, thank you, capitán," I said coolly.

Before we could leave the grave, a figure rushed toward us, black cassock rustling around his legs, hunched shoulders leading the way.

"Capitán, thank God you're here," Father José María said breathlessly when he approached us. He shook the captain's hand warmly, and I realized the two men must already know each other. "This is a great travesty that's been committed here, beneath God's own eyes, on sacred ground. I hope you'll find the culprit swiftly and serve justice as it is due."

"Father, it's good to see you, even under these circumstances. We'll do our very best, of course. Did you know the girl?"

José María glanced down at the body for the first time, his face twisting with displeasure. I couldn't tell if it was because a girl had been murdered or because she'd been murdered here at San Miguel.

"No more than I knew any of the students here. A passing acquaintance. Mostly, I have contact with Professor Forster and Señora Forster, not the students." His voice was cold, unfeeling. Yet it softened, uncharacteristically, when he said: "They're young people, the students. She did not deserve this. I'll pray for her soul." He crossed himself vigorously.

"We're going to examine the murder weapon," the captain told him.

"Murder weapon?" Father José María looked surprised.

"Yes, the girl was strangled," Sánchez clarified, beginning to walk towards the entrance to the sanctuary. "The Professor believes it was done using the chains inside the church."

"Teodosio's chains," Father José María whispered. "May God help us." He proceeded to cross himself again and then look up at the heavens.

Chapter 25

WE FOLLOWED THE OFFICERS to the church, where I unlocked the door. Ignacio hadn't come out to open the church for visitors, which was a good sign. At least nobody but Bill and I entered the scene of the crime that morning. Father José María trudged along behind us.

Bill led the police to Teodosio's chains. "All the visitors to the sanctuary touch the chains," he said helpfully, "but there might still be a chance to lift some fingerprints from them."

"This is a gross desecration of such a holy place," Father José María interrupted before the captain had a chance to respond to Bill.

"I understand your indignation, Father, and I am in complete agreement," Sánchez said. "But we have no choice except to check the chains for fingerprints."

"It's not the fingerprints that concern me. Do what you must. It's the fact that some miscreant has profaned one of our most sacred spaces. It's intolerable. You must find this degenerate, capitán. It's of utmost importance! I must leave you now. This is all too much for me. If I'm needed, you'll find me in quiet contemplation in the house."

Without waiting for a response, the priest turned and fled with remarkable speed, the histrionics of his brash exit lingering after his retreat.

"Priests make poor investigators," the captain commented to Bill. "They are too emotional...like women. My wife is much the same, storming out of the room over the smallest things. We grow accustomed to such drama, don't we, Professor?"

Bill didn't have a chance to respond before Sánchez was barking orders at Ortega once again.

"Ortega, check the chains for fingerprints. Of course, Professor, this is standard procedure in a criminal investigation. You might be interested to know that the Guardia Civil has been trained in taking fingerprints since 1914. Before I was even born."

I was surprised that Sánchez seemed more interested in giving Bill a history class than looking around for more evidence of the crime committed in this very room. Bill and I hadn't seen anything ourselves when we came to inspect the chains, but that didn't necessarily mean that there was nothing to be found.

Ortega assiduously applied powder to both chains, flicking a delicate brush over the metal links, while the captain engaged Bill.

"That's very interesting," Bill replied. "Will you be photographing the body as well?"

"Of course, Professor," Sánchez said, smoothing his moustache with his fingers. "You have no need to worry. We're as scientifically advanced and rigorous in protocols for the investigation of crimes as police in any other country. Trust me, Professor. We have everything under control."

Despite his assurances, I had the distinct feeling that things weren't under control. Why wasn't he looking around the church? Why wasn't he asking more questions? Why hadn't they photographed the body already? The longer it was left alone, the more likely evidence could be lost or the body tampered with. I hated the idea of Angela's body lying out in the cemetery, completely exposed, while the captain seemed to be in no rush to gather any evidence for himself.

"I'm sorry, sir," Ortega said finally, putting his brush and powders away in a bag he carried slung over one shoulder. "The murderer must have wiped down the chains. There are no fingerprints on them at all."

"Fine, Ortega. We will photograph the body now. Professor, Señora Forster, you can return to the house at your leisure. We'll find you there when we return."

"There's something else," I piped up. Bill had perhaps forgotten about the vandalism in the church due to shock from Angela's death, but I felt the Civil Guard needed to have a complete picture of what was going on at San Miguel. "We don't know if they're related, but something strange happened yesterday when we opened the sarcophagi in the passageway. Both tombs were tampered with. We found a nest of vipers inside one and a mix of bones from at least three individuals in the other. We'd expected to find one body in each sarcophagus."

"Is this true?" Sánchez looked at Bill.

The audacity of the man, coupled with the tragic circumstances of Angela's death, had me ready to scream, but I held my emotions inside knowing I could make the situation far worse than it already was by losing my temper.

"Yes, of course it is," Bill replied, shoving his hands in his pockets. "We walked past it on the way in, but with everything that took place this morning, it slipped my mind. Beatrix is always exceedingly observant and organized."

"Fine." Sánchez smoothed the corners of his moustache with his fingers. "We'll look into it, I must insist that you return to the house now. There is nothing more you can do here."

We'd been summarily dismissed. I felt defeated, my feet heavy, held to the ground by some magnetic force. My head was insufferably light, as though detached from the rest of my body. We couldn't turn back the hands of time, but I hoped we could find the person who'd killed Angela. With or without Sánchez's help.

Chapter 26

"I THINK WE SHOULD talk with Miriam," I told Bill as we walked back to the house. We'd left Sánchez and Ortega to photograph Angela's body and take her to the morgue in Pamplona. "She knows more than she's telling us, and it could be important."

"Good idea. I'm not sure how well any of the students will respond to Sánchez. He's a bit of a tough nut, if you ask me."

"Goodness, you're right about that."

Miriam and Helen were alone in their room when we entered. Helen popped up and out of bed the moment we walked in.

"Any news? What did the police say? Do they know who did it? What're they going to do with the body?"

"There's no news yet, Helen," I told her gently. "Would you mind giving us a moment alone with Miriam?"

Helen turned to look at Miriam, who lay languidly on her bed, her face blotchy from crying.

"We'll have a chat with you after," I offered, before Helen could respond.

"Okay, I'll go see who's in the kitchen," she said, pouting slightly. "May I take Muffin with me?"

"Of course, dear," I said. "Just make sure she doesn't get into trouble."

Though Muffin was not a large dog, weighing about sixteen pounds, she overwhelmed Helen's small frame. I hoped she wouldn't struggle to get Muffin down to the kitchen. I did, however, perfectly understand the desire to keep her close given the therapeutic qualities of a warm and soft animal who gave unconditional love. Helen closed the door behind her when she left.

Bill and I agreed that it would be best if I asked Miriam the questions, though he would remain with me. The students tended to view me more neutrally than they did Bill, probably because I never officially evaluated their work. Bill was entirely responsible for assessing their efforts and sending the results to the university for their final grades.

"Miriam," I began, sitting down next to her legs on the bed. "I know how devastating this must be for you, and I wish with all my heart we could do something to make things better, but we can't. The only thing we can do for Angela now is try to find out who did this to her, and we really need your help. You knew her better than anyone. Is there something you can tell us? It might help."

Miriam shook her head.

"It's really very important, Miriam," I tried again. "The more we know, the better we'll be able to piece together what happened last night."

She shook her head again and rolled away from me, facing the wall.

"Miriam," Bill tried, his voice barely above a whisper. "It's okay to tell us what you know. Angela would want you to help find out who did this to her."

Miriam burst into tears, burying her face in her pillow and then forcefully turning back toward us. "She made me promise not to tell. Not anybody. I just can't betray her like that. I can't tell you. I'm sorry."

My suspicions were correct. Angela was keeping some type of secret, and Miriam knew what it was.

"Goodness, Miriam, you're not betraying her," I said. "You mustn't think that. She's gone now. It's not a betrayal. It could help us if you could tell us more about this secret she was keeping."

"I can't, Mrs. Forster. I just can't."

"Whatever you're not telling us, Miriam, could it have made somebody want to hurt her?"

"No! I don't know why you're here asking me all these questions. You should be downstairs asking Janis. She's the only dangerous one in this house. It's obvious who did this to Angela. You just don't want to see it!"

I was taken aback by the accusation. "Miriam, do you really think Janis did this to Angela?"

"You saw her the other night. She's bananas even when she's conscious. And she's strong as a bull. All she talks about is death and crime and how successful she'll be because she doesn't care about boys, only her career. And who knows what she does when she sleepwalks? You saw yourself. She had a knife."

"Angela wasn't killed with a knife, Miriam." I hoped to soothe her. If she was terrified of Janis, things in the house could get very complicated very quickly. "We'll talk to Janis, as we'll talk to everyone here, but it's especially unusual for people to become violent while sleepwalking."

"It was her. I'm sure of it. She's the dangerous one. Who else could've done it?"

Indeed, I thought. Who would do such a thing? I could tell Miriam wasn't ready to reveal Angela's secrets and that she made up her mind that the culprit was Janis. There wasn't much point in pressing her further. I had my doubts about Janis' guilt, but perhaps she did know something about Angela. They'd shared a room after all, and she had no incentive to cover for someone who, though never unfriendly as far as I knew, wasn't her close friend.

Chapter 27

BILL AND I COULDN'T FIND JANIS, and, after asking around, we discovered she was in the lab. She'd been pestering the others, and Archie told us that he'd thought a little time with something she enjoyed to occupy her mind might prevent arguments from escalating.

"I'm sorry if you don't want her there alone, Professor Forster," he said, his forehead creased with worry. "I just didn't feel up to supervising her, or even being in the lab at all, after everything. I can tell her to read a book or something, if you prefer."

It was the kind of privilege not usually accorded to our students, but Bill and I agreed that, under the circumstances, Archie had done well to keep her occupied.

We found her alone, examining a bone from the pelvis of the skeleton that was there the day before, when the noise startled me.

"Hello, Janis," Bill said as we entered. "What are you up to?"

Although she didn't get along well with the other students, she was always well mannered around us.

"Hello, Professor Forster, Mrs. Forster," she said, not stopping to look up. "I'm just having another look at this skeleton. I hope that's all right."

"Yes," Bill said, "it's fine. However, we did come to speak with you about Angela."

"Do you know anything about what happened last night?" I asked, watching her run her finger over the iliac crest of the innominate bone.

Janis shrugged and set the bone down with care on the table. "Not really, Mrs. Forster. I slept downstairs in the kitchen last night, just like the night before. I don't know why the other girls are so worried about my sleepwalking. My family thinks it's funny. They've never had a problem with it. I've never done anything dangerous, though. Did Miriam say I did something?"

I ignored her question. She didn't need to know that Miriam was accusing her of murder. "Did you hear anything unusual last night? After everyone went to bed. The kitchen's right next to the front door, so perhaps you heard some noises or something."

"I wish I could help," she said, looking me in the eye. "But I didn't hear anything strange. I was pretty tired, so I slept right through last night. I mean, I think I did. I don't think I had a sleepwalking episode, though like I told you before, sometimes I don't remember them. People just tell me about them the next day. That's how I know for sure. Sometimes I do remember, but it feels as though it were a dream, so I don't always know if I was up and about or just dreaming. Anyway, I don't see the big deal. Angela was always going out in the middle of the night, and Miriam never complained about that. She went out, too, sometimes. So why is it different if I do it and I'm not even awake?"

"Angela went out in the middle of the night?" Bill asked.

"Well, not all the time. But sometimes she would. I mean, I assumed she was going to the bathroom some of the times, but if I was awake when she came back, it felt like it was a long time. And some of those times I thought it smelled like smoke...I think. I'm not actually sure, to be honest. Angela was the only nice one, so I don't want to tell stories about her. I don't want you to think I'm a fink or anything like that. But she did leave our room sometimes at night. Maybe some of those times it was the bathroom, and maybe on occasion it was for a smoke outside. I couldn't say for sure. Some of the others did that, though, now and again. I overheard them talking about it. I wasn't invited, of course." She sounded disappointed that she wasn't included. "Apart from that, though, where would anybody want to go in the dark on this mountain? You can't see a thing!"

I glanced at Bill. "Goodness, so many nocturnal activities."

He looked as surprised as I felt. Maite mentioned it to me casually in the past, of course, but now it was far more important than it had been at the time. The day before, the issue was just one of young people out gallivanting from time to time, but now someone was dead. It was serious.

"Any chance Angela was sleepwalking as well?" I asked.

If we had one somnambulist, it was entirely possible we had another. Our own son had been a nighttime wanderer for many years in his youth. It wasn't so uncommon.

"I don't know, Mrs. Forster. Angela was a bit of a daydreamer anyway. I saw her just mosey off sometimes, down the mountain trail, by herself, picking wildflowers and strawberries. I don't know where she was going. I think she just liked the forest. And probably she wanted a break from Miriam. She's a bit clingy when it comes to Angela. I'm sure Angela just needed a little space."

"Is there anything else you can tell us?" I asked. "I noticed your hair was damp this morning, did you shower early before the others?"

Janis shrugged again. "I don't know, Mrs. Forster. Maybe I did, but I don't remember doing it."

She sounded genuine. Had she remembered showering this morning there would be no reason not to tell us, as her having damp hair didn't implicate her in Angela's death in any way.

"What about the tombs in the church?" I asked. "Or any other strange thing that's happened?"

Janis was strong, and she wasn't afraid of vipers. Could she have opened the tombs alone or with the help of someone else? And what about the students going out at night? Was Maite right about witchcraft and they'd gotten themselves involved in something sinister? And then there was the murder weapon. Was using Teodosio's chains symbolic, or were they a weapon of opportunity? And the button in the tomb, did we have the right to go through everyone's clothing searching for a shirt with a missing button?

"Finding the vipers was very cool," Janis smiled, as though recollecting a fond memory. Then her face grew serious. "I don't know how they got there though, Professor Forster, Mrs. Forster. But everything is a bit strange here, isn't it? Maybe the others are right, and this place is haunted."

Chapter 28

AFTER SPEAKING WITH JANIS, despite her quirks, I couldn't imagine her luring Angela into the church in the dead of night, strangling her to death with Teodosio's chains, then carrying the body out to the cemetery and staging it to be found the next morning. She certainly had the physical strength to accomplish the task, but what would her motive have been? As she'd said herself, Angela was one of the few students to be cordial to her, as her queer behaviour made her a target for some and a person to ignore for others. I found myself at a loss. I just couldn't imagine anybody with whom we'd been living these months committing such a crime. It was unimaginable.

"What are you thinking?" Bill asked me after we'd moved to the other laboratory room and closed the door.

"Goodness, I'm thinking that I don't know what to think. What are you thinking?"

"Much the same, I'm afraid."

I sighed. I was concerned that the police would do a superficial investigation and leave again. Despite Father José María's warm reception of the captain, the policeman just didn't inspire much confidence, and he clearly demonstrated a lack of concern for a foreign national who'd just been murdered in his jurisdiction.

"Why don't you show me those bloody sheets while we're down here?" Bill suggested.

I was surprised he'd remembered them. "I can. But I don't know that they have anything to do with this. Angela didn't have a speck of blood on her, and I found those sheets before she was murdered anyway."

"Something to bide our time until the return of the police?"

"Fair enough," I said and led the way to the room that contained the priests' vestments and other assorted sundry.

In the storage room, I opened the closet door and pulled the sheets down from their hiding spot. The stains had a more rusty appearance since I'd seen them last. Bill examined them, turning them over in his hands and holding them up to the dim light projected by a bulb above our heads.

"It's quite a lot of blood," he murmured. "Not enough to kill anyone, not that much, but certainly more than just a small cut."

"Goodness, I wasn't sure what to think. I just tossed them back up into the corner. They seem to have been hidden, but I can't imagine why."

"Who uses this room?"

"Probably nobody. I would think only Ignacio is supposed to be coming here. The students are quite a curious bunch though, I have to say. I wouldn't be surprised if they'd discovered this place long before I did, regardless of it being off limits to them."

"You're quite right. The students have probably gotten into every nook and cranny in the place."

"Speaking of Ignacio, he's rather an odd duck, don't you think?"

"Well, a bit, I'd have to admit, but more than that, I think he's just quiet. He enjoys his solitude. And we have most definitely disturbed the peace around here, I'm afraid."

"You're more charitable than I am, Bill. I find his behaviour to be a smidgen more than bizarre. I've said it before. I think he's got a secret."

"Do you think he did this, Beatrix?" Bill looked at me expectantly.

"I don't know what to think. Can you think of anybody else more likely to have committed a crime among the people here? I've always had the impression that he didn't care for our presence on the mountain. A murder would certainly be enough to scare most people off."

"Well, I imagine he's spent many years here alone. You have to agree we're a bit of an intrusion in a place he's used to having all to himself. He may not appreciate our presence, but that's a far cry from killing a young woman to get rid of us. He essentially works for the church, and the church has approved our work here. Why would he go against the wishes of his employer?"

"It could be just as you say, that he's more comfortable on his own. Or it could be more. I would never have suspected him of being a murderer, now I just don't know what to think. And with all the other strange occurrences....I did find it odd, though, when we met him in the woods and he had blood on his hand, yet he said he hadn't caught any animals in the forest."

"Odd but not inexplicable, I suppose. Maybe he'd hurt himself. I can't imagine how it would relate to Angela either way, though."

"Goodness, perhaps I'm grasping at straws, but I'd like to get to the bottom of all this. Remember we have to sleep here tonight with a killer on the loose. Let's go speak with Ignacio. He knows this place better than anybody. If he wasn't the one who did it, maybe he knows something that might help determine who killed Angela and if the vandalism of the tombs has anything to do with her death."

"We can give the sheets to the police and maybe they can determine if the blood is human or belongs to an animal," Bill said, opening the door of the storage room so we could leave. "And at some point, the police will speak with everyone, so in the meantime, I don't see why we shouldn't have a crack at it first. We're certainly more amiable than that captain."

I smiled genuinely for the first time that day. "Isn't that the truth!" I said, looping my arm through my husband's.

Chapter 29

BILL AND I WERE in the hallway, approaching the stairs that led to Ignacio's room in the attic, when we bumped into Helen followed closely by Muffin.

"Are you coming to talk to me?" she asked eagerly.

"Actually, Helen," I said, "we need to speak to someone else first."

"But you said you'd talk to me after you talked to Miriam," she whined, clearly not accustomed to being brushed off.

"I tell you what, Helen. You and I can have a little chat while Professor Forster attends to other matters. How does that sound?"

Ignacio might be more willing to speak openly if Bill were alone, and it could prevent a meltdown on Helen's part. Two birds, one stone.

"You can find me when you're done," Bill said swiftly, leaving no time for Helen to protest.

She pouted slightly and said nothing.

"Now let me think a moment," I pondered aloud as we stood alone in the hallway. "Where can we have a private conversation?"

"We could use the office beside the kitchen," Helen said as though nothing were out of the ordinary.

"I'll ask the priests if they mind," I said, wondering why the office would even come to Helen's mind.

Though I'd been in once or twice, we generally didn't use the office for the purposes of the excavation. It was also off limits to students. Maite explained to us on arrival that the office was used by the priests when they stayed at the sanctuary and by her to store a few things when the pantry grew too cramped. I snapped my fingers to get Muffin's attention and the three of us headed down to the main floor of the house.

I found Father José María in the kitchen staring into a cup of tea, a stern look on his face. He sat in silence, which was no surprise to me. Everyone reacted to tragedy in their own way. I asked, and he gave his approval to use the office.

"Do I need a key to get in?" I asked.

"No," José María said. "It's not locked. There's been little need to keep things locked up until now."

Of course, given the repeated thefts at the sanctuary, I knew this wasn't true. However, I said nothing, knowing that the older priest was still stewing over the events of that morning.

Helen and I entered the office. It was a large room adjacent to the kitchen, cluttered with furniture, books, loose papers, and other odds and ends. There were also two large wooden desks set up facing each other, a few bookshelves with glass doors, a couple upholstered chairs, and several more wooden chairs placed against one of the walls. Each wooden chair had a stack of books and papers leaning precariously on the seat, preventing anyone from using them for their true purpose. I didn't want to disturb the order of things, as there might have been logic behind the perceived chaos. Bill's office was much the same when he was teaching.

"We can sit at the desks," I told Helen, pulling a chair from beneath the heavy oak desktop.

Helen sat across from me at the other desk. Her elbows on the desk, she leaned forward impatiently. She was a frail girl, nothing but skin stretched taught over bird-like bones. I knew already she simply didn't have the strength necessary to kill Angela on her own and she absolutely could not have opened a sarcophagus. I'd seen her struggle in the field with nearly every tool. She couldn't lift the pickaxe above her head, the wheelbarrow toppled over if there were too much dirt within, and she required two hands to lift a hand-shovel of dirt into her bucket. Angela wasn't much bigger than Helen, petite and slight of frame herself, but nobody on the dig struggled with the tools like Helen. If Helen was involved in these crimes, she'd certainly need to have an accomplice or two.

"Well?" she asked.

"The police have taken Angela's body away, but they'll be back to investigate. I have no doubt they'll want to question all of us. Did you notice anything out of the ordinary last night? You share a room with Angela. Did you notice her go out at any time?"

"Am I a suspect?" she asked, her tone excited rather than accusatory.

Evidently, she relished being questioned. I knew she liked to be the centre of attention, in the thick of things, knowing all that was going on. Perhaps she could reveal some information that would be of use.

"No, not specifically. Though I suppose we're all suspects at this point."

"I've never been a suspect in a crime before." She reached over and grabbed a pen out of a holder on the desk at which she sat. She twiddled the implement around in her fingers nervously.

"Goodness, Helen," I reprimanded her softly. "We're guests in this office. We really shouldn't touch anything that doesn't belong to us."

"Sorry, Mrs. Forster. I fidget when I get nervous."

"Nothing to be nervous about, unless you've done something wrong."

"Oh no! I haven't done anything. Not really. Nothing related to Angela's death anyway."

"Good," I said. "Back to my question. Did you notice Angela leave the room last night?"

"No. I wish I had, though I suppose it wouldn't have made any difference. I wouldn't have stopped her or anything. Gee, to think I could've stopped her and maybe prevented this whole thing!"

"The only person who could have prevented this was the person that killed her, Helen, so don't start with that kind of thinking. There's nothing you could've done."

"I guess."

"Was Angela there when you went to bed last night?"

"Yes, she was usually first to bed. I didn't hear her go out though. My mother says I sleep like the dead —" Helen covered her mouth, embarrassed by her figure of speech. "I'm sorry, Mrs. Forster. I don't want you to think I don't care. I do care."

"I know you do," I said gently, wondering to what extent that could be true. Helen spent more time thinking about herself than anybody else. "Now, Janis told us that Angela would go out at night from time to time. She thought it was just a visit to the bathroom, but she wasn't sure. Did you ever notice Angela go out any other night?"

"Maybe, but I don't think so. As I said, I'm a sound sleeper. It takes a lot to wake me up. Sometimes Miriam has to shake me to get me to wake up in the morning. I could sleep through just about anything. Who do you think did this, Mrs. Forster? Do you think it was one of us?" She began fidgeting with her hands again, picking up pieces of paper and replacing them on the desk.

"I wish I knew, Helen. I haven't got any idea who could've done something like this. Nobody fits the bill of cold-blooded murderer around here. Now, I've also heard that some of the students sneak out at night to smoke. Have you ever gone with them? You're not in trouble if you have, but it's important to tell me in case you saw something without even realizing it."

"Oh no! Mrs. Forster, I wouldn't. My parents say that smoking isn't ladylike and I'll never get a husband if I smoke. I wouldn't want that to happen. I wouldn't want to end up an old spinster, would you?"

She giggled nervously as she absent mindedly allowed her hands to dance across the desk, stumbling over obstacles in the form of books, a

magnifying glass, an old ink pot, paperweights. I was about to repri-
mand her once more, as she was bound to break something, when her
hands located an object that made a clinking noise at her touch. We
both instinctively looked to see what she'd grabbed. Helen pulled her
hand back as though she'd touched a red hot iron, but it was no such
thing.

"Hand me those keys, please, Helen," I said, recognizing the items
she'd accidentally found on the desk.

She obediently picked up the set of heavy keys and passed them
across the desk to me. One of them looked familiar, much like the one I
carried on my belt.

"What is it?" Helen asked.

I ignored her question and produced my own, comparing the teeth
and seeing immediately that they matched perfectly. One of the keys on
the desk was the key to the church. It was on the desk, in the unlocked
office all the time. If it was always kept here, anybody could have gotten
hold of it and entered the church in the night, if they knew where to
look for it. Access to the church, I'd believed, might help us to eliminate
suspects. If anybody could've acquired the keys from the office, then we
all remained suspects. We were no further ahead.

"What?" Helen said more loudly this time. "What is it?"

"It's the key to the church," I said.

"So? You have one too. Why do you need this one?"

"Goodness, Helen. So many questions. I don't need it. I'm just surprised to see it here, that's all. I thought only certain people had access
to the keys to the church. But here they are where anybody could find
them."

"I don't see why it matters," Helen said, a pen having found its way
back between her fingers. Of course, she had no way of knowing that
Angela had been killed inside the church. "You don't actually need a key
to get into the church from here."

"What do you mean you don't need a key to get into the church?"

"There's a secret passageway," Helen stated, as though this were
common knowledge.

"I beg your pardon?"

"The passageway. It takes you from the house to the sacristy, and from the sacristy, you can get into the nave of the church. We discovered it about a month after we got to San Miguel. We don't use it though! Or at least I don't. I wouldn't know about the others. I know we aren't supposed to be over there after hours. I think Maite uses it sometimes, though. She'll be there one minute and then she's gone the next."

"Goodness, I had no idea. Why didn't any of you tell us you'd found a way into the church?"

"Oh, there are lots of things we don't tell you," Helen said, then covered her mouth as though she shouldn't have said it at all.

"I'm beginning to see that," I replied and shut my eyes for a moment to process all the information I'd gleaned so far.

Chapter 30

I FOUND BILL in our room after I left Helen. He was sitting on the bed, hunched over with his face in his hands, his glasses next to him. He looked tired, old. I felt the same way. I moved his glasses away and sat down next to him. I noticed Bill had placed the bloody sheets on the night table, ready to be handed over to the police.

"Any luck with Ignacio?" I asked.

"I couldn't find him," he said, straightening up to look at me. "He wasn't in his room, nor was he in the kitchen, and nobody knows where he went."

"His being gone doesn't make me feel any better," I said. "And I found out from Helen that there are lots of goings on around here that we don't know about."

"Such as?" Bill raised his eyebrows.

"Apparently, there's a secret passageway that connects the house to the sacristy. So anybody that knew about it could've gotten into the church without a key."

"A passageway? Why didn't we know about this?"

"That's what I said."

"Where's the entryway?"

"Inside the pantry. Helen showed me the door."

"Where's the pantry?" Bill asked.

I laughed and squeezed his hand. "You don't know where the pantry is?"

He shook his head. He knew even less about this curious old house than I did.

"It's the door between the kitchen and the office. Where Maite keeps the provisions."

"Oh." He pressed his index finger to his lips and began to tap them rhythmically. "So you can get inside the church without a key," he began again. "So anybody could've been inside the church last night, entering either by the church door or from the house. So the culprit might have gone through the passageway. But did Angela go willingly, or was she forced? Or was she already in the church and the culprit found her there?"

"And if she were there already, why was she there?"

"Meeting someone?"

"Sleepwalking?"

Bill looked at me dubiously.

"It's possible," I said in my defence.

No response.

"Janis has put ideas in your head, my dear." Bill pointed at his temple. "I think sleepwalking is unlikely. That's a long way for someone to go while asleep."

"I suppose, but not impossible now with the passageway."

"Let's look at this again, a different way," Bill said, recovering his glasses and putting them back on. "Angela and the person who killed her are inside the church. He, or she, strangles her. Then what?"

"The body," I said. "The person still has to get her body to the cemetery.

That's a long way no matter which way you go."

"What's the shortest way?"

"That would be through the front door of the church. Leave the nave, take the body through the antechamber, then through the long hallway and out the wooden door, and then up the hill and into the cemetery."

"The door's locked."

I could see Bill walking through the events in his mind. His eyes had that unfocused appearance.

"The only other option would be to take Angela's body through the passageway," I began, trying to imagine the scene myself. "Go through the nave to the sacristy, through the secret passageway, through the house, out and around the side of the house and the church, and finally into the cemetery. It's much farther. And you'd risk being seen or waking someone in the house. It's not easy to carry that much weight either. Angela was petite, but she didn't weigh nothing. And dragging her that distance would surely have left extremely obvious marks on the body and in the dirt in the excavation area."

"So we come back to the fact that the person who murdered Angela needed to have a key, because they most likely used the church door to get to the cemetery."

"Yes," I agreed, rubbing my neck to try to reduce the massive tension accumulated since the morning.

"So only people with access to the key could've committed the crime," Bill said hopefully, looking over at me. "That narrows things down a little."

"Well, not really," I told him. "That was the other thing I found out when I was with Helen. There's a key to the church in the office, which is kept unlocked. So anybody in the house could've had access to the key and used it to get Angela's body from the church to the cemetery. I'd initially have believed the students wouldn't go into the office without permission, so they would never know about the key. But I'm beginning to see that the students are up to all sorts of things that we don't know about. Excursions in the night, smoking, sneaking about through secret passageways. How were we so oblivious, Bill?"

"Let me help you with that," Bill said, motioning at my neck but ignoring my question. I turned away from him so he could massage the knots in my neck and shoulders. "So where does that leave us?"

I sighed. "Square one." I didn't want to cry again, but I could feel the tears brimming in the corners of my eyes.

"Just a moment!" Bill shouted, abruptly ending the brief massage and shocking me out of the depths of my tribulations. "I've just thought of something."

"No need to shout, dear. I'm just beside you."

"Sorry. It's just something you said. The body. A dead body is difficult to move. Not everyone would have the strength to move a dead body all the way from the church to the cemetery. I think we can both agree at this point that the killer moved the body from the nave, through the antechamber and hallway, then out the front door, and that the secret passageway wasn't used to get Angela's body out of the church."

"Agreed," I said, wondering where Bill was going with this train of thought. Was he suggesting we could narrow down the suspect list based on strength alone? It was a possibility.

"But even that's quite far, as you said. Most people would be physically incapable without great strain. Especially if they were alone. But what if the killer had something with which to transport the body?"

"Such as?"

"What do we use to transport heavy loads every day?"

I gasped. He was right. The killer would not necessarily have needed to drag Angela's body or even carry it through the church to get it outside.

"The wheelbarrows," I said. "We need to look at the wheelbarrows."

"Precisely!"

Chapter 31

ON OUR WAY to the tool shed to examine the wheelbarrows, we were intercepted by the captain and the sergeant.

"Professor Forster," Sánchez began. "We've taken the body to the morgue. It's a weekend, you understand, so they're not certain when they'll be able to perform the autopsy."

"Isn't it rather crucial to get the results of the autopsy as soon as possible?" Bill asked. "It can only serve to aid the investigation."

"This is Spain, professor. We cannot rush things. This is the way things are. I'm sure you understand."

Vuelva usted mañana, I thought. Come back tomorrow. A well-known essay, written last century, came to mind that explained the way things worked in Spain much of the time. Today wasn't a good day; one should come back the next. And so on and so forth. Delays were inevitable.

"So what do you propose in the meantime?" I interrupted.

Generally calm even in extraordinary circumstances, I could see Bill's cheeks were flushed, and I knew he was getting angry. I wasn't sure that it would get us anywhere except on the wrong side of an officer that already seemed not to take things very seriously. We couldn't afford to alienate him, given our situation.

"We'll question everyone on the premises about the events of last night," the captain said, glancing at his watch.

I looked at my own and realized it was already two o'clock in the afternoon. It was long past our normal lunchtime, we'd been so preoccupied we hadn't even noticed.

"We've made some additional discoveries while you were absent," Bill began.

Sánchez held up his hand.

"Professor," he said, "you've been very helpful in identifying the murder weapon, but you must now leave the investigation to the professionals. No need to play amateur detective now that we're here."

"But," the sergeant began, "maybe the Professor —"

"Notes, Ortega! Notes. Just that. No talking, just notes. How many times do I have to tell you?"

"A la orden, mi capitán."

I felt sorry for the poor sergeant and wished he were handling the investigation alone. It was clear that Sánchez didn't care much for the junior officer and left no room for him to contribute to the investigation.

"Now, we'll interview you and Señora Forster first. It's just a formality. I don't really believe that you or your wife did this. Your wife couldn't have done it alone, and you, sir, do not seem the type."

"Is there a type?" Bill asked, sounding defeated.

"There's always a type," the captain said with a conspiratorial wink.

"Wouldn't it be best to keep an open mind?" I asked. "Really, anybody could have done it."

"Señora, you must not worry. Trust me. I'm very good at reading people. We'll have this solved in no time. Where can we conduct the interview?"

"I suppose it would be all right if we used the office again," I suggested. I didn't think anyone would mind under the circumstances.

The captain nodded, and we walked in silence to the house. Inside the office, Sánchez ordered Ortega to clear off the chairs and arrange them around the desks. Sánchez poked around at the desk while the sergeant piled books and papers on the floor.

"Quite messy in here," the captain commented. "This would never pass at the garrison."

The Civil Guard was military in nature, and I imagined that life was highly regimented for anybody who signed up for service.

"Let's get started," Sánchez said as soon as Ortega placed the chairs next to the desks.

We all sat down, Ortega with his notepad and pen before him.

"When was the last time you saw the victim?" Sánchez began, leaning back in his chair and looking at Bill.

"I suppose it would've been after dinner," Bill replied. "Angela was unwell in the morning, but she did join us for dinner. After dinner, she worked with Beatrix in the kitchen, along with some of the other students, and then Patrick, another student, played some music for us before we went to bed. Beatrix and I retired to our room after that, and I imagine the students weren't long behind us."

"So they're not supervised at all hours?"

"No, they're all adults attending university. They can do as they please in their free time, with the exception of a few rules." Bill sounded a bit defensive, as though the captain was accusing us of being negligent parents.

"And what are these rules?"

"No alcohol, no drugs, no smoking in the house. No girls in the boys' room and vice versa. Everyone should be back in their rooms and quiet by eleven o'clock. No entering rooms that are off limits. No engaging in anything but platonic relationships. I think that's about it. Beatrix, did we have others?"

I shook my head.

"Eleven o'clock?" Sánchez scoffed. "Many people have their dinner at that time or later here." *

"Of course," I said, knowing very well that we did things earlier than the locals. "But we need to keep everyone on the same schedule here. I don't imagine Maite would want to have people dining whenever it pleased them."

"It was only a comment, Señora Forster. No need to get defensive."

Again, I bit my tongue.

"Who, exactly, was here last night?"

"The students," I told him. "There are eight of them; ourselves; our teaching assistant, Archie; Maite, a local woman who helps with meals; Ignacio, the sanctuary's caretaker; and fathers José María and Pedro."

"Quite a full house. So you didn't see the girl or anybody else between when you went to bed and when you discovered the body this morning?"

"I didn't." Bill looked at me. "Did you, Beatrix?"

I thought about it for a minute. Even on my last trip to the bathroom before getting into bed, I hadn't seen anybody. I shook my head.

"That should be enough to get started," the captain declared, rising from his seat.

"You don't want any more information?" I asked, surprised that he didn't want us to talk about the characters of the students. "Nothing about what people here are like?"

"Not to worry, señora. You'll see I can make my own determinations about people."

I pursed my lips but said nothing.

Chapter 32

I'D HOPED THAT Bill and I would be left to our own devices after the
captain finished interviewing us, but that wasn't to be. Sánchez insisted
that we be present to help with interpretation, as neither he nor Ortega
spoke any English. He made a point of adding that although Bill was
expected to translate, I should remain in case anybody should become
overly emotional. At least, I thought, we'd hear what everyone had to
say. Bill suggested he might want to speak with Miriam first, as we'd
done, since she knew Angela better than anybody else. I was concerned
he'd not be open to the advice, but he accepted the recommendation.
Bill went to find Miriam and let the others know not to go anywhere, as
they'd each be interviewed by the police.

Miriam's eyes were red and puffy when she entered the office. She
sniffled and dabbed at her nose with a soggy handkerchief as she sat
down. Her dark hair was tangled and messy. My heart went out to her,
the poor thing. I sat down beside her, adjusting Muffin into a comfortable position on my lap, and squeezed her arm gently. Miriam patted

her lap to coax Muffin over to her, and I scooted the dog in her direction. Miriam was going to need all the support she could get.

"Señorita Berger," the captain began, leaning toward Miriam. "Tell me what happened last night after dinner."

"Well, after dinner, Angela, Patrick, Eduardo, and I helped Mrs. Forster with illustrations in the kitchen. Then Patrick played some music for us. After that, Angela said she wanted to go for a quick walk before bed to clear her head, even though it was rainy. She likes wandering around the mountain, says — *said* — it gave her space to think and breathe. I stayed in the kitchen with Helen. I don't know where the rest went. When Angela came back, we got ready for bed as usual."

The process was slow, as Bill was interpreting everything that was said.

"You're sure she was alone?" the captain asked.

Miriam glanced at me, then looked down at the floor. "Yes."

"Did you hear Angela leave in the night?"

"No."

"So you saw her just before going to bed, and that's it?"

"Yes." Miriam stroked the patch of black fur on Muffin's back, running her fingers quickly and repeatedly over the same spot.

"Miriam," I prodded her gently, "it's important that you tell the captain everything."

"Señora Forster, leave the questions to me. Please, just let your husband translate. Do not add your own commentary."

"It's just that —"

"Just translating. That's all I need. Perhaps you're too emotional to be here. Perhaps you'd like some tea in the kitchen."

Sánchez produced a cigarette case from his trouser pocket, pulled a white cylinder from the contents, and placed it in his mouth. He snapped his fingers, and Ortega obediently lit the cigarette with a lighter.

"I think we're done here," Sánchez stated. "Thank you, Señorita Berger. You may leave."

I was appalled. If the man would just let me speak, perhaps Miriam would reveal what she was hiding. Of course, the captain didn't know she was hiding something, nor would he allow me to tell him she was keeping a secret for Angela.

"Who's next?" Sánchez asked Bill.

"Just a moment," I intervened, switching rapidly between Spanish and English. "Miriam," I said sternly, "It's imperative that you tell us the whole story, even if it means breaking your word to Angela. It's incredibly important that we find out who did this. We've spoken to Janis, and it seems very unlikely she would've done something like this in a conscious or semi-conscious state. So if we don't get the whole story from you, it's unlikely that we'll solve Angela's murder."

Miriam burst into tears. I hadn't meant to be harsh, but I wanted her to see how desperately we needed to know everything. At this point, only she knew what Angela had been doing in her free time.

"He wouldn't have hurt her," she sobbed.

"What —" the captain began.

I held my finger up to silence him. This time he didn't object. Perhaps he sensed this information was important, even if he couldn't understand what was said.

"Who wouldn't have hurt her?" I asked.

"I don't know who it was. She wouldn't tell me his name. She was worried they'd both get into trouble, but she told me he loved her, and I believed it. He wouldn't have hurt her. I know that."

"Why don't you start from the beginning, Miriam, and Professor Forster will translate for the officers?"

Miriam began to cry even harder, gasping for air. She grasped the fur on Muffin's legs, pulling the long hairs unconsciously as she tried to gain control over herself. I rubbed her back and, from my pocket, handed her a fresh handkerchief that I'd retrieved earlier from my room, intended for my own use.

"There, there, you poor child," I soothed her. "You're doing the right thing."

Bill told Sánchez what Miriam said while I tried to get her to take deep breaths.

"I don't want to get anybody in trouble," she sputtered, moisture collecting around her nose.

"Nobody will be in trouble, Miriam," I said. "Except the person that hurt Angela."

Miriam nodded. She inhaled deeply, her shoulders shuddering as she exhaled. "I'll tell you everything I know," she said, folding and unfolding the handkerchief in her right hand. "It started just after we arrived here. She'd go off on walks by herself. She's always been like that, so I didn't think much of it. But then she told me that sometimes she wasn't alone. That she was meeting someone. She told me she loved him, and that after the field school was over and a little time passed, they were going to be married. She'd never tell me who he was. She was worried he'd be in trouble, that their relationship would jeopardize him, and that she'd be in trouble too. She didn't want to get kicked out of this program. We all knew that any kind of relationship would be frowned upon, by you and the university. She didn't want to risk anybody finding out. And, there's something else..."

"What is it, Miriam?" Bill asked.

She hesitated, shaking her head. "I don't want to say."

"It's important," I pleaded with her.

This was our first breakthrough. We needed her to tell us what she knew. She looked at me, tears in her eyes once more.

"She was pregnant," she whispered.

"Goodness," I said, shocked by the news.

I tried to process everything that Miriam just revealed. Angela had been seeing someone, someone we knew but whose identity she'd hidden, and she was pregnant. Suddenly, there was a possible reason for her illness and it had nothing to do with witchcraft.

"Miriam, were you really sick yesterday?" I asked.

She shook her head.

"I wasn't. I just said I was sick to make it seem that Angela wasn't the only one. I was worried you might figure things out if she was the only one sick. Helen just said she was sick too. She didn't know anything about Angela being pregnant. She just likes to fit in with everyone else. There was nothing wrong with her."

"So Angela was suffering from morning sickness?"

Miriam shook her head again, her face pinched with grief.

"That's what she thought. At first. It seemed normal that she was nauseous. But she had a lot of pain, and then she started to bleed. I don't know, she said she thought she lost the baby."

"A miscarriage," I said. "It's not uncommon for the baby to be lost in the first few months of pregnancy. What happened after that?"

"Well, she hid the sheets somewhere downstairs. She didn't say where. She snuck fresh sheets from the linen closet and remade the bed when nobody was around. Her pyjamas were stained but she didn't want to throw them out, so she stuffed them into the bottom of her luggage to wash when nobody was around. She told Helen she'd gotten her period and that she stained her pyjamas, so that night Helen lent her a nightgown to wear. Helen was the only one that brought multiple sleepwear options with her. I would've given Angela something of mine, but I didn't have anything. Just one pair of pyjamas and my digging clothes."

That explained why I couldn't remember Angela wearing the white nightgown when I saw her in the morning. The poor girl, so unwell, having a miscarriage all by herself and far from home. What a terrifying experience it must have been.

"So the girl was a bit of a floozy," Sánchez interrupted callously. Bill was interpreting for him. "Not much wonder she ended up —"

"¡Basta ya!" Bill thundered, slamming his fist on the desk. Everyone fell silent and turned their wide eyes to my husband, who rarely raised his voice. "There shall be respect. You're here to investigate a murder, not pass judgment on the dead."

I turned toward the captain, fearing his response to Bill's outburst. My gaze flicked from the pistol at his waist to the cold look in his eyes as they locked with Bill's. Suddenly, Sánchez laughed, his belly quivering beneath the tight belt.

"Forgive me, Professor," he said. "Perhaps young ladies' morality is judged differently where you're from. Here, a woman's virtue is her value. But you're right. I'm not here to judge the girl. I'll leave that to the priests and their commander-in-chief. Anyway, what young man didn't find himself in love with a girl like that in his youth?"

He took one last puff of his cigarette, allowing the smoke to escape from his lips slowly, deliberately, and then he stubbed the cigarette out on the wood of the desk.

Chapter 33

WE SENT MIRIAM BACK to her room, giving her instructions to rest. I needed a moment to consider what we'd just learned. I couldn't imagine Angela having a secret rendezvous with any one of the young men of our acquaintance. She'd always been so quiet, so amenable to the rules, never complaining, never causing a fuss. Yet it would seem that she had, in fact, been sneaking around with someone. I did not expect that from her, perhaps one of the other girls, but not Angela.

Then again, perhaps my own perspective was poisoned by the same societal norms that pervaded the captain's own beliefs. Nice girls didn't get pregnant before marriage. What did this say about the progress of society and its views of unwed mothers? Had we more charitable views, would Angela still be alive? Was she killed because someone knew she was pregnant? The father, perhaps? Was he afraid the scandal would ruin his reputation or future prospects? It wouldn't be the first time a woman had fallen victim to the man who'd professed to love her before she got into trouble. Or was Miriam right, and they really had loved each other? Then, in that case, who killed Angela? Someone who was wildly jealous of this relationship? And was her death related to the vandalism of the sarcophagi? Was someone trying to scare us off the mountain and had gone to extreme lengths? There were still so many questions, and so few answers. The next step would be to determine who the father was and whether he knew Angela had a miscarriage. At least in this, all the women at the sanctuary could be eliminated as suspects.

There came a soft knock at the door to the office.

"Entre," Sánchez said curtly.

We'd all been lost in thought.

Maite slowly opened the door and popped her head around the corner. "I apologize for interrupting, but I've prepared lunch for anybody who'd like it. I know it's late, I just . . . I'm very sorry. I understand if you don't wish to eat anything. I thought I'd check just in case."

She looked fearful, as though the Civil Guard came to question her specifically. I doubted she had any motive to hurt Angela, but Sánchez might have other ideas. Time would tell.

"Señora," the captain was suddenly all charm. "Please, come in. We'd gladly partake of the meal you've prepared. I've no doubt it will be lovely, and a welcome break at that."

"It's only a simple meal," Maite said timidly, then disappeared from the office.

She was normally a straightforward, bold person. Not reserved at all. For many people, the Civil Guard sparked fear in the heart. Their reputation for being heavy handed preceded them, and I knew Maite held no love for this particular arm of the law. I couldn't blame her. Sánchez inspired little confidence in my mind.

LUNCH WAS A QUIET, sorrowful affair. Nobody spoke, except the captain from time to time, exclaiming that the soup was particularly good or trying to draw Maite out of her deep silence. It was no use. Maite was in her fifties, with grey hair and heavy creases around her eyes and mouth, she was still a very attractive woman. The captain was apparently well aware of this fact, and despite being married, he felt no shame in very publicly trying to make a pass at her. His disregard for her discomfort was obvious. After the things he'd said about poor Angela, I was appalled. But then, hypocrisy was most often lost on the hypocrites themselves.

After the meal was finished and the students and Maite began to clear the dishes away, Sánchez remained at the table. He produced the cigarette case once more and began to smoke. I didn't bother to remind him that one of the rules had been no smoking in the house. I imagined he believed our rules to be trivial and his right to act as he pleased incontestable. He was right about the latter. There was little we could do about his behaviour.

"Everyone was present at lunch?" he asked.

"No," I said, mentally taking note of the absentees. "Miriam didn't come down."

"This I understand," Sánchez said.

I wondered if he was capable of empathy after all.

"And Ignacio," Bill said quietly, as though less attention would be paid if he kept his voice down.

"Ignacio?" The captain asked, leaning forward over the table. "Remind me, who is this Ignacio?"

"He's the caretaker of the sanctuary," Bill said. "He lives here all year round, keeping the grounds, the building, the animals."

"And he wasn't at lunch?"

"No. We haven't seen him all morning."

"Suspicious," Sánchez said, drawing the word out. The cigarette dangled from his fingers. His moustache twitched at the corner of his mouth. "Very suspicious."

His eyes seemed to glisten through the halo of smoke.

Chapter 34

"I HAVE SOMETHING to tell you," Father Pedro whispered in English in the hallway outside the kitchen.

Bill and I left Sánchez and Ortega in the kitchen, excusing ourselves for a moment before a planned resumption of the interviews in half an hour.

"What is it?" Bill whispered back.

Father Pedro beckoned with his hand for us to follow him and he led us outdoors. Nobody was nearby, but in the crisp mountain air, voices had a tendency to carry. We walked away from the house to some stone benches that were positioned to give a view of the valley.

"What do you want to tell us?" Bill asked again.

"It's about the Guardia Civil," Pedro said, pulling down the sleeves of his cassock. "I know him."

"Which one?" I asked.

"The younger one. Javier. I've known him since childhood. We were once good friends, but I don't see him often anymore, not since I joined the church and he the Guardia Civil."

"I didn't notice you talking to him," Bill said. "Did something happen?"

"No, nothing like that. He's a good person. The Guardia Civil has a bad reputation among many people, but not all are bad." Pedro glanced over his shoulder toward the house, but there was nobody there. "The captain, however, is, how do you say it? Notorious, that's the word. He is notorious here in Navarre...well, depending on who you ask, of course. For this reason, when I saw Javier, I pretended not to know him. I'm sure he understands, though I've not spoken to him yet. If the captain knew he was a friend of someone here, I'm certain he'd send for a replacement. I think it's best if he remain part of the investigation. A witness to the process as such. I trust that he'd want this case solved properly."

"You're concerned the captain won't carry out a thorough investigation?" Bill kept his eyes fixed on Pedro's face.

"That or worse."

He didn't elaborate as to what "worse" might entail.

"What do you mean by 'worse'?" I didn't really want to know, but I couldn't help asking.

"I don't mean to frighten you, it is not uncommon for the police to torture confessions out of people. As foreigners, you have some protection against these practices, but those of us from here are not so lucky."

I shuddered at the thought of anyone being tortured to obtain a confession, even if they committed a serious crime. It was an inhuman practice we often associated with times of war, not countries at peace promoting themselves as fun-filled tourist destinations. There was an ugly side to authoritarian regimes, and it was easy for visitors to ignore what life was really like for the local people.

"But it was clear that the captain knew Father José María," I said, pushing images of torture out of my mind. "Should he not recuse himself if he knows somebody involved?"

"José María knows many people," Father Pedro said, taking the stick that suddenly found itself in his lap and tossing it, half-heartedly, away from him. "So does the captain. The standards are quite distinct when one finds oneself in charge. And the captain is very much in charge."

Bill grunted. "Quite true."

"So that you're aware," Pedro continued, brushing some dust from the stick off his black cassock. "The captain is a devoted supporter of Franco. On that, he and José María are quite in agreement. It's not uncommon here, as many in Navarre supported the uprising that started the Civil War. Any comments deemed in opposition to the Caudillo will be taken quite seriously by him."

"We understand," Bill said. Our political beliefs were no secret to Pedro. "We don't want to get into trouble with the law. We'll be careful to watch our tongues, won't we, Beatrix?" He winked at me.

I smiled and adjusted my glasses. "Goodness, I'll do my best." I laughed apathetically, knowing Bill was trying to make me feel better, but I could sense the gravity with which Pedro spoke. I'd be wary of Sánchez, as Pedro suggested.

"Anything else we should know?" Bill asked.

"About the captain?"

"About anything," I said delicately. The situation was difficult for everyone.

Pedro fell silent for a moment, looking out across the valley at the cliff face opposite, where the rough, grey limestone met the lush, emerald grass. Only the fittest would climb to the top, ascending a near vertical kilometre of trail to reach the church of San Donato, which graced the mountain of Beriain.

"It's a terrible thing that's happened here," he said, clutching the cross that hung from his neck. "It causes me great distress that someone would take the life of a young woman. How must her family feel? They can only be devastated by such a tragic occurrence. My heart and prayers go out to them."

I gasped and looked at Bill. I'd been so caught up in the turmoil of the day I'd forgotten that we still needed to contact Angela's family. I looked at my watch. It was now mid-morning in Toronto. Bill nodded and the three of us rose in silence.

Chapter 35

BILL MADE THE PHONE CALL himself from the telephone in the sacristy. It took several minutes to reach the correct overseas operator, who then connected him to the Sorensen family home in Toronto. The conversation was brief, the tragic news, the static on the line, and the expense of a long-distance call. When Bill hung up, his face was ashen, his appearance fatigued.

"They said they needed some time to decide whether or not to come over and return with the body," he told me.

"It will be a difficult decision," I said, trying not to imagine what I'd do if one of my children were killed in a foreign country.

Bill nodded.

We walked back to the house, stopping briefly to collect Muffin from a hole she'd dug near the entrance to the sanctuary. The air was still, with only the cries of vultures circling nearby to disturb the mute solitude of the mountain. Not even Mauricio, Margarita, and the donkey brought by the priests the day before dared shatter the quiet that shrouded the atmosphere at San Miguel.

THE MOMENT WE RETURNED to the house, the captain's voice broke the silence.

"Tengo buenas noticias," he announced proudly. "Sargento Ortega has located our missing man."

"Where was Ignacio?" Bill asked, removing his glasses and wiping the corners of his eyes with his index finger.

"Hiding up the mountain. Ortega found him wandering around with a pig. Dirty creatures."

"Well, the pig is his pet," Bill said, "so that makes sense."

"Or is it suspicious, Professor?"

"Not particularly, capitán." Bill sighed, pushing his glasses back into place. "Ignacio spends a great deal of his time with Francisco, away from everyone else."

"Francisco? Who might that be? Nobody has mentioned a Francisco to me," Sánchez said sharply. "A family member?"

"Nearly," Bill smiled a little. "It's the pig. The pig is named Francisco."

"What?" Sánchez looked stunned. "He named the pig Francisco?"

"It's a common name here, is it not?" Bill asked, shrugging his shoulders and taking a cue from Maite.

"A common name for people, Professor. People, not pigs. Never mind that. We'll interview him immediately. No need for your presence, Professor. No interpretation is needed in this case."

The captain marched swiftly down the hall, and a moment later, we heard the door to the office slam. The smoke from his cigarette lingered in the air.

"Goodness, this does not bode well," I said to Bill.

"No, it does not."

As much as Ignacio was a bit queer and I had my own suspicions about his activities, we'd lived with him for more than two months.

I couldn't imagine him as the father of Angela's unborn baby. He tended to avoid company rather than seek it out. Frankly, I questioned what she might have seen in him. He was neither pleasant to look at, nor did he have pleasant manners. Relationships needed some basis upon which to flourish, and I could divine none here. Regardless of my feelings about Ignacio, and despite the captain's desire to interview him immediately, I believed that determining the identity of the father of the baby was the crucial next step in solving Angela's murder. I had to admit, though, that deep down, I hoped none of us was the perpetrator of such a heinous act. In this case, Maite's superstitions held a certain appeal. If witchcraft were at the heart of all that happened at San Miguel, Angela's miscarriage, the vipers and mixed-up bones in the church, and, ultimately Angela's murder, then perhaps everyone here was as innocent as I hoped. Unless, of course, they'd gotten themselves involved in malevolent rituals at the sanctuary. At this point, nothing made sense anymore. We needed some concrete evidence rather than flimsy hypotheses and indiscriminate speculation. Witchcraft or not, someone was responsible for Angela's death.

Chapter 36

THE TOOL SHED was nothing more than a small, ramshackle structure, built from untreated, warped pine boards. Given the dramatic changes in weather to which the mountain was prone, I imagined that this little shed was replaced frequently. Untreated wood didn't take kindly to fluctuations in temperature and humidity caused by shifts from direct sunlight to heavy rains and dense snowfall; it couldn't last long. Inside the shed, occupying every available space, were tools that belonged to the sanctuary and that we'd appropriated this summer for our excavation. Pickaxes, shovels, buckets, and wheelbarrows.

Bill pulled the wheelbarrows out of the shed one by one, using clean gloves to handle them. There were three wheelbarrows, dusty with dried brown clay from the cemetery. They were heavily rusted, the paint bubbling and peeling in patches. We examined them in silence, searching for anything that could suggest that the perpetrator used one to transport Angela's body from the church to the cemetery, thus eliminating the burden of carrying or dragging the body a long distance.

"Beatrix," Bill called. "I've found something."

"What is it?" I asked eagerly.

"Look," he said, pointing at the wheelbarrow in front of him.

I leaned in. A few strands of long blond hair were trapped between the handle and the basin of the wheelbarrow.

"Goodness, Angela's hair," I murmured, knowing very well it had to be her hair, as she was the only person at San Miguel with long blond hair. "I suppose this confirms that the killer moved the body using the wheelbarrow. Strange that her nightgown wasn't dirtier, don't you think? The wheelbarrows aren't exactly clean."

"True, but we didn't actually see the back of the nightgown. Only the front. The back might have been quite soiled. I suppose we'll never know. The captain isn't going to share that kind of information with us."

"At least now we know that anybody capable of getting her body into the wheelbarrow could've committed the crime alone," I said. "I would think there are a few of us who'd struggle to do even that. I don't think I could've lifted Angela's body into the wheelbarrow by myself. She wasn't a husky girl, and forgive my poor choice of words, but dead weight is difficult to manipulate. I think my back would certainly have made it impossible."

"True," Bill said, taking the gloves off his hands and scratching his beard. "Now, if we could just determine who the father of the baby was. It seems to be the vital missing piece of the puzzle. I'm afraid that despite Miriam's belief in his innocence, the prime suspect has to be the man that Angela was secretly meeting. He'd have the motive, if he didn't want her pregnancy to become public. If he were already meeting her secretly, then he most likely had the opportunity as well. Then again, if the tombs are somehow related to what happened to Angela, then the father of the baby seems a lot less likely to have been involved in her death. I just can't see how the two are related, except that they happened in close succession here at San Miguel. There's just something odd about the placement of the vipers in the sarcophagus, the way Angela was killed with Teodosio's chains, and then how her body was displayed in the cemetery."

"Don't let your archaeologist's brain get the better of you here, Bill," I warned him. "Not everything is ritualistic, despite what Maite might believe about witches. Though I don't like it any better than you do, an everyday, average person could just as easily have committed a murder and tried to make it look like something it wasn't."

"You're right, of course, dear," Bill. "Even if the father of the baby didn't kill Angela, perhaps he could tell us who did, or at least provide some motive for the crime. If what Miriam said is correct, he must have known her well enough."

"I certainly hope he can shed some light on all of this."

Chapter 37

SHOUTING FROM THE HOUSE roused us from the momentary iner-
tia brought about by ascertaining a new piece of information. I wondered what more could possibly have occurred in our short absence. We
rushed through the tall grass toward the commotion, only to find the
captain triumphantly pushing Ignacio along before him. Ortega trotted
briskly a step behind the captain. Ignacio's hands were cuffed behind
him, his brow damp with sweat that caused the fine strands of hair to
stick to his forehead. His eyes were wide with fear, and he appeared
excessively thin in contrast to the substantial body of the captain.

"Professor, I have your assassin for you," Sánchez announced boast-
fully, again pushing Ignacio forward.

"What do you mean?" Bill asked, his forehead creased with apprehension. "Did he confess?"

"He did indeed. I told you I'd make quick work of this."

I couldn't believe it. A confession. So easily? It seemed unbelievable.
I looked carefully at Ortega's face as he passed. He caught my gaze and

shook his head. It was barely discernible, yet I knew he was trying to tell me something. Had Ignacio indeed confessed? If he were the killer, why confess so quickly? Was he consumed with remorse for his crime? Or was there something else afoot here? Had the captain coerced his confession? Had he resorted to torture, here at San Miguel?

Behind the officers and their captive came a stream of people: most of the students, Archie, Maite, the priests, and a small dog weaving in and out of the crowd. We all followed the Civil Guards to their car, a grim parade of dismayed astonishment.

I wondered what motive Ignacio might have had for killing Angela. He couldn't have been the father of the baby, could he? He was more than twice her age. I never once saw them exchange even a glance. I was ashamed to judge so harshly, I couldn't help wondering once more, what a beautiful young woman, with her whole life ahead of her, would see in an aging caretaker that seemed to have few social skills and a sincere lack of appetite for human company. Stranger things have happened, to be sure, but I couldn't accept this. I felt nearly certain that the father of the baby played some role in Angela's death, killer or not.

The captain brusquely shoved Ignacio into the back of the car and slammed the door. He made a theatrical bow to the onlookers and waved as though he were the Caudillo himself, bidding his well-wishers a warm adieu. In contrast, the sergeant politely nodded his head and got into the driver's seat without a word.

"I wouldn't have expected it of Ignacio," Father José María said gloomily, as the group turned in unison to return to the house. "But then, how much did any of us really know about him?"

"I'm not completely convinced," Bill whispered to me as we walked back with the rest. "Yet, who else could it be? I'm baffled by all of this."

"I'm not convinced either," I told him. "Something about the way Ortega looked at me. He was trying to tell me something. Confessions don't come that easily. Look how long it took us to get Miriam to tell us what Angela was up to. The whole thing is fishy."

At the house, Bill gave the students instructions to rest until it was time for dinner, which would be later than usual and at which point we'd reconvene in the kitchen. He made it clear that both he and I would be available if anybody needed to speak to someone about the events of the day.

"Tea?" Bill asked me as the others began to disperse.

"Goodness, yes, please," I said, realizing how desperately I wanted to sit down for a moment.

I was surprised by someone taking my arm, firmly but not roughly. It was Maite. She looked upset.

"Por favor," she begged. "May I speak with you both?"

I nodded. Tea could wait.

Chapter 38

WE FOUND OURSELVES once more in the office. Maite was distressed, pacing back and forth in the room while Bill and I sat down. Finally, Maite took a seat too.

"What is it, Maite?" I asked, concerned by her sudden uneasiness.

"It's about Ignacio. I'm certain he didn't commit this crime. He wouldn't have done such a thing."

"How do you know?" Bill asked.

"I know he didn't do it, but I don't know for certain. How do I explain?" She inhaled abruptly and forcefully. "I mean, I wasn't with him last night, but I'm convinced that he wouldn't have done this."

"The captain said that he confessed," I reminded her gently.

"They have ways of getting people to confess, Beatriz," Maite said vaguely, looking at her hands. "They have ways. God knows I'd confess to anything they wanted." She looked up again, observing each of us momentarily. "I'll tell you everything I know if you promise not to tell anybody. I trust you both. I know you're good people, Father Pedro says I can trust you, but it could be very dangerous for Ignacio if you revealed what I am about to tell you. It wouldn't matter if Ignacio were innocent of Angela's murder, he'd end up in prison anyway. It's important to find the real killer so he doesn't spend the rest of his life in prison, or worse."

"As long as it doesn't affect our ability to find and bring Angela's killer to justice," I said, "then yes, we promise not to tell anybody."

Bill nodded his assent.

"Ignacio is my brother," she began slowly, her voice barely above a whisper. "Almost nobody knows this. Father Pedro's the only one. Not even Father José María knows. Nobody in the village knows because we didn't grow up here. We're from the north, near the coast. After the war, I needed to leave my own village. Women who'd supported the Republican government against Franco's Nationalists were harassed. I wasn't political; my father was both a teacher and a known Republican. As they'd already executed him and there was nobody left for the revenge they sought, not even my mother, who died heartbroken after my father was killed, they chose me to suffer. They shaved our heads to mark us. They paraded us through the streets. They forced us to drink castor oil so we couldn't control our bowels and would soil ourselves in public. It was humiliating, even worse, some were imprisoned, tortured, and executed. It was terrible. I guess I was one of the lucky ones. Ignacio wasn't around when this happened. At the time, I believed he was probably dead, among the many nameless victims of the war. I'd received no notice of his death, but that wasn't unusual. When my hair grew to a reasonable length, I obtained false papers and moved to Huarte-Araquil in the valley. I wanted a fresh start. People didn't ask a lot of questions in those years, unless they were the police. For most, it was better not to know your neighbour's secrets. The people in the village are good people, but we mostly keep to ourselves. It's safer for everyone that way. I made a new life here and tried to forget the past."

She paused to wipe a tear from her eye. I knew that talking about this must be difficult for her.

"I'm sorry," she said.

"Don't apologize, Maite," I said, reaching over to squeeze her hand. "Whenever you're ready."

She nodded. "Many people left for France during and after the war. Some continued to fight fascism in France against the Germans. Some came back, and those who believed there was still a chance to defeat Franco moved into the mountains where there were already guerilla fighters, coming down to attack units of the Guardia Civil or trains or to undertake whatever sabotage might disrupt the dictatorship. They were few, but for many, they kept hope alive. I didn't know, but Ignacio escaped to France and upon his return, he joined one of these groups. 'Maquis,' we call them. They continued this way for years. People hoped that the war in the rest of Europe would spill over the Spanish border, that when the allies rid Germany of Hitler and Italy of Mussolini, they'd come to save us next. We hoped they'd rid Spain of Franco. They never came. We waited and they never came. The maquis kept on, but eventually they were so few, hunted by the authorities and shot on the spot if they were found, that they disappeared."

Maite stopped. She remained silent a moment, turned to look at the door, and then resumed her story.

"Ignacio found me through an old friend in our village. I still wrote to her, and she knew where I was living. One day I came home to find him sitting at my kitchen table. I was so excited, you can't imagine. I'd believed him dead all those years. Almost two decades passed since I'd last seen him. We talked all night and into the morning. I almost forgot to go to work that day. I was employed as a cleaning woman at Santa María de Zamarce, the monastery in the valley, and at Father José María's residence. Father Pedro hadn't arrived yet when I started, but Father José María had already lived there many years. I knew that Father José María was of the old ways and that he admired Franco for promoting traditional Catholic values in Spain, whatever the cost. He feared these values were under threat when the Republican government was elected in 1936. They'd tried to change traditions too much, too quickly, and many feared change more than they feared violence and war. Father José María, despite his harsh exterior, is a generous man. He wants to protect the traditional ways in Spain, but he helps people when he can. I don't love him, the way I love Father Pedro, but I respect him. He gave me the job at Zamarce, which gave me independence. I told Ignacio we must never tell anybody about our relationship because, if they decided to condemn one of us for our past, at least the other wouldn't be found guilty by association. The next day, I made him leave in the middle of the night and told him to be at the church in the morning, where he'd plead poverty and beg for sanctuary, offering to work for his keep."

Ignacio's position as caretaker at the sanctuary began to make sense. His desire to avoid contact with others and his ability to remain isolated in the mountains for long periods also became understandable.

"Father José María took pity on him and offered him work here at San Miguel. He was glad to have it, and though I couldn't see him often, I was grateful to have him nearby. Just knowing he was safe made me feel better."

"Father José María and Ignacio don't seem to get along well," I interjected, wondering at the antagonistic relationship between the two men.

"It's true. Even though Ignacio depends upon the generosity of Father José María, he seems incapable of not riling the old man up. Just small things. And I've warned him of the danger, but he can't help it. I suppose it's his only source of entertainment up here. Mostly, it's Francisco that bothers José María. Ignacio does a good job. That's why José María puts up with his peculiarities. It doesn't stop him from voicing his opinion loudly, though. He has many strong opinions, but as I said, he's a generous man. He wants to help. He is strict for show, I think, though he has become sourer with age. I think his body pains him greatly, but there's no escaping old age."

I knew that to be true, all too well. I almost smiled at the thought of Ignacio gaining pleasure from irritating Father José María. It really wasn't difficult to aggravate the older priest, as I'd come to learn first-hand. I did sympathize with his pains, however. I knew how they could wear a person down and make one ill tempered.

"I'm very sorry to hear all this," I said. "It's an unfortunate story, and I wish you didn't have to live through these experiences. How does this prove that Ignacio wasn't involved in Angela's murder?"

"That's not the whole story," Maite said, looking up at me with a sigh. "There's more. I don't know everything, and it's difficult to explain. You noticed that he's secretive, that he keeps to himself?"

"Yes, we did notice," I said.

"Maybe I should show you," she said. "It'll be easier."

Chapter 39

MAITE PULLED A KEY from the pocket of her apron, and with a quick twist of her wrist, we were granted entry into the room on the second floor that I'd previously failed to access. Before she shut the door, Maite carefully scanned the hallway to make sure nobody followed us. She eased the door closed, the latch clicking quietly, and then she locked us in. The room contained an assortment of furniture, some in use, some stacked against the walls as we'd seen in the room adjacent. In contrast, this room was clean, no cobwebs dangling in the corners, no dust coating the surfaces of the furniture. It was clear it was regularly occupied. There was an old army cot pushed up against one wall, with rough grey blankets and old stained sheets. A desk, next to the window, held a large radio transmitter along with books and pamphlets. Old books lined the shelves, neatly organized with spines facing out and titles in a language I recognized as Basque but was unable to understand. Prior to leaving for Navarre, I'd learned a little about the history of the area but didn't attempt to learn Basque, having been told it was difficult to pick up and rarely used in public given the potential repercussions.

"This is where Ignacio spends much of his time," Maite said. "This is why he's so secretive, why he keeps to himself, why he finds it difficult to trust people."

"I don't understand, Maite," Bill said, looking around the room. "What does he use this place for?"

"Look," Maite pointed to the books I'd noticed. "These books are written in the Basque language. They weren't permitted under the law. Until this year, we weren't supposed to speak Basque, study Basque, or even have Basque names. When Franco first came to power, he banned every language spoken in Spain except for Castilian, what you call Spanish. I know I've told you this before, but I say it again. Some people didn't even speak Castilian when the war ended. They were forced to learn a new language and abandon the languages they'd spoken their entire lives. Basque went underground in many places, spoken and taught in secret. Things have improved greatly in these past years. Franco has other concerns and has loosened his grip, so the languages have been resurfacing over the last decade. They've just begun to publish a Basque section in the newspaper this year, and Basque can once again be taught in schools. They're much more tolerant here in Navarre about the language because, unlike where I come from, it's not considered a traitorous province. Much of Navarre didn't oppose the uprising in 1936. Before, the authorities looked the other way when they wanted to, but they could also have used it as an excuse to arrest someone. So Ignacio continued teaching some people from the village in private, here at the sanctuary. Though, with your visit here to San Miguel, he's not been able to continue except with one pupil, whom you know well. He teaches him here in this room. Ignacio trusts him with his life, as do I. He'd never betray us."

It wasn't difficult to guess who that pupil could be. When he lived in Toronto, he'd told us about the language, how he'd not been able to learn, and how he wished he could speak it. It seemed that Father Pedro found someone to teach him. I was certain this was something he'd keep secret from his mentor.

"If it's permissible to teach Basque again, Ignacio wouldn't be arrested just for that, would he?" I asked, wondering why Maite was so afraid for her brother's safety if the language laws were relaxed.

"There's more," Maite continued. "If it were just about the language, it wouldn't be so dangerous. There's much more than that. How do I explain?" She smoothed her hair back to the tidy bun she wore at the nape of her neck. "Ignacio belongs to an underground organization that seeks freedom for the Basque people from Spain and France." She motioned with her head to the radio. "It's an illegal organization, as many organizations currently are, and if anybody found out about this, Ignacio would undoubtedly go to jail. It's common for prisoners to be tortured, as you know, but also sometimes even executed, depending on the crime. The grises, the armed police, and Franco's secret police, are dangerous and feared by many even more than the Guardia Civil. Franco is most afraid of communists and Basque nationalists, and he'd go to great lengths to crush people who fall into either category."

"Doesn't the church protest against the torture and executions?" Bill asked. "They have a strong voice here in Spain. Franco claims to be a good Catholic. So if they spoke out against it, wouldn't he have to stop these things from happening?"

"Some of the younger clergy do. Father Pedro went to Barcelona last year to protest against the torture, but nothing changed. The old guard still supports Franco, even when they torture and execute people. This is Spain, Professor," Maite added sadly. "Here, not even God can be saved. They assassinated him."

"What was that?" I was surprised by her pessimism; she was usually so lively.

She seemed defeated. "Oh nothing. It's from a poem that has stuck with me. One of the social poets. I don't know that I agree with what Ignacio does here, but he's my brother, and I couldn't bear to lose him again." She began to weep, brushing the tears away with the heels of her hands.

"We won't tell anyone," I promised her, putting my hand on her back. "Ignacio won't be placed in more danger on our account."

"But now he's in jail for something he hasn't done," she sobbed. "He isn't a violent man, Beatriz. He told me how much he regretted the killing during the war and the years after. He's part of this organization, and though they break the law, sabotage things, spread illegal propaganda, they haven't killed anyone. They seek to agitate, motivate young people to action, to antagonize the dictatorship. He wouldn't have killed Angela. I know this. I know him."

"Maite," I said, looking her in the eyes. "Angela was having a secret relationship with someone here. She was pregnant. Did Ignacio tell you anything about a relationship with her?"

Maite gasped, shaking her head. "No," she said forcefully. "If she was seeing someone, it wasn't him."

"Are you certain?" Bill asked. "We only ask because it's imperative we find out the identity of the father. It could help to demonstrate Ignacio's innocence."

"I'm certain," Maite stated forcefully. "One hundred percent. Ignacio will never have children. It's impossible. He was injured during the war, and because of that, he can't have children. So he couldn't be the father of Angela's child. Of this, I'm certain."

I looked around the room once more. Just like Angela, Ignacio was living a secret life, and we were blissfully unaware. How many others here had secrets to reveal?

Chapter 40

"IF ONLY THE FATHER of the baby would come forward," I lamented to Bill once we'd retreated to our bedroom. "It would make things a lot easier. We can question all the men in the house until we're blue in the face, it doesn't mean he'll confess."

"At least we can rule out Ignacio," Bill said, sitting on the edge of his cot.

We both still believed that finding out the identity of the father had the potential to be the decisive element to finding Angela's killer. A pregnancy out of wedlock would certainly unravel the lives of those involved, and depending on the stakes, it was enough to push someone over the edge, regardless of the role the father played getting to that stage. The question was whether the father knew about Angela's miscarriage. It was possible he didn't, increasing the likelihood that he might himself be the killer. Of course, if Angela's lover killed her, a connection between her murder and the vandalism of the sarcophagi was nebulous at best. Still, it seemed wise to solve the mystery of Angela's secret relationship and then worry about tying up loose ends.

"We'd better get started soon," Bill said. "It will soon be dinner time, and I think everyone would be better off if they had something to eat, us included."

I nodded. "Where do we start? I think we need to look at opportunity, motivation, and actual ability to carry out the murder."

"Well let's go one by one, shall we? We can start with Roger. He's biggest and strongest, and he wouldn't have a problem putting Angela into the wheelbarrow. In fact, he might not even have needed it." Bill looked at me expectantly.

"Perhaps that says something in itself," I replied. "Why not just carry her out if he could? It would've been easier. However, looking at whether it was likely he had a relationship with Angela, I'd say that he could attract the attentions of a young woman. And there was something Angela or Miriam said. I can't quite remember what it was, but it made me suspicious there might be something there. He certainly had opportunity; we all lived together. As for motivation, if he were concerned we might send him home from the excavation or that his family would be angry when they found out, it could cause someone who's already struggling with all these major stressors in life to lash out."

"Well, I think we can agree that all the students, and Archie, and Ignacio had opportunity. Even the priests, though not here as often, came to San Miguel from time to time. Every one of us had the opportunity."

"Very true," I said, staring at a gap in the wooden floorboards. A world of dust and debris accumulated in the crack, and I wished I had my vacuum cleaner handy to make it disappear. "Next there's Patrick. I'm sure many young ladies would find him attractive, though he's very quiet and not so assertive as Roger. I've seen the way the girls look at him when he's singing. I sensed some unspoken bond between him and Angela the other day, but I couldn't say exactly what it might be. Yet, he has much the same kind of personality as Angela. Dreamy, you might say. And I wonder if that would push them away from each other rather than toward. Does that make sense?"

"I don't know, Beatrix. Opposites attract, but so do similar personalities. Patrick isn't quite so strong as Roger, but he could get Angela into a wheelbarrow on his own. What about Archie?"

"Surely not Archie, Bill." I felt guilty just considering any of our students or Archie as possible suspects. "We've known him a long time. He's a trustworthy young man. He's only just gotten married to a lovely woman. Do you really think he'd put his marriage along with his position here and at the university in jeopardy like that?"

"He certainly has a great deal to lose by getting involved with a student." Bill stood up from the bed. He began to pace in the small area beside the bed. The stress of the day was wearing on both of us. "But it wouldn't be the first time we've seen something like this happen at the university. And should his wife find out about an affair, she might be inclined to leave him, and he'd go back to being a poor doctoral student. Money is a strong motivator, and he's strong enough to move Angela's body into the wheelbarrow. But you're right: it's difficult to believe it of Archie. As you say, we know him, and we trust him. What about the other two, Eduardo and Graham?"

"Eduardo's father makes him a special case." I watched Bill walk back and forth in front of me. The pacing was making me anxious. "Please, Bill, sit down." I patted the edge of the cot where he'd been sitting before. He sat down as instructed, but I could tell his mind was now doing the pacing instead of his legs. "Of course, I suspected him of tampering with the tombs at his father's behest. However, convincing his son to get a student pregnant and then kill her is too evil, too conniving, for even Domingo Reyes Iglesias. He's sneaky and unethical, but he's not that malicious. That doesn't eliminate the possibility that Eduardo had a genuine relationship with Angela, and I can't see his father involved in that aspect of what's happened at San Miguel. The sarcophagi, yes. The murder, no. Eduardo would also struggle to get Angela into the wheelbarrow, I think. Same for Graham. He's not very strong, and my gut tells me Angela would not have been attracted to him either."

"Just the thought of Domingo using his son to undermine our excavation makes my blood boil."

"I know, dear," I said. "I just think that he'd never go so far as to involve himself in the death of a student. It's simply too outrageous. And of course, we have to look at the priests as well. The thought of Father José María being involved with Angela is just as absurd as

Domingo being behind her death. José María could be her grandfather. However, if he were having a secret affair with Angela, his motivation would be strong to hide what was going on. His reputation would be ruined, and his life's work would be over in an instant. His career as a priest would be finished. On the other hand, I don't believe that Father José María would have the strength to get Angela's body into the wheel-barrow. Not with his spine the way it is."

"I agree with you on that, Beatrix," Bill said, looking up at the wooden cross on the wall above our beds. "I don't think he could lift the body, and I have a feeling Father José María would rather die than be caught up in an illicit love affair."

"And then there's Father Pedro," I said, examining the wrinkles on my fingers. The disparity between young and old grew more acute in my consciousness with each passing year. "Father Pedro is still young. He could've lifted the body, and Angela could've been attracted to him. I think Janis is a little sweet on him, so why not Angela too? In terms of motivation, though, he has far less to lose than Father José María. He hasn't been a priest for long, and he's young enough and smart enough to start over if need be. And beyond that, I feel the same way about him as I do about Archie. We've known him many years. Maite shares our opinion of him. He's trustworthy."

"Assuming what Maite told us about Ignacio is true," Bill said, reaching over to place his hand on my leg, "then he's the only one that can definitely be ruled out as the father of the child, though I would wonder about Father José María's fertility. And in terms of strength, anybody but Eduardo, Graham, and Father José María could've moved Angela's body without help or at least a significant struggle."

I wrapped my hand around Bill's and squeezed. "It's not much to go on, but it's something."

"We can't forget that appearances can be deceiving," Bill said ominously.

I looked at my watch. "There's still a little time to get started before dinner."

Chapter 41

IT WAS NO SURPRISE that Father José María was displeased when we asked to speak with him about Angela's murder. We'd found him sitting alone in the office, scribbling furiously on a piece of paper on his desk.

"The Guardia Civil have already made an arrest," he protested in Spanish, glaring at both Bill and me as we sat down. "It's not your place to conduct your own investigation just because you're not satisfied with the results, though I can't begin to comprehend why you should want to defend Ignacio. He confessed. Capitán Sánchez has informed us of this fact. What do you hope to gain from further questions?"

"Father José María," Bill began, his voice steady. "We have reason to believe that the confession might have been coerced from Ignacio. If that's indeed the case, then justice will not be served if he's imprisoned for something he didn't do. You must agree that, in this case, it's most important that justice be served. Is that not true?"

"Of course! I still can't understand why you think the Guardia Civil have got it wrong. What evidence do you have that he's innocent despite his confession?"

"I understand your confusion," Bill said. I kept quiet and let Bill conduct the interview, knowing Father José María would respond better to him than me. "Angela was pregnant, and Ignacio couldn't have been the father. So whatever he confessed, it might not have been the truth."

"The girl was pregnant?" José María spat out, incredulous. "Pregnant? How could such a thing have happened here? This is a holy place, and now it's been desecrated repeatedly. I shouldn't have allowed you to come. Look what's come of my generosity. I shouldn't have let Pedro talk me into it. San Miguel will be forever ruined by this."

"José María, I understand your distress," Bill said. "We're all shocked by what's happened here. Right now, though, it's important that we find out who the father of Angela's child is so that an innocent man doesn't rot in prison."

José María's face was twisted and crimson. His hunched shoulders heaved with each breath he took. "What are you suggesting, professor? That I might be the father? Good God, what would've possessed me to get involved with a common trollop? I'm highly regarded in this community. I would never stoop to such depths. I'd be better off dead than caught up in such a sordid affair!"

Bill was right. Father José María would prefer death over ruining his reputation. That or he was an exceptionally good actor.

"Please, father," Bill said, holding up his hands. "We're not suggesting that you were the father of Angela's child." Though we were seeking that information, it was clear a direct inquiry wouldn't sit well with the elderly priest. "We're simply speaking with everyone in the household to gain more information about what occurred last night. You were here last night, just as everyone else was, so it's not inconceivable that you might have heard something or seen something."

I could see that Bill was shifting tactics. I didn't actually believe that José María had an affair with Angela, and on the slim chance he'd been involved with her, it was unlikely he'd confess his sins to us. His indignation was no wonder. He'd probably never been suspected of relations with a woman in his life. However, as Bill said to Father José María, just because he wasn't the father didn't mean he knew nothing of the crime.

"I see, Professor," José María said, leaning back in his chair. "I apologize for jumping to conclusions. I'd assumed you were accusing me of being the father, which of course is a ridiculous notion. I do wish I could help you. If, in fact, Ignacio isn't guilty, then I'm afraid I won't be able to help you in your investigation. I know your students very little, as you're aware. You've seen how minimal my interactions are with them. And I was asleep all last night. You can ask Pedro, if you like. He can attest to the fact that I sleep very soundly. Noises do not disturb me during the night. I saw the girl last at dinner last night. There's really very little more I can add to my testimony, as I knew almost nothing of what was going on in this house. Very much like yourselves, it would seem."

His words were cutting, but they were true. We were not aware of much that was happening under our own noses. Bill nodded but didn't continue to question the priest. I wondered if our efforts with the others would be more fruitful.

I had one more question for Father José María. "There's something else, before we speak with Father Pedro," I said hesitantly, not knowing how the priest would react. "When we opened the sarcophagi and found the unexpected, Maite mentioned the possibility of witchcraft being involved."

I didn't have the opportunity to ask anything before Father José María exploded: "Witchcraft? There are no witches here. This is nothing but the idle talk of peasants. As a good Catholic, Maite should not say such things. I thought you would know better than to listen to the superstitious ramblings of an old village spinster, but I was mistaken." He rose, hovering ominously over his desk. "I will have no more part of this. Unless you find some irrefutable evidence of Ignacio's innocence, as far as I'm concerned, he's guilty."

He hobbled unsteadily over to the door. Just before Father José María departed, he turned back to us and said, inhospitably, "Just because Ignacio wasn't the father doesn't mean he had nothing to do with the death of the girl."

Chapter 42

"THAT DIDN'T GO WELL," I said to Bill after Father José María left us alone in the office.

"No, but his reaction was to be expected, I suppose. He would, of course, take any hint at impropriety on his part as a great affront to his position. I wouldn't have expected him to react otherwise."

A soft knock on the door ended our conversation abruptly. Pedro peered around the corner.

"José María said you wished to speak with me," he said, a look of concern clouding his features. He spoke in English, as he most frequently did with Bill and me.

"Yes," Bill said. "Please come in and sit down, Pedro. Did he tell you why we wanted to see you?"

Pedro tucked the cassock under his legs as he sat down where Father José María had been moments before. He kept his back perfectly straight, the kind of posture I imagined was expected of young clergy in training at the seminary.

"No, he didn't specify, and he seemed quite upset. I hope no more bad news is forthcoming, but I anticipate that you have something unexpected to reveal."

"I'll get straight to it, Pedro." I noticed Bill dropped Father Pedro's title, as though he were once again one of Bill's students. "We believe the police coerced Ignacio's confession." Bill leaned toward Pedro, who sat across from him.

"I see. What makes you suspect the confession wasn't voluntary?" Father Pedro's voice was soft and delicate. He had a way of speaking that made me feel at peace, the anxiety sapped from my body through his words.

"It's because Angela was pregnant," I said. "And Ignacio was unable to father children. Of course, we don't know the content of Ignacio's confession, if he's not the father, what motive would he have to murder Angela?"

"I understand," Father Pedro nodded sadly. "It's a question to which I'm not sure I know the answer. I take it, then, that you're going to investigate the crime yourselves?"

"Yes, Bill and I will be speaking with everyone to find out if they have any idea who the father was. We think it's quite crucial we obtain this information as soon as possible. I don't know if we'll be successful, but we hope that someone may know something."

"And you suspect the father of the child killed Angela?"

"We don't know," I sighed, taking off my glasses. "But we do think that this secret relationship and the pregnancy might have been factors in her murder."

"I see." Father Pedro's manner exuded tranquility and grief in comparison to Father José María's belligerence. "And how might I be able to help? I'm afraid I didn't know any of the students very well. José María and I come up to the sanctuary from time to time, as you well know, and I like the students very much. They're a very cheerful and curious bunch, but we're not here often enough for me to feel that I have more than a trivial association with any of them."

"Yes, of course, Father Pedro," I broke in, impatient to direct the conversation. "We know that you don't know them especially well. We don't expect you to. But did you hear or see anything unusual last night? Or have you noticed any behaviour from anyone that might make you suspicious?"

"I'm very sorry to say, Mrs. Forster, that I don't think I can help much with either of those questions. I really find it difficult to suspect any of the students of any transgression that would lead to murder. Being the father of an illegitimate child is a forgivable offence, in my humble opinion, murder is quite another thing altogether. And with respect to hearing something last night, I can't say that I did. I really wish I could help, but I slept more soundly than usual last night. I couldn't say why. And José María is a very heavy sleeper. He'd never admit it, but I believe he takes a sleeping draught at night." Pedro paused and bit at his lower lip. "Ignacio is my friend, and I don't like to think poorly of anybody of my acquaintance. He's perhaps not the father, but even I must question my friend's involvement. Ignacio had many secrets he didn't want anyone to discover. Perhaps Angela saw something she wasn't supposed to. If he didn't kill Angela, then who did? It pains me to say it, but I'm afraid there's nobody at San Miguel more likely to have committed this terrible crime."

We didn't need to ask Pedro to expand upon Ignacio's secrets, and he was right about the others. Each person seemed as unlikely to have committed this crime as the next. There was one thing that Father José María and Father Pedro did agree on, though perhaps for different reasons. Ignacio might not have been the father of the unborn child, but in their eyes, his involvement in the crime was plausible.

Chapter 43

"DO YOU THINK we're going about this all wrong?" Bill asked me.

I looked around the office at the clutter, the books, the papers, the furniture, all in disarray and worse since we'd moved additional chairs around the desks. The keys to the church were a grim reminder of the urgency of our investigation.

"I couldn't say, dear. We might be. I do think it might have been best to start with the priests. They can be counted on to be discreet about Angela's situation, even if they have different reasons for doing so. We have to speak to everyone anyway, so what does it matter in what order we do it?"

"I suppose you're right. I hope Eduardo has more information for us than the priests did."

"As do I."

Eduardo shifted nervously on a wooden chair in the office. He wiped his palms on his clean khakis and then pushed his glasses up with the heel of his hand. "I thought Ignacio killed Angela," he said, his leg bouncing up and down.

"We believe the police might have made a mistake," I told him.

"So the killer is still here?" He looked around the room as though the perpetrator might suddenly appear.

"Most likely, yes," Bill said. "That's why it's important that we find out all the necessary details."

"How did you feel about Angela?" I asked.

"I liked her," he said sincerely. "She was nice. I'd say she was the nicest of all the students. Everyone liked her. We weren't close in the way that she and Miriam were, but I honestly think she was the last person someone would want dead."

"We've heard from Maite and some of the students that on occasion people leave their rooms at night," I said. "Have you noticed this or perhaps gone out yourself at night? You're not in trouble. We just need to know. Someone out at night might have seen or heard something of importance."

Eduardo looked at me and nodded. "I do occasionally go out at night. I like to have a cigarette from time to time. It helps me to relax and get to sleep. So yes, I've been sneaking out sometimes at night. Only when I need it. I'm sorry. I hope this doesn't make you and Professor Forster think poorly of me."

"Of course we don't think poorly of you," I said. I knew very well that many young people smoked. I didn't care for the smell myself, nor did Bill, but we had no reason to cast judgment on Eduardo or any of the other students. They might have been sneaking round, but they smoked outdoors as we asked them to do. "Who else went out to smoke with you?"

"Well, sometimes I was alone, sometimes there were others, depending on the night. I think at some point everyone went out at least a few times except Janis, Helen, and Archie. Yes. Everyone except for them, I've seen everyone out at least a few times."

"What about last night?" Bill asked. "Did you go out?"

"Not last night, no. I don't know if anyone else did either. I heard someone get up last night, but I was facing the wall and I didn't see who it was. I had no reason to think much of it. I'm sorry, I can't say more. And after that I went back to sleep."

"We understand," I said. "Now, Eduardo, this is a difficult question to ask, did you have an intimate relationship with Angela? She was seeing someone secretly, and it's vital that we find out who she was seeing."

"Oh," Eduardo said, his cheeks suddenly flushed with colour. He shifted uncomfortably in his chair. "It wasn't me she was seeing. I don't know anything about that."

"It's very important that we know the truth," Bill pressed.

It was easier to compel the students to provide information than the priests. We have authority over the students, and, in a sense, the priests have authority over us.

"I promise," Eduardo pleaded. He looked on the verge of panic. "I promise it wasn't me. You have to believe me."

His sudden and strong reaction made me think he was hiding something. Beads of sweat began to form along his hairline, and his glasses slipped lower on the bridge of his nose. He was clearly distressed at being asked these questions.

"What is it, Eduardo?" I asked. "Are you hiding something? Do you know something you aren't telling us?"

Eduardo looked at me, then Bill, then down at his lap. He started to chew on a fingernail, but said nothing. I motioned with my head for Bill to leave the room. Eduardo and I already established some communication about more personal subjects, and I wondered if he'd be more open with me if Bill weren't in the room.

"If you'll excuse me just a moment," Bill said, nodding his assent to my silent request. "I need a glass of water."

Eduardo's shoulders slumped, and he exhaled sharply when Bill closed the door.

"I'm sorry, Mrs. Forster. Please don't be angry with me. Please don't tell anybody. I don't want to get in trouble. I don't want to go to jail."

"Don't tell anybody what, Eduardo? I don't know what you mean."

"I don't..." He glanced at me, then looked away. "I don't..."

"Go on, dear," I said softly.

"I don't like women," he whispered, still avoiding eye contact. "I mean, I don't like women in that way. I didn't have a relationship with Angela or any other woman. I swear. Angela was my friend, nothing more."

"Goodness, I see," I told him. "I understand now."

"Please, Mrs. Forster," he begged. "Don't tell anybody. I don't want to be arrested."

In Canada, and many other countries, homosexuality was considered a gross indecency and thus a criminal offence. Men who had intimate relationships with other men could be thrown in prison, and Eduardo was well aware of that fact. If we had barbarous laws in Canada, Spain was certain to have similar or more stringent views given the association between church and state here, and the very traditionalist views of family life held here. Eduardo had every reason to fear for his safety.

"You're not going to be arrested," I told him firmly. "I'm not going to tell anybody. I promise. Thank you, Eduardo, for confiding in me. You're a very brave young man."

I doubted that he'd be able to trust many people with his secret. It was a dangerous time to breach societal norms despite how far we'd come in other areas of civil rights. I knew his father would be outraged if he ever found out, but I still needed to know if Professor Reyes Iglesias was somehow involved in the mysterious events that took place at San Miguel.

"Eduardo," I put my hand on his shoulder. "I'm sorry, but I have another difficult question to ask you. Did your father ask you to do anything that would interfere with our excavation this summer? It's very important that we know what happened with the tombs, as it may relate to Angela's death."

Eduardo's eyes grew wide, and he shook his head vigorously. "Mrs. Forster, I swear. If my father asked me to do something like that,

I would've refused. He was angry that I came here instead of going to Mexico, but I promise he didn't ask me to vandalize the tombs. I really like this excavation, and I want to be here. I wouldn't want to get kicked out of the program, not for my father, not for anyone."

Chapter 44

BILL RETURNED from the kitchen with a cup of tea in his hand and Muffin trotting happily behind him.

"Thought you could use this," he said, passing me the steaming beverage.

"Thank you, dear," I said, breathing in the soothing aroma.

I stood up from the hard, wooden chair, my joints stiff, and moved to one of the more comfortable chairs at Father Pedro's desk. Bill sat down across from me at Father José María's desk. He said nothing, just raised his eyebrows expectantly.

"I believe we can rule out Eduardo as the father of Angela's child," I said. "And I asked Eduardo directly if his father asked him to cause mischief at the excavation, and he said he hadn't. I believe him, Bill."

He nodded. He didn't ask me how I knew Eduardo wasn't the father, and I was glad. I was tired. The stress of the day was grinding away at my ability to think clearly. The minutes ticked by, the dinner hour approaching, when we would find ourselves all together once more. And one of those people, sitting beside us, sharing the same meal, the same conversation, had killed a young woman. I shuddered at the thought. I set the cup of tea down on the desk. It was still too hot.

Bill looked at me, standing slightly to reach over both desks and take my hand. He squeezed it gently before sitting back down. "Someone must know something," he said reassuringly.

"And someone is hiding something," I reminded Bill.

"Perhaps he doesn't know we know. It's not yet common knowledge. Or perhaps he didn't even know about the pregnancy. Angela might have kept that from him. If he thinks his relationship with her had nothing to do with her death, he might try to hide it from us for fear of the consequences. We had a no-relationships rule. We might not have said that relationships between students would result in expulsion from the program, but they might believe that anyway."

"Well, let's get on with the rest, shall we?" I said wearily.

"Graham?" Bill asked.

"Why not?"

GRAHAM CAME INTO the office and sat down on one of the wooden chairs. He smiled at us and sat patiently, waiting for one or the other to speak. I realized how strange it was to see someone smile unreservedly after what happened. Graham was always well kempt. Clothes neat and tidy, blond hair slicked back. He had the appearance of a young English boy attending public school. Yet his table manners betrayed him, suggesting a far humbler upbringing than one might have guessed at first glance.

"Graham, what can you tell us about Angela?" Bill asked.

"That's a bit of a broad question, Professor Forster. I guess I'd say that she was a nice girl. She was always friendly, if a bit aloof at times. She never had anything mean to say about anybody. As far as I know, everybody liked her. That's why it is so shocking that she's been murdered. can't understand it. Eduardo told me you don't believe that Ignacio did it, that he's been framed."

"Not exactly framed," I said, "but something along those lines, yes. What do you know about Angela's personal life?"

"Personal life?" Graham looked surprised. "I'm not sure exactly what you mean, Mrs. Forster. Like was she keen on anybody?"

"Yes, that's exactly what I mean. Was she keen, as you say, on anybody? We've been told Angela was seeing someone in secret here."

"Oh, that explains a few things, then. Why didn't you just say that, Mrs. Forster?" Graham scratched at his scalp, leaving tufts of hair standing up at the back of his head.

"What do you mean by that explaining some things, Graham?" Bill continued.

"Well it's a bit of a long story."

"We have the time," I lied, hoping that he had some information of relevance.

"Well, it happened in July, when we went down to the San Fermín festival in Pamplona. Professor Forster, you gave us a day off so we could go see the bulls run and the party in the city."

"Yes, we remember," Bill said. "Father Pedro arranged for some members of his family to drive us to Pamplona. What happened there?"

"It didn't seem like such a big thing then, just a coincidence. Now, in retrospect, maybe it didn't happen by accident at all."

"What didn't happen by accident?" I asked, eager to hear the story Graham was taking so long to tell us.

"We all went over together with Pedro's family, like Professor Forster said. We left early to be there before eight in the morning to see the bulls run. And then you and Professor Forster went with Father Pedro and his family to someone's house, I remember."

Graham paused, as though recreating that day in his mind, the pickup before dawn at San Miguel, the winding road to Pamplona, the students so excited they couldn't sleep in the car despite rising early, the noise and bustle in the city streets in preparation for the day's festivities. I recalled the day vividly as well. We'd left the students to find places along the wooden barricades that separated spectators from participants in the famous encierro. The running of the bulls through the streets of Pamplona. Father Pedro's family had friends in the city with a balcony overlooking the route run by the bulls from the corral to the arena. Bill and I were invited to join them, squeezing ourselves onto the small balcony with our hosts. Though I'd felt bad about the students being left out as well as our own special treatment, there simply wouldn't have been space on the balcony for everyone. The students didn't seem to mind, though. At their age, being part of the crowd was more appealing.

"We pushed our way to the front and climbed on the barrier to get a good view," Graham said, "but we did it. We heard the shot go off and then people started to move, slowly at first, looking behind them, waiting for the bulls to come. Some had newspapers rolled up and held out so they could feel if the bull came up but still look where they were running. Then people started to shout, and we saw the bulls barrelling down the street, and then people really started to run. We saw one man fall and get trampled by the bulls, other people just fell one on top of the others, tripping over each other in their rush to escape the bulls."

"Graham," Bill said, "I'm sorry to interrupt your story, what has this got to do with Angela? We don't have that much time, you understand."

"Oh, sorry, Professor Forster, I got caught up in the excitement all over again. I'll do better. The bulls hardly lasted even a minute, I think. They just ran by, and then they were gone. It was all over. So we all just joined the crowds in the street. We were together then, all of us, including Archie. There was music and dancing and parades. Anyway, what I wanted to say was when the giants and the big heads came dancing by, the crowd got very thick, as everyone pushed back to let them go by."

As Graham told his story, I could picture everything in my mind. After we watched the bulls run by, Bill and I ate breakfast with the family in their apartment, and then they suggested we might like to go back out onto the street to enjoy the festival up close. They were kind and told us to come back to the apartment if we got overwhelmed, that someone would be at the house throughout the day, and we could rest there if we wanted. Bill and I had seen the parade of gigantes, people dressed as giants, and cabezudos, the large papier mâché heads worn as the participants twirled through the streets to traditional music. It didn't surprise me that Graham was captivated by the spectacle. Probably we all were.

"That's when it happened." Graham paused, and I had the distinct feeling it was for theatrical effect.

"Goodness, Graham. What happened?"

"We got separated. I didn't think much of it at the time, you know, because with the crowds and everything, it seemed quite normal. But now, I wonder if some people preferred to be off on their own, if you know what I mean."

"You mean Angela went off on her own?" Bill asked, removing his glasses and running his fingers down either side of the bridge of his nose, a telltale sign that he had a headache. "Is that all?"

With his excited chatter, Graham attracted Muffin's attention. She stood up on her hind legs, resting one front foot on his leg and pawing at him with the other. He quickly brushed her aside, forcing her to put all four feet back on the ground. Graham was not a dog person.

"No, there's more," he continued, distractedly picking dog fur from his pant leg and rubbing his fingers together to get the hair off. "Eduardo and I ended up together. At first, we tried to look for the others, but they'd completely disappeared. Vanished, you might say. So we decided to explore the city on our own, wandering the streets and drinking wine at the bars even though it was still morning. We had a grand time, really."

I hadn't heard Graham talk so much since we'd arrived at San Miguel. Apparently, all he was lacking was a captive audience. Though I was pleased at his excitement about the festivities, I sincerely hoped he'd get to the point of his story before Maite called us for dinner. The sands of time were diminishing rapidly.

"Graham, please stick to the parts of your story that are relevant to Angela," Bill said. "You can tell us all about your experience in Pamplona when we aren't quite so pressed for time."

"Sorry, Professor Forster. I know I get off track. Let's see, where was I? Oh, right, we all got separated. A few of us in the group had read *The Sun Also Rises*, so I thought maybe we might bump into the others at the café on the square, the one Hemingway used to go to. Café Iruña. You know the one I mean?"

Everyone knew the one he meant. It was a point of pilgrimage in Pamplona for anyone even remotely interested in twentieth century American literature. Bill and I stopped in for a coffee on the terrace when we first arrived in Spain, but during the festival, the place was too crowded for us to bother.

"Yes, dear," I replied, "we know the one you mean."

"Well, Eduardo and I went in, and I saw her at the bar. Angela, I mean. She didn't look at us, but I knew it was her because of her long blond hair and the red scarf she'd tied in it that morning. She was easy to recognize. There aren't a lot of girls with long blond hair around these parts. I expected she'd be with Miriam, except I couldn't see Miriam at all. But there was a man beside Angela, and she was talking to him. We were going to go over to them, but then some raucous singing began, and people started to shove this way and that, and Eduardo and I got pushed outside. So we went and bought ice cream and sat in the shade on the square."

"The man you saw Angela with, what did he look like?" I asked

"I don't know, Mrs. Forster, I didn't see his face," Graham said simply, as though it were of less importance than his ice cream that day.

"What about his hair colour?" Bill asked.

"Sorry, Professor Forster, I wish I knew. The man had a white straw hat on, the kind you could buy on the street to help keep the sun off your head. Everyone was wearing them. Not one of those paper cones, though. It was definitely a hat. The hats were cheap enough. I think most of us ended up with one in the end. Nobody thought to bring their hat from the dig down to Pamplona."

"What about his height?" I asked.

"Well, he was much taller than Angela. That's about all I can tell you."

That was something, I thought. If what Graham said was true, it seemed likely Angela was with her lover the day we went to Pamplona.

Chapter 45

ROGER'S LARGE FRAME filled the small wooden chair dispropor-
tionately. He was best suited to the outdoors, where, in contrast with
the vastness of the landscape, he could avoid the awkward appearance
of a fully grown adult attending a child's tea party. His presence was
almost preposterous. It was, however, certain that Roger was much
taller than Angela. He smiled, balancing uncomfortably on the chair
that had, moments ago, been occupied by Graham. I anticipated that
this would be a very different conversation.

"Roger," I began, "do you know why we asked to speak with you?"

"I suppose you think the police have got it wrong and you're looking
for a new scapegoat?"

"Goodness, Roger," I said. "A scapegoat would imply that the person
is innocent. We don't want to blame someone who had nothing to do
with the crime. We're just looking for the truth, nothing more. What
can you tell us about Angela?"

"I guess she's a nice girl. Barely gives me the time of day, and believe me, I've tried on that front. Friendly enough, in a distant sort of way. She's a real looker, that's for sure," Roger smiled for a moment, and then suddenly the expression fell from his face. "Sorry, professor, Mrs. Forster. I meant *was*. And I didn't mean to sound unfeeling. I'm really sorry that she died. She was a good person."

He looked like a puppy that's been scolded.

"So you didn't have an intimate relationship with her?" Bill asked.

"I..." Roger halted, likely to prevent the release of another heartless comment. "Sorry. I did not."

"But you would have," I persisted, "had you been given the chance?"

Roger hung his head. "I suppose I would've. But I didn't. I swear. Like I said, she barely gave me the time of day. There was nothing between us. She just always seemed distracted, you know? Off in her own world."

"Would you have been upset if she were seeing someone else?" I asked.

Roger looked confused. "Maybe a little. But she wasn't seeing anybody, was she? Are you asking me these questions because she was going steady with somebody?"

Bill nodded.

"I had no idea." Roger appeared genuinely shocked. "I didn't think that she was..."

"That she was what?" I asked. Evidently the rumour mill hadn't spread the gossip as quickly as I'd imagined.

"You know, Mrs. Forster, that kind of girl. That's why I never pushed it with her. I just assumed she wouldn't go out with anybody. I guess it was just me."

I sighed. Rome wasn't built in a day, I consoled myself. "So you never noticed Angela going off with a man?"

"No, not that I noticed. She was always going walking, I just assumed she went walking alone to get away from Miriam for a little while. I can understand that. I mean, I like to be alone sometimes too. My friends back home are great, but here I just feel the need to get away from everything and everyone once in a while. I assumed Angela was like that too. I'd never have guessed she was meeting someone."

"Tell us about what happened in Pamplona," I said.

Roger shifted his weight in the chair, the wood coming into contact with the metal frame, making it squeak. It sounded deafening in the quiet of the office.

"Who told you what happened in Pamplona?" Roger asked, his cheeks flushed with embarrassment.

"Graham told us a little about what happened that day," Bill said, "but we'd like to hear your version of events too."

His embarrassment flashed to anger as he prepared to speak. "I'll tell you what happened," he said, eyebrows puckered into a frown. "They all just up and left me in the middle of a crowd. One minute, everyone was there. The next, everyone was gone. They just left me alone. It was terrible. They pretended later that it was an accident, but it didn't feel like that."

I could see the hurt spread across Roger's face, the feeling of being a social exile. Seeing that expression of pain, I couldn't help but appreciate the kindness Angela had shown to everyone.

I tried to comfort him, leaning over to place my hand on his shoulder and give it a good squeeze. Everyone needed a little sympathy, even tough boys like Roger. "From what Graham said, it did sound like an accident. He said that he and Eduardo looked for the rest but couldn't find anybody in the crowd. Isn't it possible that's the truth?"

Roger looked at me, hope in his eyes. Had he been silently holding on to this grudge for a month? I felt sorry for him. Angela had been right. Maybe he was rough around the edges, but clearly he felt his peers' perceived rejection acutely. It wasn't my intention to mend hurt feelings in this interview, but it seemed that was the path we needed to take with Roger.

"I just thought they did it on purpose. Maybe you're right, Mrs. Forster. Maybe it was just an accident. I shouldn't have been so hard on them."

"Roger, did you see any of the others again before coming back to San Miguel?" Bill asked.

"No, I didn't, Professor Forster. I didn't want to roam the city alone during a party, so I just went to the museum in the old part of the city until it closed. Then I wandered around until it was time to go to the meeting point. I'm sorry I can't tell you more. I wish I could help."

"It's all right," I said, though I was disappointed he didn't have more information for us. "You can only tell us what you know."

It seemed appearances deceived us. Roger wasn't the outgoing, confident young man we'd believed him to be. That or he was a real Paul Newman. It did seem, however, that all this time he'd been masking his insecurities from the others. Perhaps they'd have been more forgiving of his flaws if he had given up the bravado and been more honest with himself and everyone else.

Chapter 46

BY DINNER TIME, the cat was out of the bag, as they say. Everyone knew about Angela's secret relationship and that Bill and I didn't believe Ignacio killed her. Time flew by, leaving us no opportunity to speak to Patrick or Archie before dinner. Their interviews would have to wait. Bill and I agreed that we'd continue after the meal. Someone was hiding something. That was exceedingly clear. The question was who.

Everyone came down for dinner. The only people missing were Ignacio and Angela, of course. We all sat around the table, uncomfortable in our mistrust of one another. Doubt about everything and everyone lingered in my mind, a constant sense of unease that we were missing something important.

"I don't see how we can stay in this house tonight with a murderer on the loose," Helen grumbled. With extra time on her hands during the day, she was even more dolled up than usual, with shimmering stones dangling from each earlobe, her hair styled in loose waves, and a floral, long-sleeved mini-dress that I'd seen only a few times before.

"I'm not afraid," Janis announced. "I can defend myself, if need be." She banged the knife clenched in her fist on the table, dramatically.

Startled by the noise and theatrical gesture, several others jerked to attention. I was worried that everyone would be too frightened to sleep that night. We were all jittery. It was to be expected.

"I'm with Janis," Roger declared confidently. "I'm not scared. Obviously, it was a lovers' tiff that went wrong."

"Roger," Bill reprimanded him.

Evidently, Roger's moment of vulnerability with us didn't prevent him from donning his cloak of assurance once more for the benefit of the other students.

"Sorry, Professor Forster," he mumbled.

"It'll be quite acceptable tonight, for those who don't feel safe, to stay in the kitchen," Bill said. "It's not obligatory, but we can bunk down in here. It's important that everyone feel safe."

"Will Janis be sleeping in the kitchen too?" Helen asked.

"Helen." I took my turn playing parent to quarrelling teenagers.

"Sorry, Mrs. Forster."

"I know everyone here is feeling dreadfully anxious," I said. "I don't blame you. You've lost a friend, and we don't yet know who might have committed the crime. But it's crucial that we not bicker among ourselves. Please, for Angela's sake, let's be kind to one another. There's no need for snarky comments."

The students nodded. I looked over at Miriam. She hadn't said a word at dinner, but she seemed to be eating her food, which I thought was a good sign. Her nose and eyes were still red from crying, but I felt she was holding up quite well given the circumstances. The others seemed less outwardly disturbed by Angela's death, but I knew that each of us handled tragedy in our own way.

Bill told Maite in Spanish the plan to sleep in the kitchen and asked her if she'd feel safer sleeping with everyone else. She eagerly agreed that she, too, would spend the night with the rest. I knew she'd been feeling troubled since we opened the tombs, and everything since then exacerbated her worry, but we hardly had time to look after all the students and Maite too. Father José María declined the invitation, stating that he'd be safe enough in Pedro's company under the watchful eyes of God. Father Pedro was thus left little choice in the matter. Everyone else agreed that they'd bring their mattresses and blankets to sleep in the kitchen. It would be crowded, but at least everyone might get a little shut-eye in the safety of numbers.

Chapter 47

"DO YOU THINK it's one of them?" I asked Bill after we retreated to the office to finish the last of the interviews. Bill again sat at Father José María's desk, and I sat across from him at Father Pedro's.

"I hope not, but then again, I hope it's none of the people we know. I suppose we won't have such luck. Regardless, Beatrix, we still have no idea if the father and the murderer are one and the same. Just because we identify him doesn't automatically mean that he had something to do with her death."

"I know, dear, but I can't help thinking that her relationship and her death are not a coincidence. Maybe I'm wrong, either way Bill I'm heartbroken. These things aren't supposed to happen. Not to anybody."

Bill came over, and I stood up so he could wrap me in a hug and hold me tight. He was a full head taller than I was, and he rested his chin on the top of my head. It didn't fix things, but it made me feel just a little bit better.

"We're in this together," Bill said. "Now, let's see what Patrick has to say."

PATRICK ENTERED THE OFFICE quietly, a dull look in his eyes. He didn't smile as some of the others had. It seemed more appropriate, a sober attitude, given the circumstances. He wore fashionable bellbottom jeans and an ivory cotton tunic, the ties at the neck hanging loose. He sat leaning back in the chair with his left ankle crossed over his right knee.

"Patrick," I said, "we have some questions about Angela."

"Sure, Mrs. F." He nodded. "Whatever you want to know."

Patrick had a way of speaking that was slow and lilting, much like how people from California spoke, the words drawn out as though each required great effort to produce. I wondered if it was natural or part of the bohemian style he'd adopted.

"How well did you know Angela?" Bill asked.

"Other than Miriam," Patrick said softly, his demeanor still relaxed. "I knew her better than anybody here."

"Really?" I was only partially surprised by this revelation. Though I rarely saw them in each other's company, the small physical contact I saw between them the day before remained in my memory. Had I witnessed a moment between lovers when Patrick squeezed Angela's shoulder, or was I reading into the gesture? Before Angela was killed, I'd paid only passing attention to how the students interacted. "Why is that?"

"We used to be an item," Patrick said simply, brushing hair out of his eyes with his hand. He lacked the nervous energy of some of the other students.

"An item?" Bill asked, looking over at me. He would've noticed even less of what was going on among the students than I had. "When was this?"

"Last year. We broke up before Christmas, but we stayed friends. She was a wonderful person. We just weren't on the same path in life."

"How long were you together?" I asked.

"About a year. We've known each other since starting university. We met on the first day of the first semester in our cultural anthropology class. That's why I say that I know her...I mean, knew her better than anybody else here."

"Were there any hard feelings after you broke up?" I wondered if things were difficult when their relationship ended.

"No, Angela wasn't like that," Patrick replied, lacing his fingers together behind his head. "She would never hold a grudge against anybody."

It bothered me how casual he seemed when his ex-girlfriend had been murdered. Perhaps he was pretending not to be hurt, or he wasn't someone who wore his emotions on the outside. There was a good chance, too, that he'd broken the rules and been smoking grass, or whatever it was that they were calling it, to calm his nerves. It seemed to be a common practice among the young people at university. I hadn't smelled anything that hinted at my suspicion, but his eyes were slightly bloodshot, and I guessed there were tricks to covering up the smell of marijuana.

"I don't mean Angela," I said softly. If he were broken up inside, I didn't want to be too harsh with him. He was still very young, just like the others. "I mean you, Patrick."

"Oh, right, Mrs. F. No, no hard feelings on my side either. I broke up with her, to be honest. Even if I hadn't, who could stay angry with Angela? She's doesn't have a bad bone in her body."

"Yes," I told him. "We've heard nothing but good things about her."

"Did you know that she was seeing someone here?" Bill asked.

"Roger told me. Well, he told everyone after he talked to you, so yes, I knew. If you're asking if I knew about it yesterday, the answer's no. I didn't. I suspected that something was going on, though. She wasn't spending as much time with Miriam as she did on campus, and that was bothering Miriam. But it wasn't any of my business, so I never asked her about it. It's her life. I mean —" Patrick broke off, suddenly uncrossing his legs and leaning forward. He cradled his face in his hands for a moment. "I'm sorry. It hasn't really sunk in yet."

"It's completely understandable, Patrick," I said. "We can continue when you're ready."

"I'm okay," he said. "I want to help."

"What happened at San Fermín?" I asked.

"Oh that," Patrick said, leaning back again but leaving his legs uncrossed. "Everyone was a bit on edge after that day, after we got separated from one another. Nobody did it on purpose, I don't think. It just happened, but it seemed to create tensions between people. I ended up spending the day with Miriam. We could've had a good time. It was one big party in the streets. But she was so preoccupied because Angela disappeared. She wanted to look for her. She just couldn't relax and take it easy. She was protective of Angela, but it could be too much at times. Angela is an adult, not a child...was, I mean."

"Do you know Miriam well too?" I asked him.

"Yes, all three of us started at university together, and we've had a lot of the same classes since then. So we know each other pretty well."

"Is it possible that Miriam was jealous of Angela's relationship?" I asked, wondering how upset Miriam was that day in Pamplona.

Patrick paused before he answered, roughing up the shaggy hair at the back of his head. "In a sense, she could've been," he finally said. "Not so much jealous that Angela was seeing someone but upset that she was spending less time with her. Does that make sense?"

"It does," I said. "Thank you, Patrick."

He squinted as though he were trying to look through me. "You don't believe she did this, though, do you?"

"It's unlikely, but we don't know, Patrick. We have to look at all the possibilities, you understand."

Chapter 48

"HAVE A SEAT, ARCHIE," Bill said when Archie entered the office, hesitating nervously just inside the door.

"Thanks, Professor Forster," he said, taking one of the wooden chairs. He was yet another tall young man, which didn't make our task any easier. "What can I help you with?"

"I'm sure you know by now that we're speaking to everyone about Angela because there's reason to believe that Ignacio may be innocent," Bill said, removing his glasses and setting them on the desk.

"Yes, I do. The rumour mill is working away out there, you might say." Archie tugged at his earlobe and waited.

"What can you tell us about her? How well did you know her?" I adjusted my posterior in my chair. Despite the leather padding on Father Pedro's chair, my buttocks had lost feeling.

"I really liked Angela." Archie laced his fingers together in his lap. "She was motivated to do well, studied hard, listened to instructions, was careful with her work in the field and the lab. I'd say she was an ideal student. My only complaint as her supervisor was that sometimes, while she was excavating the skeletons, she'd sort of drift off, get a dazed look in her eyes, and stare off into nothingness. I guess that makes perfect sense now. If she was in love with someone, then she was probably daydreaming about that."

"So you weren't aware that she was seeing someone?" I asked.

"No, I had no idea. I spend lots of time around the students and I couldn't say I knew any of them that well. Angela included. I probably know Roger best, since he's also a grad student, but we don't spend much time together. I like the students, but I know that professional distance is important in my position. I wouldn't want to end up with a reputation at the university. It would be very bad for my future endeavours. Archaeology is my whole life, Professor Forster. You know that."

Archie rubbed his hands over his thighs, clad in dark denim. I guessed that his palms were sweaty.

"I know, Archie, but we have to ask these things," Bill said kindly. I knew he had a soft spot for the red-haired young man sitting next to him.

"I understand."

"Tell us what happened in Pamplona," I said.

"In Pamplona?" He arched his eyebrows and scratched the back of his neck. "When we went for the festival?"

I nodded.

"I'm not sure there's much to tell." He leaned forward and rested his arms on one of the desks. "I purposely separated myself from the rest of the group the first chance I got. It wasn't meant to be malicious, but I knew the others would be drinking and partying, and I didn't want to get caught up in it. Alexandra doesn't really like me to drink. Even if she's not here, I wouldn't want to do something behind her back. I went off on my own, and I had a really good time, if I'm honest. I don't really see what this has to do with Angela, though."

"We ask because Graham saw Angela with a man in Pamplona,"

I said, "and we're trying to find out who that man was. Did you see Angela or any of the others after you were separated?"

"I can't say I saw Angela, but I did see Janis and Helen. They were talking to some locals in the street outside one of the bars. Well, now that I think about it, Helen was doing the talking. Janis looked quite annoyed, actually. I don't think she wanted to be there, I'd guess that her choices were stick with Helen or go off on her own. As much as Janis pretends to be tough and independent, I think it's just an act. I think she wants to be part of the group. She just doesn't know how. That's my opinion anyway. I don't know for sure. I've never talked to her about it. Otherwise, she'd just have left Helen, don't you think?" Archie looked at me and then Bill.

"You could be very right about that, Archie," I said. "Janis is difficult to read. Is there anything else you can tell us that might be helpful?"

"Actually, there is, and I was going to tell you before, things have been quite chaotic here today. They'd already taken Ignacio away, so I sort of forgot about it."

"What is it, Archie?" Bill asked, mimicking Archie and leaning forward over the desk.

"Well, I was up last night. I needed to use the bathroom. Normally I sleep right through, but not last night. The other guys were asleep as far as I could tell. But when I went out into the hallway, I ran into Ignacio. He was terribly pale, and I got the feeling he was afraid of something. He didn't say anything at all, just went past me as though I weren't even there, and up the stairs to the attic. He just looked so scared. It made the hairs on my arms stand up."

Chapter 49

"GOODNESS, I JUST DON'T KNOW what to think anymore," I said once Bill and I were alone in the office. I was exasperated.

No response.

"Bill, did you hear me?" I stood up and went around to his side of the desks. I gently touched his shoulder to rouse him from his thoughts.

"Hmmm? Did you say something, Beatrix?" We were about eye level when he was seated.

"I did. I don't know what to think."

"Oh, yes." Bill wrapped his arm around my waist. His physical presence was comforting, something tangible to hold on to in dark times. "Obviously, we have to assume that someone is lying to us. Angela's baby wasn't immaculately conceived. This isn't a biblical story. A real man of flesh and blood got her pregnant. Therefore, someone hasn't told us the truth. One of the men we interviewed, or Maite. Who's to say which one?"

Bill took his glasses off the desk and polished them on the tail of his untucked shirt. He hadn't begun the day with it untucked, but we'd both become increasingly bedraggled as the hours wore on. I wasn't a vain woman; still, I didn't wish to see myself in a mirror for fear of what would be staring back at me.

"What about Graham's story?" I asked. "Do you think that was the truth?"

"I do, but let's be sure and ask Eduardo. He should be able to clarify things, unless he, too, is hiding something. And if Miriam can confirm Patrick's story, then Archie and Roger are the only ones that were separated from the rest of the group."

"I would say we've become quite mistrustful, dear."

"Yes, I think you're right about that. I want to believe them all, but we need to be pragmatic."

EDUARDO FOLLOWED BILL into the office, chin tucked and hands shoved deep in his pockets.

"Eduardo, dear, there's no need to be afraid," I said, motioning for him to sit down. "We just have a few more questions for you, nothing to be worried about."

"Yes, Mrs. Forster," he replied mechanically, taking a seat where he'd been before dinner.

"Graham told us a little about what happened the day you all went down to Pamplona for San Fermín. Could you tell us what happened after you got separated from the others?"

"Oh," he said, looking up at me for the first time since entering the room. "Yes, I remember now. I hadn't thought of that at all until you just mentioned it. It was a bit of a bummer that we all got separated, but it was nobody's fault. It just happened. Graham and I went to the café in the square, the one that's famous because of Hemingway. It was incredibly crowded. You could hardly get inside the door. Graham pointed out that he could see Angela at the bar, and we were going to go over to her, all of a sudden, the people started to sing and dance and we just plain got pushed out of the bar back onto the terrace. We decided it wasn't worth the effort to try to get back in. It was just too busy, so we left. We didn't see Angela again until everyone met up to go home."

"Was Angela with someone at the bar?" Bill asked.

Eduardo paused to think, pushing his thick-lensed glasses up. "Is that what Graham said? I suppose she could have been with someone, I didn't notice to be honest. There were a lot of people there. It was really crowded. Graham could be a bit taller than I am, I guess, so maybe he could see better. All I could see was her blond hair and the handkerchief she'd tied into it. I recognized it from that morning."

"Thank you, Eduardo," I said. "That's very helpful."

"All right, Eduardo, you can go now," Bill said. "Thank you for your help."

"I wish I could do more," Eduardo said sadly. "Angela was my friend. I want this person to be caught, even if it turns out to be one of us."

"SO IT SEEMS LIKELY that it was Archie who Eduardo heard leaving the room last night," I said, thinking out loud once we were alone.

"Yes, we can find out tomorrow if the others noticed him leave or not. We should have clarified that with them when we had the chance, but it's hard to keep all the details straight."

"It sounds as though Graham's story is the truth," I said. "It's entirely possible Eduardo either couldn't see the man Angela was with or simply failed to notice him."

"Agreed," Bill said, tapping his lip. "It seems Angela was with our mystery man in Pamplona. We'll have to check Patrick's story with Miriam, and of course there's no way to check Roger or Archie's stories if they were alone."

I stood up. My eyelids were so heavy it felt as though small weights were pulling them down. "I think we ought to go to bed and sleep on it a little. We can come back to it in the morning, Bill."

"That might be the best plan we've had all day," Bill said with an exhausted, somewhat sad smile.

I tried to smile back, but I couldn't help feeling nervous about going to sleep with a killer in the house. It wasn't going to be easy. I almost wished I could get my hands on some of Father José María's sleeping draught.

Chapter 50

A SHRILL SCREAM wakened those of us who'd been sleeping in the kitchen. The sound of bodies rustling around, a dog barking, blankets being thrown off, a bench being scraped over the ground, footsteps on the stone floor, all of it resonating in the dark.

"Ow!" an unidentified voice cried.

"What's going on?" someone yelled.

Another person began to weep audibly.

"Turn on the lights, will you?" I heard Roger say.

"I'm trying! It's pitch black in here."

Finally, after what seemed an eternity, the lights came on.

"What on Earth is going on?" Bill demanded, his hand hovering over the light switch. "Who screamed?"

Muffin continued to growl. I hushed her, but my own heart raced uncontrollably in my chest. What could it be this time?

"It was me," Helen sobbed, her shoulders heaving beneath the crocheted yoke of a pink cotton nightgown.

"Why did you scream, Helen?" I asked her. "What happened? Was it a dream?"

Before she could answer, both priests burst into the kitchen.

"What happened?" Father Pedro asked, in breathless English. He looked rather silly in his navy striped pyjamas, far less formal than when he wore the priest's cassock. "I heard someone scream."

"We're just trying to get to the bottom of it," Bill said. "Is everyone present and accounted for?"

We all looked around.

"It's Janis," Eduardo said. "She's gone."

"Goodness," I huffed, pressing my hand against my chest. "Where can she be?"

"I felt her, in the dark," Helen whined. "She stepped on me. I know it was her. It woke me up, and then I felt something brush against my arm, like a ghost."

"I told you she was the one that killed Angela!" Miriam shouted reproachfully. "And now she's wandering around here somewhere. She could kill us all!"

"¡Esto es un escándalo!" Father José María exclaimed, dishevelled and wrapped tightly in one of the grey blankets we all used at night. "A sinful circus in a most holy place. I won't be a part of this. Pedro, we'll go back to bed. You've woken me from my sleep for nothing."

"The Professor may need our help if one of the girls is missing," Pedro protested, now speaking in Spanish. He looked tired, with pale skin and dark circles around his eyes.

"Do as you wish. You can find me in bed. Asleep. Or, if I'm most fortunate, God will be merciful and the murderer will have slain me by the time you get back."

Father José María never missed an opportunity to be melodramatic. He should've been a Shakespearean actor, I thought, not a priest.

"I insist that you all stay here," Bill said to everyone else. "Mrs. Forster, Father Pedro, and I will look for Janis. Please, stay here and calm yourselves."

He repeated his instructions in Spanish for Maite, who looked petrified, her lips drawn and her eyes gaping, but she said nothing. I handed Muffin to her, an unspoken gesture of empathy, and she gratefully accepted, hugging the warm, furry being to her chest. Father Pedro, Bill, and I left the kitchen.

"Janis," I called out in the empty hallway. "Janis, where are you?"

"I can check the bedrooms and the lab if you like," Father Pedro offered. His accent was more pronounced, the words difficult to form at this hour of the night.

"Good, Beatrix and I will look outside," Bill replied. "If you find her, be aware that she's a somnambulist. If she's still asleep, it may not be a good idea to wake her."

"Is she dangerous?" Pedro asked cautiously.

"We don't believe so," I told him. "But be careful, nonetheless. Should we have Archie accompany you?"

Pedro shook his head. "Don't worry. I'll be fine."

Bill and I walked to the front door, a cool blast of air welcoming us into the night. Bill fiddled with the flashlight. It was a beastly old thing our son brought back from the war and left at our house. Suddenly, he stopped.

"Bill?" I whispered.

No response.

"Bill!" I said, pinching him firmly on the arm. "What is it?"

"What?" He looked surprised, wrenched from his reverie. "The passageway," he mumbled as though that explained everything.

"What about it?"

"Maybe she went that way."

I looked at Bill, the hair on his head standing straight up, his pyjama shirt and bottoms rumpled. I no doubt I was a perfect reflection of my husband, hair mussed from the pillow and bedraggled in my matching sleepwear. Bill and I had reached the stage in our marriage at which some might believe we shopped at the same stores. We were certainly quite the pair to behold tracking down a sleepwalking student in the middle of the night.

"Goodness," I said, pushing thoughts of our appearances aside. "I can't say I like the idea of going down there now."

"No, nor do I, but Janis might have gone that way."

"Or another way, Bill. There's no way to know where she went. She's most likely asleep."

"It's just a feeling I have. I can't explain it."

"All right, dear. But make sure that flashlight is working first!"

THE DOOR TO THE PASSAGE was located at the back of the pantry. Among the stacked bags of lentils and jars of preserves, I could discern a door with a brass handle. I'd never noticed it until Helen showed me where it was located. With Maite preparing all the meals, there'd been no reason for me to go into the pantry. I took a deep breath. It wasn't the thought of encountering Janis asleep and brandishing a kitchen knife that made me apprehensive about what lay beyond that door. It was what else might be there, lurking in the shadows, that concerned me. After all the work we'd done with the dead, I didn't believe in ghosts, at least not in the traditional sense of filmy white beings haunting the living. Yet on the off chance they did exist in one form or another, there were good odds they'd be in an ancient place like this. All the students' talk of the house being haunted must have gotten to me. The house had been here for enough centuries to accumulate its fair share of lingering spirits.

"Ready?" Bill asked, the flashlight projecting a faint beam on the door handle.

"Can anyone ever be ready to step into the unknown?"

"If the students can do it," Bill said adamantly, "so can we."

He always enjoyed a mystery more than I did.

"Goodness, Bill, the students did it during the day, not in the middle of the night."

"You think."

"Very true."

"Anyway, Beatrix, this passage would be this dark no matter the time of day. Don't tell me you've developed a sudden case of nyctophobia."

Bill laughed. He was right. Fear of darkness was irrational, yet I felt justified in my apprehension, all things considered.

"All right, let's get on with it, then." I clenched my teeth and steeled my nerves.

The door squealed in protest, as Bill, slowly and with great effort, pulled it open. Before us loomed an opaque darkness that even the light Bill held out before him couldn't fully penetrate.

Chapter 51

IN MY YOUNGER and more adventurous years, Bill and I had swum in a cave in Mexico. Cenotes, they were called. The only source of light had given out, momentarily, leaving us engulfed in an obscurity so deep I realized in that moment that I'd never experienced true darkness before. As I heard bats swooping low over my head and felt the wind of their wings, I held on to Bill like a child clings to a blanket in the night. Now, I clung to him again, though the flashlight allowed us to see just ahead. Beyond that was nothingness. I grasped the back of his pyjama shirt firmly in my hand. I had braved many things in life, but I didn't relish this experience.

The passageway seemed to last forever, with stairs at either end. Yet despite my preparedness to bolt at the first unfamiliar noise, the journey through the corridor was uneventful. We found the door at the end of the hall that gave us access to the sacristy. The air in the sacristy itself, though damp smelling, was cool after the stifling atmosphere of the passage from which we'd emerged. I breathed an audible sigh of relief.

"That's better," Bill said, brushing some dust from his shirt sleeves.

"Indeed," I said.

Bill led the way to the nave of the church. We carefully descended the stone steps, the muffled sound of our slippers slapping against the ground echoing from the high ceilings in the silent expanse of the old building. We walked past the pews, careful not to bump into anything, although at this point, we knew the layout of the church well. We stopped at the infamous chains. Bill shone his flashlight on them. They hung limply, impotent without the strength of flesh and blood to pull them taught. Next, Bill shifted the beam into the chapel, across the pews, over the altar, and toward the missing stone in the corner. The dragon slept more soundly than we did, I thought bitterly.

"Nothing here," I said.

"No, but I have an idea where she might be."

"Goodness, care to share, dear?" I asked, looking at my husband expectantly.

"Follow me," he said, walking on, the beam of light bouncing erratically off the walls with each step he took.

Down more steps, we strode into the antechamber, then round the corner and into the spacious hallway, where the sarcophagi were located. Though there was the possibility they were related to Angela's death, with our efforts to determine the identity of the father of her child, we'd let our attempts to solve the mystery of the commingled bones take a back seat. There were still so many lines of investigation open that we'd become enmeshed in a tangled web of intrigue that ranged from the bizarre to the tragic. I still found it difficult to believe that anybody we knew could've harmed Angela, and yet Maite's alternative hypothesis was equally as unfathomable. Even if witchcraft were practiced nearby, why target San Miguel above any other source of human remains and youthful victims. I pinched myself on the arm. Hard. It wasn't the time to become embroiled in the investigation. It was paramount we find Janis. I just hoped she was all right.

Bill led me directly to the first sarcophagus we'd opened, the smashed stone lid still lying in pieces on the floor. He shone his flashlight into the stone box, and there she was. Janis lay within, her hands crossed over her chest, her eyes closed.

I gasped, holding the air inside my chest while we both stared at her, the light illuminating her rosy skin. We waited, in silence. When her chest rose, I let the air come rushing out of my lungs.

"Goodness!" I exclaimed. "I thought..."

"Me too," Bill said. "A nasty case of déjà-vu."

"How did you know to find her here?"

"It was just a hunch. She asked me several times during the field school if she could lie down in one of the empty graves in the cemetery. I told her not to, that it wasn't appropriate or professional. I wasn't really sure why she had such a strong desire to do it. It seems her subconscious found a way to make it happen."

"Goodness, Bill, couldn't we have come around the other way?" I chided him. "If you thought this was her destination, we didn't really need to go through the passageway, did we?"

Bill smiled. "It wasn't that bad, was it? Plus, she might still have been in the passage. She didn't have that much of a head start."

"Whatever you say, dear. Now, how are we going to get her out of there?"

"Can't we just leave her? She seems to be sleeping peacefully. More peacefully than anybody else."

"No, I suppose we can't. Can we?"

Chapter 52

"JANIS," I SAID SOFTLY, careful not to touch her. "Janis, can you hear me? It's Mrs. Forster and Professor Forster. We've come to take you back to bed."

I didn't want to startle the poor child, though with her penchant for sleeping in the graves of the long dead, I wondered what would, in fact, frighten her.

"You still don't believe she was involved in Angela's death?" Bill asked.

"No, I don't think so. Do you?" I wasn't certain about anything anymore, though I still struggled to believe that Janis would brutally strangle Angela. Janis was strong enough and put on a tough act for the others, but was she a cold-blooded killer?

"No," Bill sighed. "The somnambulism is strange, yet I can't imagine she'd actually harm someone."

"I don't know what her motive would be either. From what she's said to the other girls, she isn't interested in pursuing a relationship. So she'd have no reason to be jealous of Angela's secret liaison, assuming she even knew about it. I really don't think she did. What other motivation would she have?"

"All the girls are bright," Bill said, "but Janis outperforms the others on tests, so I doubt that competition would be motivation either. Miriam might be convinced, but I'm not."

"Janis, dear," I tried again. "Janis, we need to take you back to bed. You can't stay here. It's very cold. You'll catch your — Oh, goodness, never mind. Come on now, Janis. Time to go."

Janis' eyelashes fluttered slightly, and then she opened her eyes, squinting at the light that shone directly on her face.

"Bill, not in her eyes," I scolded.

He moved the light to shine on the wall behind her.

"Janis, are you awake?" I asked.

She nodded.

"Do you know where you are?" I wondered if she had any idea how far she'd come.

She looked around, her eyes scanning her own body, the stone tomb, Bill's face, then mine.

"Am I in the tomb?"

"Yes, you are."

"How did I get here?"

"That's a very good question," Bill said.

"Janis, you've been sleepwalking again. You've come all this way in your nightdress. You must be freezing. Let's get you back to bed."

Janis flushed. I wasn't sure if she was embarrassed by being found in her nightgown or for being caught sleepwalking again.

"I'm sorry," she muttered. "I really didn't mean to. I don't want to cause a fuss, really. I swear I only do it sometimes. Even if the other girls say I do it every night. It's not true. I don't sleepwalk every night. Only some nights."

It was in that moment, when Janis uttered those words, jejune as they might have seemed on the surface, that I realized what we'd been overlooking all along.

Chapter 53

"BILL," I WHISPERED, leaning away from Janis. "I know who Angela was seeing."

"Who?" Bill's eyes were wide, his mouth forming a little O of surprise.

"Just wait. Let's get Janis back to the house, and then I'll explain everything."

I didn't want to go back through the dark passageway to get to the house, but Janis was barefoot and dressed only in a flimsy pale blue cotton nightdress. I worried that taking her around outside, through the damp grass and chill air, might see her catch a cold. Indoors was cool enough. We had no choice but to retrace our steps through the church, into the sacristy, and down the long passage bathed in inky blackness. We ushered Janis back to the kitchen, where all eyes turned toward us as we entered. Father Pedro had already returned. He nodded and smiled when he saw us. The others gazed upon Janis, either with mirth as she stood before them in her feminine nightgown or with enmity by those who'd already internalized her culpability.

Bill insisted that they all go back to sleep, that Janis's absence was caused by a disturbance to her slumber. That it was nothing out of the ordinary. He sent Father Pedro back to his own room, thanking him for his help. Bill then made an excuse for us to leave the room, telling the others we'd be back shortly.

We found ourselves back in our room, the beds not slept in. We sat down on Bill's side, directly on the taught canvas, as we'd taken our mattresses and bedding down to the kitchen the evening before. I was thankful for a moment of peace.

"What did you realize?" Bill asked eagerly, taking my hand.

"Although we've said ourselves that everybody is a suspect, we've perhaps held some above suspicion for no other reason than their profession."

Bill gasped, as he himself realized our error. We'd interviewed the priests, but we'd simply assumed they were telling us the truth. Perhaps one had, but I knew now that the other was lying. We'd also not directly asked either of them if they were involved with Angela. We'd both been blinded by the black robe of piety.

"But," Bill said, as if pleading for their innocence, "just because we didn't suspect them doesn't mean that either one of them was the father of Angela's baby."

"Well, one of them is, Bill. Of that, I'm nearly certain. Pedro has been hiding something from us, as much as it pains me to say it. It makes perfect sense. Janis said to me that she didn't sleepwalk every night. That she only did it sometimes. It made me think of what one of the girls, I can't remember which one, said about Angela and her nocturnal outings. She didn't do it every night. Why not? If her secret lover had been here every day, as most of us are, would she not have gone out every night? Or at least nearly every night? But if her lover were an occasional visitor, then she wouldn't sneak out every night, only those during which the man in question was present. It makes sense that she would go walking every day, to create a routine that everyone was accustomed to, and to make it difficult for anybody to guess she was meeting someone. Or if they did know, to figure out who she was meeting. But at night? Why go out alone at night unless she had a good reason to?"

"Good Lord, you're right. Pedro and José María only stay some nights, not every night. I never really considered that Pedro might've been involved with Angela."

"A priest's cassock sometimes acts as a cloak of invisibility for the wearer's sins."

"True," Bill squeezed my hand harder. "But it is more than that. It's also how much I care for him and trust him."

"We both do, Bill, but I think our friend has betrayed both our trust and that placed in him by his offices."

"Do you think he killed her?" Bill asked, his voice expressing his desire to believe in the goodness of his friend.

"I don't know, dear. But I have little doubt now that he was the father of Angela's unborn child. Given how the church and many others would view this relationship and its consequences, it would certainly give him motive."

Chapter 54

VOICES FROM THE KITCHEN told me that nobody went back to sleep as instructed. I couldn't blame them. I understood that now it would be nearly impossible for anybody to get to sleep. I wouldn't have been able to fall asleep either, not with everything that happened. When we opened the door, everyone turned to look at us. The lights were still on and bodies seemed to occupy every available space, some sprawling on their mattresses laid out on the floor, others sitting at the table. Maite appeared to be making tea at the stove.

"Any news?" someone called out.

"No," Bill said. "We have nothing new to tell you. I'm sorry."

"So we still don't know if Ignacio did it?" Roger asked.

"Or Janis," Miriam said.

"We don't know anything new at this time," I insisted. I didn't see the point of creating a panic by telling them that the priest they liked best was having a secret affair and might have killed his lover. "We shouldn't speculate, as it only causes unrest."

"Can't we have the police come back?" Helen asked.

"We can try," Bill said, "but the police believe that they've arrested the person who killed Angela. There's no reason for them to come back. Mrs. Forster and I are just making sure they got it right."

"But you think they didn't," Miriam said, sitting up on her mattress and hugging her pillow to her chest, "or you wouldn't still be questioning people."

"We know you have a lot of questions," Bill said, smoothing some of his unruly hair down against his head. "So do we. There are still many things that remain unclear, and we'd like to make sure that all the questions we still have are thoroughly resolved. I sincerely wish we could give you all the answers you want, we simply don't have them. It's important to be patient. We want this settled as much as you do, but we can't read minds."

Nobody said anything more.

Bill and I decided to speak with Pedro in the morning to avoid rousing suspicions during the night. We settled down onto our mattresses in the kitchen with everyone else. I didn't anticipate anyone getting much rest that night, but soon enough, after the lights were turned off, the soft and rumbling sounds of slumber filled the room. I myself lay awake wondering if Father Pedro, such a polite, kind, young man, could have committed such a horrible crime. Was his reputation as a priest worth the life of a sweet girl in the prime of her youth?

Chapter 55

"YOU KNOW, DON'T YOU," Father Pedro said, his cheeks ablaze, his gaze distant.

We found ourselves once more sitting on the stone benches facing south toward the opposing mountains across the valley. It was still early in the morning, and the clouds hung low, obscuring the village of Huarte-Araquil beneath them. We could see the top of the Andia mountain range, towering above the puffs of pure white cotton candy from our privileged position in the Aralar mountains. The views were breathtaking, but we were about to have a difficult conversation.

"We know you were seeing Angela," Bill said in English.

"I was," he sighed, looking down at his hands. "I'm so sorry. It pained me greatly to hide this from you both. You've shown me so much kindness over the years, and I've repaid that kindness with dishonesty. I'm truly ashamed. I should've said something, I know that. It was wrong to pretend I knew nothing. I swear I don't know who killed Angela. If

I'd known something, anything at all that would've helped, I would've told you what was going on between us. I was afraid of what you might think of me. I didn't think that telling everyone would help find Angela's killer, so I kept quiet. It was dreadfully wrong, and I'm sorry for it. I just don't know who could've done such a thing. I loved her and would have done anything for her. I would never have hurt her. I was going to leave the church so we could be married. I swear, this time I'm telling you the truth. Can you possibly believe me?"

Tears began to well in his eyes. I noticed he was digging his fingernails into the soft skin of his forearm. I often did the same when I was trying to keep my emotions tucked deep inside. It was difficult to fathom how he'd hid his grief so well from everyone until now, but self-preservation seemed to have a way of taking the reins and ensuring the truth stayed hidden deep within.

"Did you know about the baby?" I asked gently.

He nodded. The sun was still low in the sky, its golden rays illuminating the clouds and casting a heavenly glow across the mountains.

"Yes. I was planning to return to Canada with her, where we'd be married. We had every intention of keeping the child and raising it ourselves. I would've found some work, somewhere. We were going to make the best of it."

"And did you know that Angela had a miscarriage?" I probed further.

He turned toward me, guilt enveloping his dark eyes. "I felt so awful that she went through that alone. I should've been there for her, but she didn't tell me until that night. We met, and she told me about being sick during the day. It didn't change anything, though. I was still going to leave here and marry her. I loved her more than anything."

"Pedro," Bill said kindly. "I think you'd better start from the beginning. Tell us everything that happened. Someone killed Angela, and it's imperative that we find out who really did it. Maybe you know more than you think."

I could tell Bill believed Pedro's story, and I was relieved. I believed him too. I couldn't fathom how the man who'd shared so many dinners with us in our home could have brutally killed one of our students. Had he lied to us? Had he broken his vows? Yes, that was clear. Breaking one's promise to God and killing someone were two different matters.

"I never really wanted to be a priest," Pedro began, leaning forward and grasping the cross he wore around his neck. "I knew that when I was in Toronto, when I met you. But when I returned here, I felt I had little choice. My family has money, but they intend to pass the family business on to my older brother, not me. They're also very religious. Many people around here are. They let me go away to be educated, on the condition that I return and join the church. They pressured me to become a priest, and to be honest, I didn't know what else to do, so I went along with it. I didn't agree with the church's allegiance to Franco. It seemed wrong. Some of the older priests are very traditional, but I soon realized that other priests, many of them young, are more progressive, like me. They wish to see change in the church, and they want to end the oppression of the Basque people, bringing back the language and culture here. But it's not just here. There are priests like this all over Spain hoping to push back against the dictatorship and the wrongs that it commits against the Spanish people. They're what we call worker-priests, as they go out into the fields with the labourers and do the same backbreaking work as the most humble farmhand. Last year, I travelled to Catalonia to join priests there in protest against the torture of political prisoners. In the end, I didn't mind being a priest so much, as long as I felt I could do some good with my work...to help create the changes that new generations want to see in this institution. I hoped to be more tolerant than generations past. And within the church, I found some, like myself, who saw a future free of the strict doctrine that punishes rather than forgives. Things are beginning to change."

Pedro's words didn't surprise me. He'd had a similar mindset when he lived in Toronto, and it seemed that his religious training hadn't altered his fundamental beliefs.

"I took my vow of celibacy seriously," he continued. The long sleeves of his cassock had ridden up his arms. Sitting beside him, I could see that little crescent impressions marked his wrist and disappeared under the fabric of his robe. I noticed scabs, too, from where he'd pressed so hard that he'd drawn blood. I guessed that he'd been using this tactic to conceal his emotions since Angela's body had been found the day before. "It was part of the profession I'd taken up, and I had accepted that, though it wasn't always easy. Everything changed, though, when I met Angela. She was so different from any other woman I'd known. We met accidentally, or at least met alone accidentally. You'd introduced everyone to me and José María. Then, I bumped into her in the woods one of the first days you were here. I was just out for a walk, and I found her searching for an *eguzkilore*. Maite told the students about the thistle that means so much to the Basques, and Angela wanted to find one for her. I offered to help."

Father Pedro's voice dropped off. His gaze fell on the slope of the mountain before us, and he seemed lost in his memories of meeting Angela. I remembered the day that Maite asked us to explain the *eguzkilore* to the students. Bill interpreted for her as she described the thistle that grew close to the ground and translated literally from Basque to English as "flower of the sun." Mother Earth gave the Basques this unusual plant to hang at the entry to their homes to protect them from the evil spirits that came on moonless nights. The spirits had to count the hairs on the leaves of the thistle before they could enter the house. There were so many that daylight came before they finished counting and chased the spirits away. I'd seen silver thistles before on my travels in southern France, nailed to front doors and used to predict the weather, but Maite was the first to explain that in Navarre and the Basque Country, the silver thistle was meant to protect against evil. I wasn't aware that Angela went looking for an *eguzkilore* for Maite. I only wished that the mythology of the plant had worked and we'd all been protected from the evils of this world.

"Go on, Father Pedro," I encouraged him gently. There were tears on his cheeks, but he seemed less distraught, as though finally sharing his burden was a great relief.

"We started talking...about everything," Pedro said, his voice catching slightly in his throat. "We talked for a long time. She was incredibly beautiful. It hadn't been my intention, but I fell in love with her that very day, and she with me. I couldn't help thinking that God had intentionally put her in my path. Now it seems I've been punished for what I did. I'll never forgive myself."

"You must not talk like that, Pedro," I told him, rubbing his back gently. "You weren't the one that took her life."

"I wonder if she's dead now because of our relationship, though I don't think anybody knew about it. Angela promised me she'd told nobody but Miriam, because she sometimes needed her to cover for her absences. Miriam wouldn't have told anybody about our relationship. She loved Angela, and she wouldn't have betrayed her trust. Angela never told Miriam my identity just in case, but I suppose it might not have been so difficult for her to guess if she really wanted to. We did try to make sure it wasn't too obvious, in case anybody else was suspicious. Angela went walking most days, even if I couldn't meet her, but she only went out at night when I was around, making sure to smoke with the others if they were outside to hide her real motives for being out of bed. She actually hated smoking, but it was a good excuse for being up after dark. The other students were often wandering in the mountains during the daytime as well, so it would've been more difficult for Miriam or anybody else to know who I was based on a simple process of elimination of who was present when Angela was absent. We didn't want it to be that easy. However, you'd have to ask Miriam if she knew the whole truth, because I don't know how much she knew."

I did believe that Miriam and Angela were very close, as Father Pedro said. We'd seen how fiercely Miriam tried to protect her friend. She'd claimed not to know the identity of the person Angela was seeing, but she might have still been trying to protect both Angela and Pedro. She wouldn't have been the only one to lie to us.

"When did you see her?" Bill asked.

"We met frequently in the forest. After she'd finished work, she'd tell everyone she was going for a walk. On days when I was in the valley,

Angela would walk partway down the mountain, and I'd walk the rest of the way up. We didn't meet every day, as that might have made people suspicious. But we met often. On my visits here to the sanctuary, it was easy enough for us to get away and meet somewhere. Everyone was already used to Angela going off alone, and nobody paid attention to me. If I stayed the night at San Miguel, we could sneak out. José María sleeps like a bear, so I didn't need to worry about him noticing I was gone. Angela always had some excuse planned in case the other girls noticed. Helen slept soundly, and Janis simply didn't care, at least not from what I understood."

"Could anyone have seen you when you met?" I asked.

"I don't think so," Pedro said sincerely. "We never saw anyone else."

"What about Ignacio? He was always in the woods. Might he have seen you?" I thought back to the time Ignacio had been out hunting in the woods, or so he'd said.

Pedro shrugged. "I never saw him, not when I was with Angela."

"Pedro," Bill said, "why didn't you say anything when Ignacio was arrested?"

"I know. I should have told you everything. But I was still shocked by what happened. When they took Ignacio away, I honestly wondered if he could've done it. I didn't know why he would've, but who else? He was my friend and tutor, and it was hard for me to believe it of him. At the same time, he was also the most likely to have done it, wasn't he? If Angela found out what he was doing, he might have been afraid she'd tell someone. I know Maite told you about Ignacio. I didn't want to believe he could've done something like that, but I couldn't think straight. So I did nothing. I was afraid that if the Guardia Civil knew about my relationship with Angela, they'd think I killed her to cover up her pregnancy and save my reputation. I knew I hadn't done it, so it had to be someone else. I just couldn't think who it might be. I knew Ignacio killed during the war and the years after, so it wasn't so much of a stretch to believe he might kill again to protect himself."

"I wonder if Ignacio himself could shed some light on all of this," Bill said. "We never had a chance to speak to him. Do you think your friend, Ortega, could get us in to see him?"

"I can try if you think it'll help," Pedro offered. "I can call him. I just want to find out who did this. My life is ruined. The only thing I can do for Angela now is help in whatever way I can."

"Before you call Ortega," I interjected, placing my hand on Father Pedro's arm to keep him from standing up. "Is there any connection you can think of between Angela's death and the vandalism of the sarcophagi?"

Father Pedro frowned at the question, pausing before he answered. "I can't think of anything. None of this makes any sense to me. I can't imagine what Angela's death would have to do with the bones in the church, but perhaps I am simply blind to the things I don't want to see."

Father Pedro was right. Sometimes we didn't see the things that were too painful to comprehend.

Chapter 56

FROM THE SACRISTY, Pedro called the garrison to speak with the sergeant.

"He's sending a car to pick us up," Pedro said after he hung up.

"What about the captain?" Bill said, smoothing the hair on his head. "He won't like any of this."

I realized neither of us had seen a comb since we discovered Angela's body.

"It's our lucky day," Pedro smiled weakly. "He's not in."

"Good," I said. "We don't want to get that nice young man in trouble."

"I hope this conversation with Ignacio clears up a few things," Bill said. "Like why he confessed to the crime in the first place."

"There's always the chance that he confessed, Professor Forster, because he was the one who did it," Pedro said, nervously clenching his cassock with his hands. "I don't want to believe it any more than anyone else, but if not him, then who?"

Bill nodded. It was a question we simply couldn't and, to a certain extent, didn't want to answer.

We had enough time to return to the house prior to being picked up by the Civil Guard. Bill decided it would be best to send the students back to work under Archie's supervision, with strict instructions that the wheelbarrows shouldn't be touched under any circumstances. They would have to use their buckets to remove dirt from the excavation area. It was better not to have them stuck inside all day wondering whether the killer had been caught. Idle hands and minds often led to strife within a group, and it was best to keep them occupied. They were already very much on edge, and for many, a distraction might be welcome.

Father Pedro said he'd like to accompany us to the garrison, but he'd have to come up with an excuse to tell Father José María, since it was Sunday and the mass would be given that morning. Bill and I decided we should have one last chat with Miriam before she joined the others at work outside if she felt up to it. Given Pedro's story, perhaps Miriam knew more than she was telling us.

FATHER JOSÉ MARÍA was using the office to prepare for the mass that morning. We left Father Pedro to explain his absence at the religious service, and Bill and I decided to sit in the kitchen with Miriam. The room felt vast and empty with just the three of us sitting at the table. The others went outdoors to work, except Maite, who graciously left us alone, saying that she needed to feed Francisco and the donkeys.

"Miriam, Father Pedro has confessed that he was seeing Angela," I told her. "Did you know that he was the one Angela was meeting in secret?"

Miriam took a deep breath, flipping some unruly curls over her shoulder. "I didn't know for sure, but I suspected," she said quietly, sitting across from us at the kitchen table.

"Why didn't you tell us what you knew or thought?" I asked.

"I didn't know for sure, Mrs. Forster. I didn't want to get him in trouble. That would've been the worst thing I could do to Angela. I knew she loved him and he loved her. I knew he wouldn't have killed her, so what did it matter who he was?" She became flushed and tears rolled down her cheeks. "She was my best friend. I couldn't betray her like that. I didn't think it would matter who he was, and like I told you, I didn't know for sure anyway. She never actually told me. I just guessed because of when she went out at night."

"This is very important, Miriam," I continued. "Do you think anybody else suspected what was going on?"

"No!" Miriam stated emphatically. "No! I didn't tell anybody. I didn't even hint at it. I'm sure nobody knew. Angela was very secretive about it. I don't think anybody could've found out unless somebody had been following her, which makes no sense. Who would do that? And why?"

Although Miriam had hidden Father Pedro's identity from us, it seemed she really didn't know more than what she was telling us now. Her words made me consider a new possibility, though. Had someone been following Angela? Or perhaps following Father Pedro? Was this a case of unrequited love turned to fatal jealousy? And if it was, who was the object of this unreciprocated desire? I recalled the fleeting moment from when we first arrived at San Miguel, when Father Pedro told us the story of Teodosio. Had I not noticed Janis blush under his gaze? I defended her, considering her incapable of such a terrible crime, yet she was strong enough to kill Angela and move the body. She might also have had the strength to tamper with the tombs. She certainly wasn't afraid of snakes. With the right motive, as passionate jealousy could be, anybody could fall victim to their emotions. And her hair was wet the morning we discovered the body. Had she washed it to hide some evidence? I couldn't help wondering. I glanced at my watch and realized we wouldn't be able to speak with Janis until after we met with Ignacio. I just hoped nothing bad would happen in our absence.

Chapter 57

IN THE CEMETERY, the students were hard at work, crouching over the exposed skeletons, carefully carving the dirt away from the bones with fine wooden tools to avoid damaging the fragile remains. Archie went around checking each student's work, ensuring that they were doing things properly, not scratching the surface of the bones or removing too much dirt so the bones became loose before we could take a photograph. It was a delicate procedure, but we trusted Archie to make sure it was done right. I knew Father José María would be aghast by the excavation continuing on a Sunday, especially in full view of his flock, but both Bill and I believed that the students needed to be occupied even if that was frowned upon. Let José María's wrath fall where it might.

Leaving the sanctuary to meet the police officer who'd drive us down the mountain, we crossed paths with the faithful who'd come to worship at San Miguel. Father José María would lead the mass, of course, and according to Pedro, he hadn't been pleased about the younger priest's absence. It was no surprise. Father José María's respect for tradition was expected, and he believed without question in the sanctity of religious services. Pedro, on the other hand, had other priorities that I imagined he hadn't yet confessed to his mentor.

The people filed past us, some dressed in fine clothes, frilly dresses for the little girls, short pants and high socks for the little boys. The women wore hats and carefully pressed dresses. The men wore suits with glistening shoes. These were the people who'd arrived by car. Those who'd walked up the mountain or arrived by horse, mule, or donkey wore more humble clothing. The kind that couldn't be ruined by rubbing against a saddle or getting caught on branches in the forest. The kind of shoes a little mud couldn't hurt.

As we descended the steps against the flow of people who paraded happily, carefree in their manner, toward the church, I stopped and looked back. I could see José María's crippled form meeting the congregants at the entrance. He was invariably greeted with a smile, which was not returned, and many bent their heads to kiss his hand. A demonstration of reverence for his position.

The people greeted Father Pedro as he passed by them, joking with him about shirking his duties on a Sunday. They addressed him in a jocular fashion, not so formal and stuffy as what I'd witnessed with the older priest. We reached the widened culmination of the dirt road that led up to the sanctuary, a flat, unpaved surface that served as a parking lot for those who arrived by car. There, we encountered the altar boys, already dressed in white robes and ready for the liturgical service. Hidden among the cars, they passed a cigarette from one to the next. They couldn't have been older than ten or eleven. I laughed and winked at them as they attempted to hide the cigarette under my watchful eye. Father José María certainly wouldn't have approved. I was becoming more like Ignacio, taking pleasure in the things I knew would irk the priest.

THE WINDING ROAD carved into the forest, descending toward the villages in the valley on the north side of the mountain. Bill and I sat in the back of the police wagon while an especially stern young officer drove us to the garrison of the Civil Guard. He said nothing as we drove, and the rest of us followed his example. The car kicked up dust us as we sped along, with the driver braking hard at each turn and then speeding up again. It wasn't like the pleasant Sunday drives we used to take out to the country, but it was better than riding up and down the mountain on a donkey.

The garrison was a simple red brick building surrounded by a ten-foot wall crowned with barbed wire. An enormous Spanish flag rippled in the wind above the main entrance. The red and gold stripes were emblazoned with an ominous black eagle bearing a coat of arms upon its breast. Various official cars, all painted green and white, were parked in front of the building. Our driver pulled up, parked, and then beckoned for us to follow. Inside the building, painted entirely in a drab cream colour, we were met by Sergeant Ortega. He thanked the junior official who'd driven us and dismissed him.

Ortega looked around to confirm nobody was there before shaking hands warmly with Pedro and exchanging pleasantries. There was nobody else around, so they didn't pretend to be strangers.

"Me alegro verlos." Ortega lowered his voice despite the absence of other people. "The captain's investigative methods are neither thorough nor orthodox, if you understand me. The Guardia Civil is highly hierarchical, and there's little one can say against the methods of a superior officer. There was little I could do for the investigation, you understand."

We nodded. This wasn't the only police force in the world to use unorthodox methods.

"I'll take you to Ignacio," he said.

We followed his tall, uniformed frame down several corridors, all the same off-white colour as the reception area. The interior of the building had a clean, uncluttered, hospital feel to it. Sterile, I thought. Ortega led us to a small room, with a modern metal table and matching chairs. Ignacio was already seated at the table, his hands resting on the table. His wrists were ringed with bruises, a purplish blue halo adorning his skin.

"Do you want me to stay?" Ortega asked politely.

We all looked at each other. We hadn't discussed the presence or absence of the police. In fact, we hadn't planned much for this interview at all. Yet for Ignacio to be open with us, it was essential that Ortega be absent. Even if he hadn't murdered Angela, he could be arrested and jailed for his other activities.

"It's up to you," Bill said finally. "The objective is to find the truth. He might be more willing to talk without an official presence, if I may be so bold as to say so."

"I'll leave you alone," Ortega said, looking at us meaningfully, "but you'll let me know if you find out anything important?"

"Of course," Father Pedro told him.

He looked relieved that his friend wouldn't be joining us. I imagined that wasn't solely because of Ignacio. It would be difficult for him to tell Ortega about the relationship he'd had with Angela. There were many closely guarded secrets in this room.

We all turned simultaneously toward Ignacio as Ortega closed the door. He'd been silent since our arrival, but he looked pleased to see us. Maite wouldn't be able to visit him under the circumstances, and I expected that he had nobody else that would come to see him. He looked worse for wear, his long hair tangled and unwashed, his clothes wrinkled.

"We've come to hear your side of the story," Bill said quietly. "Maite has told us everything she knows, so there's no need to hide the truth."

Ignacio nodded. He looked at his hands splayed on the top of the metal table. There was dirt and blood embedded beneath his fingernails.

"Did you kill Angela?" Pedro blurted out as he collapsed heavily into a chair opposite Ignacio.

Ignacio looked surprised, as though he couldn't imagine why anyone would ask him such a question. He held up his hands. "No. I swear I didn't do it."

He turned his head slightly away from us as he spoke, and I realized he was again hiding his gold tooth from view.

"Then why did you confess, Ignacio?" Bill asked, pulling out a chair for me and then sitting down himself.

We all sat across from Ignacio, staring at him expectantly. He looked uncomfortable, embarrassed. He fidgeted, pushing his hands under his legs and rocking back and forth, a little boy being reprimanded by his teacher for misbehaviour.

"I said I did it," Ignacio admitted. "I only confessed because of what the captain did."

"What did he do?" Bill asked.

"He..." Ignacio looked up at us, then down at the table again. "He threatened to kill Francisco if I didn't confess to what I'd done. I told him what I thought he wanted to hear. I said I killed her, but I promise, I didn't do it."

I sighed. He put his own life at risk for his pig. Capital punishment was still legal in Spain, and certainly the murder of a young, foreign woman would grab attention in the headlines. Ignacio wasn't a particularly sympathetic defendant. The lucky ones, if those condemned to death can be deemed lucky, faced a firing squad, or so I'd heard. But mostly they were garroted, an iron collar tightened around the neck until the victim asphyxiated or the neck broke. Dismally similar to how Angela had been killed. It was a cruel and unusual death to be sure. Ignacio must have known the risks, but he'd confessed to save Francisco.

"I only said it to stop him," Ignacio continued. "I thought things would be sorted before there was a trial. You do believe me, don't you?"

"We do," Bill said. "But believing you means that someone else killed Angela, and now we have to find out who. It's not an easy task. There are no likely suspects. Everyone appears as innocent as everyone else. All trails have led to more questions, and we're no closer to finding out who committed this crime."

I didn't find an opportunity to discuss my suspicions about Janis with Bill. It would have to wait until we were back at the sanctuary.

"I've made a terrible mistake," Ignacio lamented.

He cradled his face in his hands, elbows resting on the table. I felt sorry for him. His life was not an easy one, and he'd suffered in solitude for many years, with little more than the company of a pig. For him, that pig was family as much as any person could be. The captain preyed on his weakness and been successful in getting an admission of guilt. But of what value was a false confession?

"Maite showed us the radio you use to communicate with others in your organization," Bill began. I wasn't sure where Bill was going with this line of questioning, but I didn't want to interfere. Ignacio was always more comfortable around Bill than me, and I knew he'd be more forthcoming if I let Bill guide the conversation. "It's strange that we have never heard you making a transmission."

"After you came here," Ignacio said, "I started communicating only during the night to be sure that nobody was using the rooms adjacent. That's why you couldn't hear me."

"So you're regularly up in the middle of the night?" Bill asked.

"Yes."

Bill interlaced his fingers on the table. "Did you ever see Angela out at night?"

"No."

"What about Pedro?" Bill gestured at the priest. "Did you see him at night?"

Ignacio looked at Pedro, confusion clouding his features.

"No," he said, shrugging. "Sometimes I spent the entire night in that room, with the radio. I have a bed there."

"Yes, we saw it," Bill said. He paused and began to stroke his beard.

He said nothing more, so I turned to Pedro: "Tell us what happened the night Angela was killed. When did you see her? Where? Tell us everything."

Pedro looked apprehensively at Ignacio.

"I was in love with Angela," Pedro told him.

Ignacio nodded and said nothing. His expression didn't reveal whether he had prior knowledge of the relationship.

"I saw her in the evening after Patrick played for everyone," Pedro continued, clasping his hands together tightly on the table. "She'd been sick, so I told her to use the passageway and meet me in the church rather than meeting in the woods as we usually did. I knew nobody would be in the church at that hour. It was late. All the students knew about the passage to the church, but Angela told me they were too afraid of being caught to use it much. And the thrill of the secret passage had worn off anyway."

Father Pedro paused, pulling the sleeves of his cassock down over his wrists. "I'd been with José María in the office. He was reading. I told him I was going out to see the sunset because I knew he wouldn't be inclined to follow me. He was more interested in heavenly delights than Earthly ones. He barely noticed me leave, he was so engrossed in his book. Nobody saw me go into the passage. I made sure. Angela was already waiting for me in the chapel when I arrived. She told me she'd lost the baby. We talked about the future, about getting married. Then I left her in the chapel and returned to the house. I never saw her again after that. I found out she was dead with everyone else, when you told us yesterday morning."

"Ignacio, did you use the radio that night?" I asked, seeing that Bill was still processing some thought that had come into his head.

He nodded.

"Did you see Angela?" I leaned forward.

Ignacio shook his head.

"Did you see anyone that night?" Bill rejoined the conversation.

Ignacio shrugged his shoulders. "When, Professor?"

"During the night. After everyone went to bed."

"No..." Ignacio replied hesitantly, tucking some long grey hair behind his ear.

"Ignacio, this is important," I interjected. He needed to realize the risk he was taking. I could tell he was hiding something. "You need to tell us everything, even if it's small. Your life's at stake here."

Ignacio began to fidget again.

I decided to take a firmer approach. "Right now, the only person who will suffer for your silence is you. You may not receive the death penalty, but you'll spend the rest of your life in prison."

Ignacio looked up at me.

"There will be nobody to look after Francisco," I pushed. "And what about Maite? She's devastated that you're here in prison."

"I did see something that night," he said finally. "It happened so fast, I wasn't sure if it was real. You won't believe me if I tell you."

"We can't believe you if you don't tell us," Bill said.

"I saw...I saw a ghost." He shuddered. Ignacio must have seen the apparition just before he bumped into Archie, I thought. That's why he'd looked so afraid.

"A ghost?" Bill asked, his tone incredulous.

"I knew you wouldn't believe me." Ignacio looked away from us. "I shouldn't have said anything."

"What did it look like, the ghost?" Father Pedro asked, suddenly joining the interrogation.

Ignacio looked up at Pedro as though to determine if Pedro were making fun of him. "It was just a glimpse. In the stairwell. It was white, all dressed in white."

I pictured Angela in the grave, dressed in a white nightgown. Could he have seen her the night she died? Had he mistaken her for a ghost?

"Was it Angela?" I asked.

Ignacio shook his head. "No, I'm sure it wasn't her. It was a man."

I tried to remember what colour Janis's nightgown had been. Pale blue. Would Ignacio have confused her for a man with her stocky build and short hair? In the darkened hallway, could her pale blue nightgown have been mistaken for white? It was all possible. Ignacio looked ashamed. He was hiding something still. I could feel it.

"Do you know who it was?" I asked, wondering if the ghost was actually our murderer, a person of flesh and blood, not a spectre.

"I think..." Ignacio stopped. He scratched at his scalp beneath his greasy hair. "I think it was Teodosio," he whispered.

"Teodosio?" Bill asked.

Ignacio frowned. Bill's disbelief was audible but not mocking. It was clear, however, that the scientist in him refused to believe Ignacio's story. Ignacio didn't take it well. Perhaps because he himself could hardly believe his own story.

"What makes you think it was Teodosio?" Pedro asked.

"Because of what I did," Ignacio whispered. "He must have been angry."

"What did you do?" I asked.

"I'm very sorry," he mumbled. "Really, it wasn't personal. I needed you all to leave, to recover the sanctuary for myself and my work. So I opened the tombs."

"Pardon me?" Bill sounded surprised, but it shouldn't have come as a shock.

We'd talked repeatedly about how we'd disturbed Ignacio's peace at San Miguel. With Maite's revelation of his activities, it should've been clear to us that he had the motivation to disturb out work. He'd wanted us to leave, and we'd been so distracted by Angela's death and finding the father of her child that we hadn't been able to complete the simplest of equations. We'd looked every which way, from Eduardo's father to Maite's witches, except the right way. If we hadn't been able to see that Ignacio had meddled with the sarcophagi when it was so obvious, then how would we be able to figure out who'd killed Angela?

"A few snakes weren't going to scare us off," I told Ignacio, feeling angrier at myself for not seeing what was going on in front of me than I was with him.

"It was stupid," he moped, hanging his head. "I thought that if things were ruined and you thought that something sinister was behind the mischief, you'd think it wasn't worth continuing, that you'd have less work to do. Just collect the bones and leave. I didn't want to do anything that would hurt anyone, or even scare anyone too much. It was just meant to ruin the work and make you think there was something disturbing going on at San Miguel."

I immediately thought of our conversation with Maite. She'd been so convinced that witches were responsible for the vandalism. Had she known all along that Ignacio was trying to get rid of us and drummed up this story to help his cause?

"Ignacio," I tried to keep my voice steady, but I felt deceived. "Did Maite know what you did to the tombs? Was she involved in this with you?"

Ignacio shook his head vigorously, the strands of hair falling loose from behind his ears. "No, I promise that she had nothing to do with this. I knew, though, that she would suspect witchcraft when she saw the vipers and the bones the way they were. She's my sister, and I've known about her superstitions for a long time. I knew she'd see what happened as a bad omen and believe that something supernatural was going on. I knew she'd be worried."

I felt relieved. I didn't want to believe that Maite lied to us, after everything, but many of us would do much more for family if we were asked.

"Why now?" Bill asked. "We've been here for months already. More than half our time here has gone by."

I could tell he was trying to control his anger.

"I'm sorry. It was stupid. I shouldn't have done such a thing. hoped you'd decide to leave the project, that Teodosio's remains were beyond recovery or that something bad would happen if you continued at San Miguel. The cause is more important than your project, you see. I received instructions to establish a safe place to stay for others in the organization if they needed to hide. I just couldn't do everything I needed to do with all the students around all the time. It was impossible."

Clearly, Ignacio had no understanding of archaeological work and what archaeologists perceived as important. Finding Teodosio might have been the ultimate objective of the church, but it had been far from Bill's sole interest in San Miguel. Archaeologists were no longer the treasure hunters of the early days of the field. Now the common people were deemed as important if not more than the wealthy people with status. How could one appreciate the overall society, the everyday life of any population, if one focused solely on the riches of the minority of a culture rather than the reality of the majority in any civilization? Archaeology was unable to leave the gold-digging, grave-robbing stereotypes of the past behind. As for witches, scientists were hardly the superstitious type to be scared off at the first sign of dark powers. In fact, any anthropologist would be inclined to stay to understand the rituals and complexities of the society they studied, modern or ancient, especially if witches were involved.

"Ignacio," Bill began, his voice relaxed once again. "There were at least three bodies in the second sarcophagus we opened. Where did the bodies come from?"

Ignacio paused for a moment, looking at Bill. "Well, one body came from the tomb where the snakes were. One body was already in the other tomb. And the third body came from a hiding spot beneath the altar inside the church."

This was an unexpected twist. A third body inside the church? How long had it been there, and to whom did it belong? I knew instinctively that Ignacio wouldn't be able to provide these answers.

"Tell me everything you know about the third body," Bill demanded.

"I was cleaning in the church one day and found an old wooden box hidden beneath the altar. There were bones inside. I decided when I opened the tombs that more bones would make it seem worse than it was, so I added the bones from the box to the mix."

Bill let an audible rumble of exasperation escape from his lips.

"How did you lift the tomb lid by yourself, Ignacio?" I asked.

I knew his answer would leave us no closer to finding Angela's killer; it was simple curiosity that made me ask the question. We'd needed several strong young people to lift the lid safely. How could he have done it alone?

"I made a pulley system with ropes to lift the lid up and keep it up while I removed the bones and put the snakes in. At first it didn't work, but with a few fixes, I made do. I could work on it at night after the church closed to the public. I knew I wouldn't be disturbed. I just cleaned up the materials after each evening and set things up again until it worked."

How ingenious. Had we known, we could've used Ignacio's clever system and avoided smashing the lid of the sarcophagus. Of course, we weren't aware of his tinkering until it was too late.

I watched the others as they all sat in silence for some minutes, each wrapped up in his own thoughts. I knew Bill was fuming over the tombs. Pedro was most likely in deep turmoil, consumed by thoughts of Angela. Perhaps Ignacio regretted the decisions he'd made these last few days. I, on the other hand, kept wondering who or what Ignacio saw that night.

"There's something else I want to know," I said, interrupting the stillness of the room.

Everyone looked at me, waiting for my next question.

"On Thursday, we met you in the woods, Ignacio," I began. "You'd been shooting, and you told us you hadn't caught anything. Yet you had blood on your hand. What happened? Did you hurt yourself? Did you catch something and didn't want to tell us?"

Ignacio glanced up at me and then away when our eyes met. "I did kill something in the woods that day," he admitted. "I wasn't out hunting for food, though, so I didn't want you to expect meat at dinner that night. Sometimes, we need to pass things from one person to another without having contact. Much of the organization runs on anonymity to protect everyone from arrest and so that even under torture, we couldn't reveal the identities of other members. Sometimes, in order to pass something on without meeting the other person, I kill an animal and leave it near the package I need to transfer. The vultures will eventually find the animal and circle above before consuming the carrion. I'll have already indicated the night before via radio that there's something to be picked up, so those waiting know to watch for the vultures and follow them to the place indicated. We don't like to have a standard drop spot because patterns are how the police catch you. That day, I left an animal and a package to be picked up. That's why you saw blood on my hand."

I didn't ask what was in the package. It seemed of no relevance to Angela's death. I shivered slightly, however, at the thought of people sneaking through the woods, probably armed, searching for dead animals and mysterious packages, all just steps away from where we ourselves went up and down the mountain. What would've happened if we mistakenly bumped into one?

Chapter 58

THE DRIVE BACK to the sanctuary was as quiet as the ride down. The same austere young man that brought us to the garrison took us back. He said nothing, and nor did we. I looked out the window, watching the beech trees whip by in rapid succession. Every now and again, we came across an open pasture where a stocky Basque mountain horse grazed peacefully alongside a little Pottoka pony on the lush subalpine grass. The landscape was so tranquil, it made me feel miles away from the troubles of the past days, though the respite was temporary. As we drove toward the sanctuary, a gloomy foreboding descended on me. I sighed heavily despite myself as I got out of the car, thanking the young officer before I closed the door. I stared up at the church. The Romanesque architecture, the isolation of the sanctuary, had been welcome when we arrived. Now the silhouette of the building seemed dragged from an ancient and unforgiving past of religious fervour and violent punishments. I thought of the thieves who'd had their hands cut off and hung on the church for all to see. This place had seen too much blood spilled already.

We could see the students still working in the cemetery as we approached the church. Just the day before, we'd found Angela's body in one of the graves. Now the students dug for the bodies of those that had lain peacefully for many centuries. Death was universal, but it was some comfort when it was a result of natural causes, or at least a death that occurred a thousand years before. Ortega confirmed at the garrison that the autopsy of Angela's body hadn't been performed yet, though we expected not to learn much new information from it.

As we climbed the steps up toward the church, I blurted, "I believe we're in need of a fashion show."

The men halted, turning to stare at me as though I'd lost my mind.

"What do you mean, Beatrix?" Bill asked, his tone thick with skepticism. "A fashion show?"

"Well, I don't believe for a minute that Ignacio saw Teodosio's ghost, do you?"

Father Pedro sounded unconvinced: "It's not so unbelievable after everything that's happened, is it?"

"Goodness, Father Pedro, I don't believe in ghosts, and neither should you."

As I admonished Pedro, I felt momentarily ashamed for my own thoughts of spirits and spectres the night before, when I was faced with the sinister passage. However, in the light of day, I no longer questioned my belief that ghosts were a figment of more colourful imaginations.

"I still don't understand what you mean by a fashion show," Bill said. "What's that got to do with a ghost, real or not?"

"Well, think about it for a minute. Ignacio saw somebody in the stairwell in the night. Dressed in white. If it wasn't a ghost, it was obviously a person. And probably in the middle of the night, that person would be wearing their nightclothes. If we can determine who it was that Ignacio saw, then we may be one step closer to either the killer or a witness at least."

"That's sensible," Bill said, shading his eyes from the sun. "So you want to see everyone's pyjamas. I doubt anyone will object. They don't have to wear them, just bring them out for us to see."

"Exactly," I said. "And if someone does object, well, there may be a very good reason for it."

Bill smiled at me. "Let's get to it then."

I looked at Pedro. The colour drained from his face as though he himself had seen Teodosio's ghost.

"What is it, Pedro?" I asked.

He bit his lip and pressed his hand to his face. "Oh no," he sighed softly. "There won't be any need for a fashion show."

Chapter 59

"GOODNESS! BILL, get him some water, quick!"

Pedro slid to the ground, one hand on the railing to prevent a serious fall. He muttered incomprehensibly, and his forehead was damp with sweat.

"Pedro, are you all right?" I asked.

No response.

Bill came running back with some water he had fetched from the students. I pushed it to Pedro's lips. The moisture seemed to revive him, and he took the bottle and drank from it greedily.

"Pedro, are you all right?" I repeated.

He looked at me, his dark eyes focusing slowly on my face. "I'm not sure," he mumbled. "What just happened?"

"You've fallen, but you haven't hit your head. Have you hurt anything else?"

He looked around. We were surrounded by curious eyes. The students formed a semi-circle around us. Pedro shook his head. "Perhaps my ego a little," he mumbled in Spanish.

Always an opportunist, Muffin licked the young priest's face while he was at her level, and Father Pedro patted her head. Then, he took a deep breath, stood up, and brushed the dust off his hands.

I looked at him carefully, examining his face.

"You know who killed Angela, don't you?" I whispered, my back to the students so they wouldn't hear.

He nodded his head.

"I think so," he said. "There's someone who wears a long white tunic to bed and doesn't normally get up in the middle of the night."

"Father José María," I whispered.

I hadn't noticed José María's nightwear, nor had I needed to. Pedro's reaction told me everything. He'd been so shocked, the person in question had to have been someone close to him, someone he would've never suspected of foul play.

"I think we'd better go and speak with him," Bill said, keeping the circle closed to the prying eyes and ears of the students, despite only one of them being able to understand us.

"Do you think he's dangerous?" I asked no one in particular.

"I don't know," Pedro said darkly. "Animals can be dangerous when cornered."

"What's going on?" Helen shouted from behind me. "Why are you whispering?"

"Goodness," I turned to face Bill. "This is going to be complicated."

Chapter 60

"¿CÓMO HA PODIDO hacer algo así?" Father Pedro shouted at the elderly priest. He gripped the back of the office chair, his knuckles white from the intense pressure. "It was...pure evil. Pure evil. You will burn in hell for this, of that I'm sure!"

Father José María looked up from the sheet of paper he was writing on. We'd found him seated at the desk in the office after Pedro burst through the door. His expression was calm, almost frigid. He stood up, his shoulders hunched over the desk, and waved a hand at the empty chairs, inviting us to sit without saying a word. I was worried Bill might need to restrain Pedro, but he made no attempt to lunge across the desk. I envisioned myself doing something of the sort, instead, I sat down on one of the chairs. It was clear now that Father José María was the man who killed Angela. A man who'd been a respected member of the church for decades. But questions remained: Why did he do it? And how did he do it? He didn't have the strength to do this alone.

"There's no need to shout, Pedro," José María said, as though Pedro overreacted to the discovery that his mentor killed the woman he loved. "I'll tell you what you want to know. It was for your own good, you see. I was protecting you, of course." He sat back down and interlaced his fingers in front of the wooden cross that always hung around his neck.

"Father José María, we know you killed Angela," Bill said, taking a seat in one of the wooden chairs. "There's no point in denying it."

"I'm not denying it," José María said, staring at Bill. "You've caught me." He held up his hands dramatically, palms toward the ceiling.

"What happened that night?" I blurted, unable to sit down. "Why did you do it?"

"I did it to protect you, Pedro. You're young and you've made mistakes, but I didn't want you to ruin your future because of some harlot. You have a bright future ahead of you, and I didn't want her to destroy that."

Father Pedro rose, his face scarlet with rage. I reached over and put my hand on his arm.

"Pedro," I pleaded with him. "I know you're outraged, and you're completely justified in it. But please, it's important to hear what he has to say. Ignacio's freedom depends on it."

Pedro slumped back into the chair as though his muscles had all gone slack. He hunched over and hung his head forward, gripping it in his hands. I knew he must be suffering greatly. First, he'd had to hide his feelings from everyone, having nobody to share his grief, and now he was being asked to stay calm when confronting the man who'd brought about this horrible tragedy. I was concerned he might break down completely, but we needed to hear what Father José María had done — and his motivation for doing it.

"Go on," I said, trying to remain composed, though my insides boiled in torment. "Tell us what happened. How did you know about the relationship?"

"I found out that night. The silly boy didn't realize that, because the office and the passageway are adjacent, you can hear the door open from here. I heard him go into the corridor that leads to the sacristy. Since he'd just lied to me, some absurdity about the sunset, I wanted to know why. So I followed him. I could hear their conversation from outside the chapel. She had been pregnant and lost the baby. That was good. There'd be no evidence of the affair. It would have been the perfect moment for Pedro to end things with her, to return to his true path, his path toward God. Instead, he believed himself to be in love. Obviously, she'd bewitched him. Led him into a trap. And now he wanted to move to Canada, to leave the church, to marry a little vixen who'd fooled him into committing a great sin. The whole thing was disgusting. I left and returned to the office, and nobody was the wiser. Before bed, I saw her alone in the hallway. I told her to meet me at the chapel at one o'clock in the morning to discuss something about Pedro. She agreed, and I went to bed as always."

"Then what?" I asked, finally giving in and sitting down. My back ached and I needed to rest my feet. "Did you plan to kill her?"

"I did not," he said, his face revealing no emotion. "I snuck out when Pedro was already asleep. I knew he'd not wake that night because I slipped a few drops of my sleeping draught into his water just before bed. Then, I went to the chapel, where she was waiting for me. I tried to talk some sense into her. Told her to leave Pedro, that his destiny lay with his faith. I told her that she'd only ruin him, destroy him. She was already ruined, a used rag, good for nothing. He didn't need to go down the same dark tunnel as her. But she refused. When we start treating women like men, educating them, allowing them to work, then they start behaving like men and think that they can do as they please, that no man is their master. When their roles in society should be restricted to wife and mother, caregivers to the men who will form the nation."

I felt the urge to strangle the man myself, but that wouldn't have helped us. We needed him to confess to the police to make sure that Ignacio wasn't punished for something he hadn't done.

"Please, Father," Bill begged. The creases between his eyebrows were deep and his eyes sorrowful. We were all at the end of our tethers. "Stick to the facts."

"She wouldn't see reason. She said she was in love. This was obviously the devil's work. The devil disguised as a beautiful woman to trick
Pedro into diverging from his path. Just as he tricked Teodosio. Pedro
couldn't see it, but it was plain to me. The devil takes many forms. We
know this well. I had to stop her from ruining him. I told her to kneel so
I could absolve her of her sins. When she resisted and tried to get away,
I pushed her. She lost her balance and fell back, hitting her head on the
stones at the entry to the chapel. She sank down to the ground and tried
to crawl away from me, feeling her way forward as though she couldn't
see. I knew then that I couldn't let her go. She would tell everyone what
had happened and both my and Pedro's lives would be over. The girl
crawled over to the chains, and I knew Teodosio would give me the
strength I needed to banish the devil from San Miguel. I wrapped the
chains around her neck, pulling them tight. Then, as though Teodosio
were there to aid me, she fell forward, her own weight strangling her.
All I had to do was hold the chains."

Pedro began to sob, his shoulders heaving. He didn't look up at Father
José María. I imagined the stooped priest attacking poor Angela, weak-
ened greatly by the events of that morning. She'd hardly have been able
to fight back to save herself, especially after hitting her head. I blinked
back my own tears. There was no blood at the scene of the crime, and
Bill and I hadn't lifted Angela's body to see the back of her head, yet had
the autopsy been performed sooner, we might have had this additional
information about how someone was able to overpower this poor young
woman.

Father José María continued: "I felt I'd desecrated the church that
I loved so dearly, despite it being the devil himself I'd killed. I couldn't
leave the body there, and I couldn't carry her outside either. It was too
far, and I wasn't strong enough. That's when I remembered the students transporting dirt to and fro at the excavation. I snuck back into
the house, took the key to the church from the office, and went to get
a wheelbarrow from the tool shed, bringing it into the church via the
front door. I struggled to get the wheelbarrow up the stairs. I simply
couldn't lift it and drag it up. Then, by the grace of God, one of your

students appeared, like an angel. At first, I was frightened. She must have walked right past the girl's body where I left her, lying under Teodosio's chains. I had no intention of being arrested for doing what was necessary. Yet she seemed to be in some kind of trance. She hardly even noticed me. I asked her if she could help me with something. She didn't say anything, but I realized that she would follow my instructions. I told her to take the wheelbarrow up to the chapel. It was easy for her. She was strong like an ox. I told her to put the body into the wheelbarrow while I wiped Teodosio's chains with my nightshirt. I knew if the police realized they were the murder weapon, they'd look for fingerprints. Next, I told her to take the body to the cemetery. All I had to do was follow her. She didn't seem to be aware of what she was doing. I instructed the girl to put the body into one of the empty graves. When she put the body in, it was facing the sanctuary toward the window where the thieves' hands had been hung on display. I felt it was appropriate that in death she could contemplate her own sins and the sins of those who came before her, daring to violate the sanctity of San Miguel, this most holy place. Her own body was on display as well as a warning of the dangers of the devil. Except the two of you, nosy old wretches, found her first. I should never have agreed to let you come here. If Pedro hadn't insisted, I never would've given my permission for the excavation. It was a terrible mistake, and for that, I am repentant."

I supposed that José María's words were meant to incense us. I tried to resist my instinct to react. I looked at Bill, his hands trembled in his lap.

"What next?" I asked.

"I told the girl to take the wheelbarrow back to the shed. I went with her to ensure that it was put back where it belonged. I wiped the handles with my nightshirt. It was very cold and damp. The girl had mud on her feet and legs. I told her to go shower and then go back to bed. I let her return to the house first, then I also went back to bed. She'd done all the work, so I had little dirt on me except for some mud on my slippers." He spoke simply, as though his nighttime excursion had been equivalent to absconding with cookies from the kitchen. "As expected, nobody suspected me in the least." He shrugged. "Until now."

He was right. We'd overlooked him because of his holy calling, because of his reputation, as we had nearly done for Pedro. His lack of physical strength also left him above anything but a superficial suspicion. I never would've imagined someone would manipulate Janis to help them with their crime. He didn't need an alibi, simply an aura of righteous innocence.

"Why?" Pedro cried. "Why did you care so much that I, of all people, remain in the church? I didn't care if I was a priest or not. Why would you care more than I did? I wanted to leave, to get married, to have children. Why couldn't you let me go?"

"It was guilt, I suppose. I felt responsible for your mistakes. I felt that I'd somehow passed on something to you that made you incapable of staying on the true path that God set out for you. I felt that you were following in my footsteps. I just wanted to make sure you didn't err the way I did."

"What are you talking about?" Pedro asked through his tears. "How could it be your fault? I knew the rules and I broke them. I did it. You've never done anything like this."

"But I have, Pedro," José María said sadly. He reached across the table to touch Pedro's arm, but Pedro recoiled in horror. "I committed a terrible sin twenty-eight years ago, during the dreadful years of the war. I, too, was tricked by the devil in the form of a woman. I didn't love her, but I lusted for her, and it can be difficult to see the difference sometimes. I sinned, but God forgave me. I feel that he has forgiven me, though I still repent for what I did. She, too, begged for forgiveness, leading an exemplary life of great piety since then. I promised God that I'd care for the product of that sin and make sure that he never made the same mistakes as his father. She promised God that the product of that sin would dedicate his life to the service of the church."

All three of us gasped, the sound of breath rapidly inhaled lingering in the air around us.

"Now you see, Pedro. You are my son, in the eyes of God. Your fate was determined for you long before you were born. I couldn't let you, my son, fall into the devil's hands as I'd done myself. You would have strayed too far from the church, never to be forgiven by God, and I couldn't let that happen. Now you can be absolved and continue along your true path."

Father José María sat back in his chair and waited for us to respond, as though what he'd done was completely natural. I couldn't bring myself to speak, so I held Bill's hand in one of mine and Pedro's in the other, and I did something I hadn't done for a long time. I silently prayed.

Chapter 61

FATHER JOSÉ MARÍA'S revelation wasn't only shocking, it was also heartbreaking. His life had been a series of lies and secrets culminating in the death of an innocent young woman who'd done nothing but fall in love. Bill, Father Pedro, and I left José María in the office and left the house in silence.

"I'll go call the police," Bill spoke first. "It's best they come as soon as possible."

He marched off in the direction of the church, and I was left alone with Pedro. I did the only thing I could think of and wrapped his tall frame in a tight embrace. He went loose in my arms, leaning over and weeping into my hair. I used all my strength to hold up his weight. I didn't know if he'd ever recover from this, but I knew he needed all the support he could get.

"Pedro," I said and he pulled away from me, brushing tears from his cheeks with the sleeve of his cassock. "I think it would be a good idea for you to go home and be with your family. Your mother might have made a mistake in the past, but she loves you and you need her now. Don't be angry with her, we all make mistakes. She did her best to ensure you had a home and weren't a social outcast for what she did. Times have changed. People judge less and forgive more now than they did then."

Pedro nodded. "Thank you, Mrs. Forster. I'll call for someone to come pick me up. I don't know how I'll face them now, knowing what I do, but I believe you're right, that there's more love than hatred in my family and that I'll one day be able to forgive my mother for lying to me all these years. She did it to protect me, not to harm me."

I watched Pedro walk away from me, his shoulders hunched, his head hanging forward. My heart broke for him, for Angela, for her family, and of course for Miriam. The others would recover from the tragedy soon enough, but Pedro, Angela's family, and Miriam would forever live with an empty place in their hearts.

I walked around behind the house toward the church, wondering if I should tell Janis of her involvement in the crime. She was yet another victim of Father José María's deception, taken advantage of because of her condition. It seemed she didn't remember what she'd done, and I asked myself if knowledge of it would only further disturb an already disquieted psyche. She didn't sleepwalk for no reason, and though I couldn't speculate as to the root cause of her somnambulism, I wasn't entirely sure knowing the whole truth would help her situation. I still believed her to be non-violent, and perhaps that was enough.

As I came around to the other side of the house, I saw Maite feeding the donkeys. She'd be glad to know that we'd found the real culprit and Ignacio would be released. I knew Bill wouldn't want to press charges against Ignacio for what he'd done to the sarcophagi, but I didn't know how Maite would feel about her brother exploiting her beliefs for his own benefit. I thought that was best for them to work out between themselves. When I came into view of the cemetery, I could see Bill on the other side of the excavation area talking to Archie. I caught his eye and waved him over.

He jogged up to me, a worried look on his face: "What is it, Beatrix?" He huffed. He was in reasonable shape for his age, but there'd been no need to overexert himself.

"It's not serious, Bill. I sent Father Pedro home to be with his family. Maybe you saw him on his way to call them."

He nodded. "I did. I spoke to him just now."

"Good," I said. "Let's tell the students and Maite what really happened. Maybe leaving out Janis's involvement for now, and we can't tell them the real reason Ignacio tampered with the tombs, but they deserve to know as much of the truth as we can tell them. It'll be a shock, but I think they'll all feel better knowing they're not in any danger."

Bill took my hand, and we walked slowly over to where the students were still working on the excavation.

Chapter 62

AFTER BILL AND I told the students about Father José María's horrifying crime and that they should stop working and rest, Bill and I returned to our room.

Bill handed me one of the hot cups of tea he'd prepared in the kitchen before we came upstairs. I sat down on the cot, cradled the cup in both hands, and let the vapours steam up my glasses.

"Thank you, dear," I said, letting the heat reinvigorate me. "We've had quite the day of revelations."

"We certainly have." Bill sat down beside me. "There's still one mystery left for us to solve, though, Beatrix."

"What's that?"

"The third body in the sarcophagus. Assuming we may have Teodosio and Constanza's remains as the two skeletons that were originally in the tombs. Then who does the third skeleton, hidden in a box under the altar, belong to?"

I rolled my eyes. We'd only just found the culprit behind Angela's murder, and Bill's mind was already on skeletons.

"That's something we don't need to figure out today. When the students are ready, we can have them separate the remains based on size and taphonomic factors and have a good think as to the reasons why there'd be a body hidden in the church. However, they're not going to be ready today, Bill. Give them some time."

Bill nodded, but I could see he was already contemplating the possibilities, drifting off to the world that existed inside his mind.

Chapter 63

A WEEK AFTER Angela's murder, the students, Bill, and I slowly and unsteadily returned to the routines of the field school. Excavating the cemetery, studying the remains in the laboratory, and eating our meals together with Maite and Ignacio, who'd returned to San Miguel and become even more reclusive than he was before.

I was on my way to the kitchen late in the afternoon when I heard excited shouting coming from the lab.

"Beatrix!" Bill's voice echoed in the stairwell. "Beatrix, come quickly!"

I rushed as quickly as my legs would carry me up the stairs and into the first room.

"What is it?" I asked breathlessly, holding my hand to my ribs.

Where there'd been two tables before, there were now three. Each one had a skeleton laid out in anatomical position, though one was very obviously missing the cranium. It appeared the students, Archie, and Bill managed to separate the three individuals after all.

"Look at this!" Bill said, shoving a mandible into my hands.

I held the bone delicately, turning it over in my hands. I wasn't sure what I was looking for, until I turned it upside down, the inferior aspect of the mandibular body facing me.

"Goodness," I gasped. There were multiple, fine cut marks, made with what must have been a sharp-edged blade. "Do you think he was decapitated?"

Bill nodded, excitement making his eyes glitter. "It's certainly a possibility. There was no cranium with the skeleton, but it is odd that the mandible would be with the post-cranial skeleton and the cranium missing, even in a case of beheading."

"What does it mean?" Janis demanded. "Can we identify him just from that?"

"No." Bill turned to Janis and the other students who were now staring at him. "It's certainly not a unique cause of death or even post-mortem ritual. We wouldn't be able to determine identity based on historical documentation and cause of death alone, but perhaps with other lines of evidence in addition to the cause of death, we could hypothesize as to someone's identity given sufficient commonalities."

"So what famous person was beheaded? A saint maybe?" Graham piped up.

"One saint does spring to mind," I said, only half seriously.

All eyes turned to me.

"Why San Fermín, of course!" I was only joking. I didn't think the students would believe we'd somehow found the remains of a martyred saint hidden at San Miguel, but the audible surprise and excitement suggested otherwise.

"Now look what I've started," I whispered to Bill.

No response.

Epilogue

"PROFESSOR FORSTER, can you confirm that you found Teodosio de Goñi and San Fermín's remains at San Miguel?" someone in the audience asked.

Bill stood at his lectern before a large crowd that turned out to hear him speak about the excavations that summer. The lecture hall was darkened, and I dared not turn around to determine the identity of the speaker for fear of dropping a stitch. I'd started knitting a sweater for my youngest grandchild, and I hoped to have it finished by Christmas. As I strained my eyes to see the loops of wool on the needles, I finally accepted defeat. Knitting in the dim theatre was a mistake. I finished the row and set the bundle aside. It could wait for a more opportune moment.

"I cannot confirm with absolute certainty that we encountered the remains of Teodosio and Constanza. Of the three individuals found inside the church, two were male and one was female. As I said previously, we did encounter a robust male individual from one sarcophagus with skeletal modifications to the pelvis that may be consistent with wearing heavy chains around the waist for many years. Is it him? Possibly, as the skeletal modifications are consistent with the legend of Teodosio. But he died well over a thousand years ago, if he existed at all. Thus, it's impossible to be certain. We must always take into consideration, when dealing with the oral transmission of legends, especially legends that involve mythical creatures, that the characters described, however human, may never have existed at all. Or at the very least, if they did exist, we know that their life events were greatly embellished. Was the legend of Teodosio a fictitious romanticization of the life of someone who lived and died at San Miguel? Someone whose name and history was long ago lost in the historical records? This seems more likely as we know this was typical in the medieval period." Bill paused to blot some moisture from his forehead with his handkerchief. The lights in the hall always produced a great deal of heat for whomever was centre stage. "In terms of the third individual," he continued, replacing the handkerchief in his pocket, "there is evidence of decapitation. In and of itself, it's not sufficient to make a case that we have the remains of San Fermín, whose very existence, by the way, hasn't been confirmed. For all three individuals, we've taken bone samples to be sent for carbon dating, which may help us narrow down the time periods during which these people died. Perhaps with additional evidence from radiocarbon dating, we'll have additional evidence to either support or refute the hypothesized identities of these individuals. Until that time, the identities are conjecture only and the truth remains a mystery. I remind you, as well, that San Fermín was certainly not the only saint to have been beheaded."

The audience chuckled, and I smiled at the thought of poor, hapless Ignacio, now living in tranquility once more with Francisco at the sanctuary, coming across a box of mysterious human bones when cleaning one day.

Many people attended Bill's lecture that day, filling the hall completely, save a few seats here and there. My belief was that morbid curiosity always drew a good crowd. Anticipating the true reason behind the success of the lecture, Bill addressed the tragedy of that summer in ambiguous terms at the beginning of his speech and asked that, out of respect, questions be limited to the subject of the excavation itself. I was in complete agreement. This was not a media circus but a space for academic advancement, and there was no place for digging into the private lives of those who were no longer with us.

Of course, Pedro had been shocked more than anyone by Father José María's revelations that day at San Miguel. He'd never suspected the father that raised him wasn't his biological father. I couldn't imagine what it was like, first to lose the person he loved most in the world, then to learn that his whole life had been a lie, and then, finally, to be manipulated by a man who wished to correct his own failings through the life of his offspring. It turned out Pedro's mother never told her husband about the affair with the priest, pretending the child was the legitimate offspring of the matrimony. He'd never known his son wasn't related to him by blood. In the wake of the tragedy, it didn't surprise me that Pedro wished to escape from the place that brought so much pain and confusion to his life.

Bill's voice broke through my thoughts: "If there are no further questions, I'd like to pass things over to the Department of Anthropology's newest graduate student, Pedro Mendoza Aguirre, who will talk about the history of San Miguel in the medieval period."

The audience erupted into enthusiastic applause. Everyone knew Pedro's story, or at least some part of it, making him an object of great sympathy and curiosity at the university. Especially among the young ladies on campus, I must say. The professors, too, entertained themselves, gossiping about the handsome former priest whose life was the stuff of a gothic romance novel, or so my sources on the inside told me over afternoon tea as we all sat around my sunroom prattling on and sneaking cookie crumbs to Muffin, who waited on tenterhooks. There were no secrets in the ivory tower. "The Curse of Teodosio," they called it, silently thanking whatever god they believed in that the misfortune had been someone else's.

Acknowledgements

First and foremost, I would like to thank my parents, Lois Barlow-Wilson and Malcolm Wilson, for always supporting me, even in the wildest of my endeavours, and my family Niall Wilson, and Ross and Gloria Barlow for a lifetime of encouragement. I am grateful to Debra Bell at Radiant Press, who took a chance on a debut novelist, and Paul Carlucci for his skillful editing and perceptive advice. In no particular order, thank you to Emma Bonthorne and Fran Valle de Tarazaga for sharing their extensive knowledge of Basque history and culture and without whom the excavations at San Miguel de Aralar (2016-2018) would not have been possible; to Michel Fernández and the rest of the Aditu Arkeologia team, who always looked out for me when I was far from home; to my MA archaeology supervisors, Dr. Angela Lieverse and Dr. Tamara Varney, for sharing their knowledge of all things skeletal; to Dr. Ernie Walker and the professors of the Department of Archaeology and Anthropology at the University of Saskatchewan, who provided my formal training in archaeology, biological anthropology, and forensic anthropology; to Dr. Kenneth Brown at the University of Calgary, who sparked a lifelong love of the Spanish language and culture, and introduced me to the history of the Spanish Civil War; to the team of the Asociación para la Recuperación de la Memoria Histórica (ARMH) for sharing their insight, over the years, into the horrors of the Spanish Civil War and Franco dictatorship; to Guy Vanderhaeghe, at the University of Saskatchewan, for sharing his wisdom on the craft of creative writing; to the professionals at the Miami-Dade Medical Examiner Department for an unforgettable learning experience; to Arantza Santibáñez García for her creative input; to all those who dedicate themselves to making San Miguel the incredible, tranquil, and welcoming sanctuary that it is today. Last, but not least, I would also like to thank Rachel Reardigan and Iván Santibáñez García for their unconditional support, advice, and ready ear through this journey.

DANEE WILSON grew up on the prairies in Regina, Saskatchewan. She completed a BA Hons in Spanish at the University of Calgary before moving to Spain to teach English. Inspired by the unidentified remains entombed in El Valle de los Caídos (The Valley of the Fallen), and hoping to work in the recovery and identification of victims of the Spanish Civil War, Danee returned to Canada to study archaeology at the University of Saskatchewan, where she received a BA Hons and an MA. During her studies, she travelled to Spain each summer to volunteer in the search for victims of Franco's regime. In 2016, Danee began work as Assistant Director of a small archaeology company in the Basque Country, and spent three field seasons excavating the medieval cemetery at San Miguel de Aralar in Navarre. After more than three years abroad, Danee once again returned home to Canada, completing a post-graduate diploma in public relations and communications management from McGill University. She currently resides in Toronto, Canada.